REKINDLING MOTIVES

Elaine Orr

Copyright © 2011 Elaine L. Orr

All rights reserved.

ISBN: **1467923095**
ISBN-13: **978-1467923095**

ACKNOWLEDGMENTS

Thanks to my husband, James W. Larkin, for permission to use some of his wonderful poetry, and to my late father, Miles D. Orr, for the use of his. In dozens of trips to East Coast beaches as a child and adult I got a sense of life in those towns, especially on trips after Labor Day. I owe thanks to every boardwalk vendor and B&B host I stayed with. If not for the Ottumwa, Iowa Ecumenical Lord's Cupboard and the Ottumwa area Hy-Vee stores I would know much less about how people band together to help those who do not have enough food. I wish every community had such dedicated volunteers and businesses.

REKINDLING MOTIVES
By Elaine Orr

REKINDLING MOTIVES
Copyright 2011 by Elaine L. Orr
Cover Design by Miss Mae

Poetry by James W. Larkin includes: Homesick Dreams
Copyright 2011 by James W. Larkin
Poetry by Miles D. Orr includes: The Lava Poem
Copyright 1994 by Miles D. Orr

All rights reserved.
This Create Space edition is licensed for your personal enjoyment only and may not be copied in any form. Thank you for respecting the authors' work.

Discover other books in the Jolie Gentil Series.
Appraisal for Murder (first of the series)
Rekindling Motives (second of the series)
When the Carny Comes to Town (third in the series)
Any Port in a Storm (fourth in the series)
Trouble on the Doorstep (fifth in the series)
Behind the Walls (sixth in the series)
Vague Images (seventh in the series)
Ground to a Halt (eighth in the series)

The following are in ebooks only
Ocean Alley Adventures (boxed set of books 1-3)
Jolie Gentil Translates to Trouble (boxed set of books 4-6)

www.elaineorr.com
www.elaineorr.blogspot.com

CHAPTER ONE

I WOULD RATHER have walked barefoot over shards of glass on the boardwalk in January than go to the Ocean Alley High School reunion. However, Scoobie and Ramona combined their charms, so on the Saturday after Thanksgiving I was in the so-called ballroom of Ocean Alley's largest hotel, Beachcomber's Alley. I'm such a wuss.

The 'ballroom' is actually a large multi-purpose room that is the site of the high school prom, but can just as easily be used for after-funeral gatherings for prominent townspeople. For the latter, the room is not adorned with crepe paper in high school colors nor does one wall have a series of poster boards, each sporting dozens of pictures of former classmates in various poses – all appearing happy, popular, and cool. Since this was not how I spent eleventh grade, my only year at Ocean Alley High, I was not in any of the photos. I know because I looked.

There were pictures of students at high school football games posing with the school mascot (a large crab), and others showing students eating lunch on the beach. There was also one of Scoobie. He was lying on the small brick wall that bears the school's name, and the caption is, "Enjoying the spring clouds." Since Scoobie spent a lot of time stoned, he would have been higher than the clouds, which was likely the point.

"You're Jo-lee Gen-teel, aren't you?" A woman who did not look at all familiar was approaching, hand extended. Since she had mispronounced my name (Jolie Gentil is pronounced Zho-Lee Zhan-tee; the "J" and "G" are soft, and the "L" on the end of Gentil is silent) I knew she was not someone who knew me well.

I smiled weakly, scanning the space behind her, hoping to see Scoobie or Ramona. "It's pronounced Zho-Lee, but yes, that's me."

"I'm sorry," she continued. "We didn't really know each other in high school, but I've been reading about you in the Ocean Alley paper. I get it mailed to me in Connecticut. You've had a rough couple of weeks."

Tell me about it. Since coming to Ocean Alley to stay with my great Aunt Madge to decompress after the end of my marriage, I had found a dead body and nearly been killed by a man who was angry with my ex-husband. I had made him angry, too, but in all fairness, that was not my fault.

"Yes, it's been...wild." I shook her hand as I looked at her name badge. "So, your name is really Gracie Allen?"

She was tall, slim, and dressed in a stunning burgundy dinner dress that clung to her like a bathing suit. She looked nothing like the photo of the round-faced girl who was on her name badge. Her laugh was contagious, and I smiled as she explained. "My maiden name was Grace Fisher, and I married Jeremy Allen. I get a kick out of being Gracie Allen, so I told the committee to put my married name on my badge."

I nodded. In a way she looked a bit like the iconic radio and TV actress, but without the curls. I had not shown up for the junior class pictures, so the reunion committee made my badge from a photo that had recently appeared in the local paper. It was not my best picture.

"It's good you have a sense of humor," I was unsure what else to add.

"Actually, I wanted to talk business with you for a minute. I heard you do real estate appraisals."

"I do." I saw dollar signs. "I work through Harry Steele's company."

She waved a hand. "I know all about that. It was..."

"In the paper," I finished for her.

"Right. Jeremy and I have to sell my grandparents' house. I have no idea what it's worth."

I didn't understand why she wanted my help. Usually a real estate agent helps the seller set the price, and the appraiser is not called for until after there is a contract with a potential buyer. "Umm, you won't really need me until after you have a contract," I began.

"I know how it's usually done. But this real estate agent we're working with has suggested a price that seems awfully high." She frowned slightly. "We don't want to sell it under market, but if we price it too high it won't sell quickly. I want to be done with all this estate stuff."

A warning bell dinged in my brain. Ramona's uncle, Lester Argrow, has a well-earned reputation for listing a house for more than the market will usually bear. He wants a higher commission. This has put him at odds with Harry Steele, though Lester and I get along okay.

I was saved from an immediate response as the lights in the room dimmed and a portable spotlight aimed toward the center at the far end of the ballroom. Gracie and I turned to watch Jennifer Stenner, one of my competitors in the appraisal business and a former cheerleader, step into the light.

She was wearing a dress of what I (hardly a fashion maven) would call party-dress material. As Jennifer welcomed everyone to the tenth reunion of our Ocean Alley High School class, I scanned the room again for Scoobie and Ramona. While I wouldn't put it past Ramona to forget, even though we had talked about the reunion the day before, I had really expected Scoobie to be on time. In the two weeks since we made the papers for solving a murder, he has made a point of seeing me on the boardwalk every day or stopping by Aunt Madge's Cozy Corner B&B.

Jennifer had just awarded the prize for coming the longest distance to a couple who now live in London. Their prize was a large plush dog dressed in school colors, making me glad I wouldn't win anything. It was big enough that it would need its own airline ticket, so I figured it would get left under a table.

"And now to the most successful Ocean Alley graduate of our class, Annie Milner." There was more applause for Annie, whom I knew to be an attorney who worked in the county's Office of the Prosecuting Attorney, so I turned to see if she was in the audience. As I did so, my eyes met those of a very pregnant woman who had apparently been trying to get my attention. She waved and pointed toward the back of the room, and started walking that way. Feeling it would be rude to ignore her, I whispered to Gracie, "I'll catch up with you in a few minutes."

Gracie, busy clapping for Annie Milner, didn't seem to hear, which was fine with me. I threaded my way through the crowd, trying to remember why the woman looked familiar. She was about my height, which is five feet, two inches, and had light brown hair. Her only remarkable feature was the watermelon that preceded her.

When we were a few feet from each other, she started to laugh. "You don't recognize me, do you?"

"Ohmigod, Margo." I threw myself at her and hugged. Or tried to anyway, in spite of the watermelon. Margo was my best friend in eleventh grade, the only person other than Scoobie who knew that I was staying with Aunt Madge while my parents 'worked things out' in their marriage. I told everyone else they were touring in Europe.

"I'm sorry, I just didn't..." I stammered, embarrassed at not recognizing her.

"I wasn't exactly pregnant in eleventh grade." Her eyes laughed at me, but she wasn't making fun. "Although, I was kind of lucky not to be."

I felt my jaw drop. "No. You and Eddie...?"

"Just once. Then we were so scared for a month we didn't do it again until we got married."

It was my turn to laugh. "Scared straight. I should have kept in better touch. Aunt Madge told me when she saw your wedding announcement, but I didn't know you were expecting." I looked at her belly. "Boy or girl?"

"I never let them tell me." She was very matter-of-fact. "The little devil kicks like a boy, though."

"So it's not your first?" I, caught up in my own life, could not imagine parenting, much less having a second child at twenty-eight.

Margo laughed so loudly we got a couple of 'keep it down' looks from people near us. She covered her mouth and we moved into the hall. "More like my fourth."

This did not strike me at all funny, and it must have shown in my expression, because she continued, with a slightly defiant look. "Eddie and I always said we wanted four, and we wanted to finish having them before we were thirty." She patted her belly.

"Lucky for her," said a familiar voice behind me, "they look more like Margo than Eddie."

I turned toward Scoobie, about to lambaste him for leaving me on my own for an hour, but the words died on my lips. Gone were his traditional unkempt look and blue jeans. Instead, he wore an old-fashioned tux, reminiscent of Rock Hudson in *Pillow Talk*, and his blonde hair and beard were neatly trimmed.

"Don't let Eddie hear you say that, Scoobie," Margo chided. "Everyone says our little Jack looks like the UPS guy. You'll get me in trouble."

As usual, Margo had taken whatever came before her in stride. Probably why she could handle three kids with one on the way. I, with no such aplomb, blurted, "Wow! You look really ..."

It was a mistake. Insecurity replaced his joviality in an instant and he interrupted. "You don't like it?"

"I do," I said, quickly. "It's just..."

"Different," said Margo, in her no-nonsense way. "But you look good."

"Thanks." He acted somewhat cocky again. "I figured since Jolie and I spent junior prom night at Pizza Hut, I'd dress for this occasion."

"Oh God, we did." I had actually been asked by a guy in math class whose name escaped me, but I barely knew him and couldn't imagine spending an entire evening talking to him. Scoobie and I had hung out a lot together, but not as an item, as Aunt Madge would say. It seemed perfectly natural to argue over who got the last piece of pepperoni pizza rather than get dressed up to see if we could get a local restaurant to serve us alcohol.

"Eddie and I went," Margo said, as she looked over me into the ballroom. "I think someone's calling you or something."

Sure enough, I heard Jennifer saying my name into the mike. "Oh, no." I felt my color rise in sync with the case of nerves I felt.

"Ha! Serves you right for being in the paper so much," Scoobie said. He gave me a small shove.

As I walked the few feet into the room, the spotlight shone on me, and I shielded my eyes. "There she is, folks," Jennifer said, and the spotlight swung back to her. Which was good, though all I could now see were blinking lights. I ran into something firm, which turned out to be a good-natured classmate.

"Go on up front," he urged.

I could feel my face turn even more crimson as I walked toward Jennifer, who was looking very pleased with herself. "And for the super sleuth," she began, as several people laughed, "we have a special award."

I stood next to her, trying to look at ease and as if it was perfectly normal for me to be in front of a couple hundred people who knew my name when I didn't know most of theirs. "I can't believe you did this." What I really wanted to say was that I would try to steal some appraisal business from her, but that would be rude.

From a small table just to one side, she took a package about the size of a shoebox and handed it to me. "Open it," Scoobie yelled from the back.

I looked at Jennifer and saw genuine delight in her face, no trace of the usual pretentious attitude that she wears about town. I struggled with the lid for a moment, and then pulled out tissue paper and looked beneath it. Tucked inside were a magnifying glass, bubble pipe, and tweed cap, which someone had inexpertly tried to fashion to look like Sherlock Holmes' hat. I took out the hat and plopped it on my head.

The applause and catcalls had me laughing in spite of myself. "Read the card," Jennifer said.

Uh oh. I recognized Aunt Madge's handwriting. She knows everyone in town, so I couldn't say I was surprised. I removed the card and read aloud, "To the best girl detective in Ocean Alley." An arrow indicated I was to turn the card over. "Now learn to mind your own business." This brought another round of laughter, and I gave a small bow and tried to edge out of the spotlight.

Jennifer would have none of that. She put her arm through mine and drew me to the center of the spotlight. "Now, not everyone knew Jolie when she was here for eleventh grade, but we're sure glad she's back." Only scattered applause for this, as people had started talking to others again. "Even," she raised an eyebrow as she looked at me in mock sternness, "if she is competition for Stenner Appraisals."

I knew she'd get her business name in there somewhere. I suddenly realized people expected me to say something. Jennifer was, after all, holding the mike in front of my face.

"I think I'd like to crawl under the boardwalk." This brought a couple of guffaws, and I remembered coming across two or three couples under there, during junior year.

"Get your minds out of the gutter," Margo yelled from the back.

Everyone laughed, and I felt the tension – my self-created tension, as usual – lessen. "It's nice of you guys to think of me, but, I have to warn you, I might use this," I held up the magnifying glass, "To see what you're up to. Watch out."

After that lame attempt at humor, Jennifer let me leave the front of the room. As she began to award the prize for most children – no doubt who would win that one – I made my way back to Scoobie.

Standing next to him, finally, was Ramona. I could understand why she was late. She had taken the time to fix her long blonde hair into a stunning French twist, but she had done it in such a way that there were strands of hair along her neck at perfect intervals. Often known for dressing somewhere between a stylish hippie and a Gypsy, tonight she was in a sleek blue evening dress that was perfect for her height of five feet six inches.

Clearly I, in a knee-length hunter green dress that I used to wear to the office, had not gotten the memo about how one is to dress for a high school reunion.

Scoobie reached for the box to examine the pipe.

"You look terrific," I told Ramona.

"I should have told you people get dressed up for this." Ramona had a kind of guilty expression,

I raised an eyebrow at her.

"But you look good too," she said, quickly.

Scoobie handed back the bubble pipe. "They should have given you a bong."

"You're the one who used to smoke that stuff, not her," Ramona said.

"Jolie. We need to finish." Gracie Allen walked up and extended her hand to Ramona. She ignored Scoobie, which made me angry. Just because he lived in a rooming house and spent most of his time on the streets did not mean she was better than he.

I was about to turn away when Scoobie caught my eye and winked. "I heard you were trying to get rid of your grandparents' dump."

She stiffened. "It's not a dump, just older and..."

"I'm sorry, that's right. I heard someone down at Java Jolt saying you were trying to dump their place."

I had to keep my lips together to keep from laughing.

"I do want to sell it," Gracie said, formally. She turned to me. "Would you be willing to come by and take a look? I'd really appreciate it. We'd pay you, of course."

Since my budget is lean, thanks to my former husband's draining our bank accounts to support his gambling hobby, I tend not to turn down a chance to work. "As long as you go through Harry Steele, I'd be happy to do it." This made Gracie happy, and I jotted Harry's number on the back of a napkin she held out for me.

As Gracie walked away the band started to play and almost everyone made a beeline for the food. I stepped back to stand next to Ramona while Scoobie joined the group loading their plates. She smiled at me broadly.

"What?" I asked.

"Jennifer said I had to be sure you came, so you'd get your box of prizes."

"Ramona! You tricked me."

"Not really," she said. "I could tell you really wanted to come. Besides, you did get a bong."

I laughed. "I'll probably use the bubble pipe with my nieces." She was still smiling. "OK, it is a good place to meet people."

I had often visited Aunt Madge in the years since I'd lived with her. My town of Lakewood, New Jersey was less than forty miles from Ocean Alley. However, Margo had moved to Connecticut, and Scoobie and I had lost track of each other, so I rarely ran into anyone I knew. If I was going to settle in here for a while, I needed to meet more people than those who lived in the houses I was appraising.

Scoobie rejoined us. His plate was piled high. "You two should get over there before all the good stuff is gone." He picked up a roast beef sandwich and took a huge bite. "Isht good," he said, between chews.

As Ramona and I walked toward the spread, someone touched my elbow. "You don't say hi when you bump into people?" asked an auburn-haired man.

"Sorry. All I saw were colored spots."

"I'm Bill Oliver." My face must have reflected my blank memory, because he added, "Math class?"

"Oh, sure. You, uh, sat across from me." I racked my brain. Was he the guy who asked me to the junior prom? If so, he looked much better now, with broad shoulders that said he worked out.

"Yep." He handed Ramona and me a plate and took one for himself.

"Hey, Bill," said Ramona, in her more typical airy-fairy voice. "You haven't been in the store for a while."

"Nope. I moved to Newark. Joined a dental practice up there."

Instinctively I moved my tongue over my teeth to be sure there were no bits of food showing. I felt like my awkward eleventh-grade self. He joined a dental practice, and I had a room in my aunt's B&B because I had less than $4,000 to my name, a car payment, and student loans.

"Deviled egg, Jolie?" he asked, lifting one off the tray with the small tongs.

"Sure." He put half a deviled egg on my plastic plate and it skidded back onto the table. "Oh well." I picked it up and popped it into my mouth.

"You're as bad as Scoobie," Ramona murmured.

"Yeah, Scoobie." Bill glanced behind him. "I heard he's had some tough times."

"He's doing better." I could hear the defensiveness in my voice as I tried to speak with the egg in my mouth.

"Scoobie says he majored in marijuana growing in college," Ramona said, as she picked up a fork. "He's getting back on track."

Bill looked dubious. "I was down here a couple of times this summer, and I saw him on the boardwalk, wearing a knapsack. Looked like it had all he owned in it."

I shrugged, which was difficult as I was trying to balance several olives and some miniature quiches. "He has a room, spends a lot of time in the library. And he writes great poetry."

"But how does he live?" Bill persisted.

I led the three of us toward some chairs in the back of the room, keeping my eyes alert for Scoobie. It occurred to me that I didn't know what Scoobie did for money.

"He's on some sort of Social Security disability," Ramona said. "But he's getting a lot better. He's thinking of taking some writing classes."

Bill's questions, which didn't seem mean-spirited, were still making me uncomfortable, so I figured I'd turn the conversation to him. "How long have you been out of dental school?"

This being a subject Bill was familiar with, he talked for several minutes about finishing undergraduate school a semester early so he could travel to Europe, going to dental school for four years, and then doing a one-year residency in pediatric dentistry, his specialty. I half-listened as I looked for Scoobie. I spotted him dancing with Jennifer. She did not look to be having as much fun as he was.

By the time Scoobie rejoined Ramona and me – after we ditched the very attentive Bill by using the time-honored method of going to the ladies room together – I had looked at pictures of Margo and Eddie's three kids and the sonogram of the one on the way, and Ramona had told me that the reason Bill stayed near the door was that he was divorced from another classmate and they had a deal not to go near each other during the evening.

This seemed quite civil to me. I, on the other hand, have no idea where my ex-husband Robby is. Since he agreed to testify against a big-time loan shark who preys on gamblers, there's a chance he'll go into the federal witness protection program.

"Listen, Jolie," Scoobie said in a low voice, "Want to help me stash some food?"

"You're not serious."

In response, he pulled a couple of plastic food storage bags from his tux pocket, and grinned. "Health department rules say they can't save the stuff, and the hotel won't give it away. They're afraid somebody would get food poisoning and sue them. Or not get it and sue."

He took my elbow and guided me toward the table. I suddenly realized that half the crowd had left. *Had I been talking to Margo that long?* "You know," I took a bag from him, "I have a reputation to uphold."

"Right. That would be the one about being in cahoots with Michael Riordan over the murder of his mother?"

"You know very well that George Winters just implied that because I hung up on him." I had since decided that it was not a good policy to hang up on newspaper reporters.

We were at the long food table, and I took in what was left. "What kind of stuff do you want?"

"I don't have a fridge, so just get bread and crackers and cookies." He poured the remains of a bowl of crackers into his large bag. "Cheese would be OK. I can put it on the window sill."

Feeling as if every eye in the room was on me, I stuffed cheese into the bag he had given me. As I zipped it shut, he handed me another one. I put cookies and a bunch of deli bread slices into it. I was reaching for crackers when a camera flashed just to my right.

"This is great," George Winters said. "Reunion attendees load up for the ride home."

"You wouldn't dare." I moved a foot toward him and he just grinned. He has a cocky grin that seems to go with his red hair. I have thought several times that I could like George if he would stop writing about me. Which it seems he won't.

"Wanna bet?" George nodded to Scoobie. "You want a picture with Jolie?"

"Sure." Scoobie draped an arm over my shoulder and I glanced at him. He looked happier than I'd seen him since I'd come back to Ocean Alley.

"Smile for your fans, Jolie."

WHEN I SAW THE *OCEAN ALLEY PRESS* the next day, I wished more than ever that I hadn't stuck out my tongue. He had taken a second picture, at Scoobie's insistence, but I knew that if the local paper printed a reunion photo, Winters would be sure it would show my screwed up countenance.

"Why were you holding those bags of food?" Aunt Madge asked as she leaned over to pick up my little cat, Jazz.

"Scoobie wanted to take home some of the leftovers." We were drinking tea at the oak kitchen table, which is in part of an L-shaped open living area. At one end is a kitchen. The bedroom and bath are in the back, behind the kitchen. Guests are upstairs, so she has some privacy.

"That makes sense. Adam is probably on a tight budget."

Aunt Madge is the only one who calls Scoobie by his given name. I glanced at her as I scanned the page to look at more reunion photos. Today her hair was almost a honey blonde. She uses temporary color so she can easily change the shade of her shoulder-length hair, which she usually wears in a soft French twist.

There she sat, widowed for more than twenty years and reading the obituary section of the paper to see who she knew, getting ready to go upstairs and change beds in her guests' rooms because her husband had left little life insurance and she, with a degree in art history, did not have a lot of job prospects. Someone else might find it sad, or at least dull, but Aunt Madge never complains about a thing. Instead, she has used her creative talent to decorate her B&B and has developed some carpentry skills. She makes built-in shelves and small end tables, and she's been working on a doll house for one of my nieces for ages.

She glanced at me and smiled. "Did you see a lot of people you knew besides Scoobie and Ramona and Margo?"

"A lot of people who looked familiar and a few that I did remember. And one woman who wants me to appraise her grandparents' house. Gracie Allen. Her maiden name was…" I couldn't remember.

"Fisher," said Aunt Madge. "It's a great old house. One of the few older homes that wasn't subdivided for apartments. Probably needs some work if she wants a decent price."

"I think Ramona's Uncle Lester is trying to talk Gracie into listing it kind of high. That's why she wants me to look at it."

"You know the story?" she asked. I looked at her blankly, and she continued. "About the house?"

I shook my head as I reached for my tea. "What kind of story?"

"You'll like it, lots of unanswered questions."

I stuck my tongue out at her and she pointed her finger at the newspaper. "You said you were going to stop that."

"What fun is a bad habit if you can't do it at home?"

Aunt Madge shook her head, but I knew she didn't mind what she has called my "somewhat impertinent view of the world."

"Mrs. Fisher, Gracie's grandmother, grew up there. Let's see, what was her name?" She paused for a moment, and waved her hand. "Doesn't matter. She was one of four children, two boys and two girls."

For a moment that sounded familiar, and then I remembered it was Margo's goal.

"Mrs. Fisher, oh, Audrey Tillotson, that was her maiden name, got married in that house. Her brother Richard gave her away, because her father had already died. Why was that?"

I waited patiently. Aunt Madge is not usually one to digress, so I figured she had a point. "Oh, of course. He died of the flu, but after 1918. Anyway, Audrey, Gracie's grandmother, was married in 1929, not long before the Crash."

"How do you know that?"

"It's part of the story." She gave me a reproachful look and continued. "Richard was apparently nervous about his father-of-the-bride type of duties. He was pretty young himself, and he helped himself to a good bit of the rum punch before going upstairs to escort Audrey down the front staircase for the service."

"Wasn't that during Prohibition?" I asked.

"They weren't after the people who had it for weddings. The press would have made police look like fools if they raided weddings. Anyway, Richard was halfway down the stairs with Audrey when he stepped on her dress and she fell forward and then missed a step. He caught her elbow, she wasn't hurt. But supposedly she was mad as a hornet, and so was the groom."

I tried to feign interest. This sounded pretty dull so far. "Doesn't sound like a story for the paper."

"Stop interrupting. The ceremony went fine, but about halfway through the reception, Audrey's husband, what was his name?"

"Fisher?"

"I meant his first name. Peter, that's it. Peter Fisher had had enough to drink that he went over to Richard Tillotson and started accusing him of stepping on Audrey's dress on purpose, to make her look bad, because Richard was mad that Audrey was getting married and leaving him in the house with their mother and the two younger children when he, Richard that is, wanted to move out on his own."

I didn't realize I'd been tapping my foot until Aunt Madge glanced under the table. I stopped.

"Audrey's mother and someone else pulled Richard out of the room because he was ready to hit Peter Fisher. Oh, did I say he'd already thrown his drink on him?"

"You left out that gory detail."

She ignored me. "So that was it, but two days later Richard was gone. Just gone."

"Gone as in he never came back?"

"That's right. After a few weeks, Audrey and her husband moved into the house. They had rented an apartment, but Audrey's mother was supposed to have a 'weak constitution,' and she really needed another adult in the house. I'm not sure why, the two younger children were close to their teens, I think."

"That's it?"

She stood up and picked up both of our empty tea mugs. "Not every story has an exciting ending. I just thought you'd like some local history."

"It's very interesting."

Aunt Madge shrugged. "I suppose not." She glanced at the door. "Would you let the dogs in?"

Mister Rogers and Miss Piggy are Aunt Madge's two shelter-adopted mutts. Both have enough retriever in them to be incurably exuberant, and they have a fondness for prunes, which Aunt Madge now keeps on the top shelf of her pantry in plastic containers. When Mister Rogers saw he had achieved his goal of getting attention he lowered his head to his front paws and, butt sticking in the air, wagged his tail so fast it was hard to keep track of it.

I slid open the sliding glass door and he and Miss Piggy bounded into Aunt Madge's large sitting room, as she calls her open living area.

Mister Rogers ran around the couch several times, Miss Piggy in pursuit. It was unusual enough behavior for them that I watched for several laps until I realized that Mr. Rogers had something in his mouth. I knelt down and clapped a couple of times. "Here, boy."

Aunt Madge was onto them now, too. "Sit!" she said, sternly. They both skidded to a stop, Miss Piggy landing on Mr. Rogers' rump. That caught him by surprise, and he opened his mouth to give a small yelp. As he did so, a tiny chipmunk sailed out, landed on the throw rug in front of him, and made a beeline for the tiny space under a nearby bookcase. It didn't look any the worse for wear. Mr. Rogers had probably held it between his tongue and the roof of his mouth rather than between his teeth.

I laughed, and my cat Jazz sailed off the back of the couch and stuck a paw under the bookcase. This stopped Mr. Rogers from doing the same, as Jazz tends to terrorize him by jumping on his back for a ride from time to time.

For a couple of seconds we looked at Jazz and listened to the chipmunk chatter at her paw. "No, Jazz." I picked her up, still laughing.

"Bad dogs," Aunt Madge said, which had no effect on them. Instead, they went to her, tails wagging, as if they expected a treat. She glanced at me. "I forgot to tell you. They must have found a nest of ground squirrels, because he had one yesterday. I've no idea where it is now."

This stopped my laughing. That and the fact that Jazz was trying to claw her way back to the floor. "You mean it's still in the house?"

"Yes. I just hope they don't make it to a guest room." She opened the sliding glass door, and the dogs went back out. "Can you imagine if one of them found it in a bathroom at night?"

"Can you imagine if I did?"

"Nonsense. At least you'd be expecting it."

CHAPTER TWO

HARRY STEELE CALLED about nine o'clock the next morning to say that Gracie Allen had specifically requested that I appraise her late grandparents' house. "I told her," he continued, "that her buyer could well end up paying for a second appraisal if the house doesn't sell quickly. She said that was fine."

"I think Lester Argrow is trying to get her to price it too high and she wants a second opinion."

There was a beat of silence before Harry said, "That's all we need. I heard that at a Board of Realtors' meeting last week he said I wouldn't know the true value of real estate in Ocean Alley if someone wrote it on a stone tablet for me."

"You know everyone thinks he's a bag of wind." Lester, who often meets clients in Burger King because his office is so small, is not a force to be reckoned with in the local economy.

"True. Even so, it won't be an easy one to appraise. The Tillotson family built it and I bet there hasn't been a mortgage on it for decades. Not too many comparables, either."

I knew that comparables, houses that are similar and can thus be used as a basis of comparison when I try to figure what a house is worth, would be hard to find for a single-family home that large and that old. Lester wants Harry to compare four-bedroom homes to a two-bedroom home Lester is selling, or something equally ridiculous, which is why Harry's appraisals are lower than Lester would like. Despite his efforts to get us to appraise a house higher so he can get a better commission, I like him. He's funny.

I told Harry I'd stop by the courthouse to see what I could find in the way of comps and he said Gracie wanted to meet me at the house at eleven. *Great*. Her presence would add an hour to the time it would take me to go through the place. It's not like I get paid by the hour. I get half of what Harry charges per appraisal. When I was a commercial realtor I made substantially more than that. But, since I'm in Ocean Alley to decompress, I'm happy with what I make.

AS I STOOD OUTSIDE the old Tillotson-Fisher home I counted the windows – nineteen – and looked for indications of wood rot. All in all it was in decent shape, with each window having both of its fairly new shutters and the paint barely peeling. It was a two-story with a cupola on top, and probably a good-sized attic. While few houses in Ocean Alley have basements, it did appear to have a crawl space, which helps prevent moisture from seeping into the house.

Whoever had last painted it had chosen a light grey and used a deep burgundy for trim. If Gracie was willing to spend a pretty penny to get it painted I figured she could add quite a bit more to the sales price. I walked onto the porch and ran my hand along the railing, shaking it lightly every few feet. Solid in most places. I peered in the front window, through a crack where the shade did not meet the window ledge, and was surprised to find the front room empty. That would make my job easier.

As I stood up a car pulled up to the curb. I raised a hand, expecting to see Gracie, and was surprised when Reverend Jamison, Aunt Madge's minister, got out of the car.

"Good morning, Jolie. Thinking of moving in?" He started up the walk toward the house.

"No, I'm waiting for Gracie so I can do an appraisal." I barely know him; in fact, I knew I had not impressed him because Harry Steele had told me I was the first young person Reverend Jamison had met and not invited to come to First Presbyterian Church.

His usually serious expression relaxed into a smile. "Madge told me you'd be over here. I stopped by the house."

"Uh. Great. Can I help you with something?"

He leaned against the railing, facing me. "As you know, I no longer have anyone to run the food pantry at the church."

Uh oh. "Don't you have a committee for that, or something?"

"Yes, but a committee needs a leader." He sighed and looked toward the street. "They are a good group of folks, but a lot of them are very senior citizens, and most of them are involved in other church committees. Watching you the last month, I gather you're fearless, which never hurts when you have to ask people for donations. So," he turned to face me, "how about running the food pantry for me?"

"Me?" My voice was unnaturally high, and I consciously lowered it to a normal tone. "I don't...I can't imagine..."

"You know a lot of people through your work and your high school friends. If you're half as well organized as your aunt you could do it with one hand tied behind your back."

The honking of Gracie's horn as she pulled up to the house caused me to jump, and I stammered. "I have a hard time managing myself most of the time. I wouldn't know what to do," my voice trailed off.

"Your friend Scoobie helps out occasionally, I suppose as a thank you for getting food sometimes." I detected a glint in his eye. "He could show you the ropes."

"Am I late? I thought I was early." Gracie hurried up the walk, a blue knit cape over her shoulders and a bright red duffle bag in one hand. "Hi Reverend, remember me?"

"I do, Mrs. Allen. You sang a beautiful solo at your grandmother's funeral."

"You've lost all credibility, Rev. I was so nervous my voice cracked on every other note." Gracie joined us on the porch.

Reverend Jamison smiled genially. "Beauty is not always in the tone." He pointed his index finger at me. "Think about it. We need the help, and your schedule is flexible."

With that, he walked lightly down the steps. "Good luck selling the house."

We watched him drive off, and Gracie turned to me. "What are you supposed to think about?"

"He wants me to run the food pantry at First Prez."

"Ha!" Gracie pulled keys from her duffle bag and turned to the door. "That's what you get for having your picture in the paper with bags of leftover food."

I stifled the urge to say something rude about George Winters and followed her into the large foyer. Once inside, the professional appraiser in me took over and I pulled my tape measure out of my bag as I looked around. The twelve-foot ceilings had beautiful crown molding that had been stained in a light cherry. It was fortunate they had never been painted.

"This is where my grandmother put the Christmas tree," Gracie said, standing in front of the largest window in the living room. "You could see it from almost a block away." She looked around almost dreamily.

"I can imagine." I leaned over to place my tape measure on the floor at the far end of the room.

"Oh, I can help." She dropped her duffle back and walked over and put her foot on the end of the tape measure. "You can just pull it over there."

I was tempted to say something about having done this a few times, but didn't. She was, after all, trying to help. I had to tune her out half the time so I could write down the measurements and look under the kitchen sink for any sign of water damage.

"And then my husband got a job in Phoenix and we were there for two years. When he got transferred back East I told him I would never move to such a hot climate again. Not even if he got a big enough raise for a 5,000 square foot house."

I realized I must not have been listening for some time, because last I remembered she had been in Memphis. At this point, we were in the upstairs hallway and I was trying to figure out how to reach the short rope that hung from the trap door that led to the attic. "Is there a step ladder or something?"

When Gracie didn't reply I glanced at her and received a brief, cold stare. With a small degree of guilt I realized I had interrupted her mid-sentence. *Can I help it if she talks incessantly?*

"There's one in the far back bedroom." She indicated the direction with her head. "My husband brought it up so he could replace light bulbs."

"I'll grab it." I was anxious to get away from her for a moment. It was no wonder I couldn't remember her from high school. I'd probably blocked her out.

Of course it was wooden, not aluminum, so I dragged the stepladder back to the hallway where Gracie stood, careful not to scratch the well preserved hardwood floor. "If you'll steady it, I'll climb up."

"Sure," she said, in what could only be described as a frosty tone. "My mother said there are a few things up there, she didn't think I'd have any problem getting them down. That's why I brought the duffel bag."

I climbed up a couple of rungs, reached the rope and gave a sharp tug. The built-in attic ladder pulled halfway down easily, so I climbed off the step ladder and Gracie pulled it aside. I finished opening the stair-step ladder to the attic. I used a falsely bright voice. "Here I go."

As I got to the top of the ladder I pulled the small flashlight from my fanny pack and shone it around the attic. In contrast to the two lower floors it was crammed with stuff, much of it covered in old sheets. It looked like a ghost convention. I sneezed.

"Bless you," Gracie said.

"Did you know how much stuff is up here?"

"I thought there wasn't that much." She paused. "I was here a couple of months ago to arrange to have grandmother's personal stuff and a few pieces of furniture moved out before the auctioneer came, but my mother said she told him not to go up there."

I shrugged in her direction. "You better come up and look. Some of the things not covered in sheets look better than rummage sale stuff." I shone the light toward a small octagonal window at one end of the large room. If we brushed dust off it there would be some natural light. "Maybe you'll find a pile of antique silver or something."

I heard her start to climb the ladder, and there was bitterness in her laugh. "I think my mother carted off all of that a long time ago."

I hauled myself into the attic, dusted off my jeans, and pulled out my tape measure. *This is going to be a real bear.* There was way too much stuff to pull the tape measure in a straight line.

I moved out of the way so Gracie could get into the attic and almost knocked over a dress form shrouded in a sheet. "Excuse me." It was involuntary, and Gracie and I both laughed.

She stood, hands on hips, and surveyed the contents. "Damn her. This is going to take a lot of work."

"Maybe you can sell it with the stuff in it. Or maybe an antique dealer would haul it out."

She sighed. "I'll still have to go through it. Actually," she moved away from me, "there was a bunch of quilts grandmother made that I never found." She turned a full circle and gave a deep sigh. "I don't know why I didn't think to look up here. As ticked as I am that my mother left me to handle this, maybe it's a good thing she told the auctioneer not to come up here."

I walked over to the window and brushed away cobwebs and grunge, which let in more light than I had expected. I wiped my hand on my jeans and extended the tape to measure the window. At the sound of metal striking metal, I turned to see Gracie opening the latch on a large trunk. "That old trunk's probably worth a lot by itself."

"Could be." She fumbled in it and drew out a stack of old magazines. "Gawd." She peered at them. "These are *Life* magazines from the 1950s!"

"Who says there aren't treasure troves in attics?" I continued working, checking the ceiling for obvious signs of leaks (there were none) and then shining my light on the floor. Solid, probably pine.

There was a loud 'plop' and I saw that Gracie had just thrown a pile of stuff down to the floor below.

"Bunch of old blankets and clothes." She shrugged. "Have to start somewhere."

I nodded. "You want to go below and I'll throw you down some of the lightweight stuff?" I figured I could make up a bit for not listening to her babble.

"That would be great." She looked around. "I'll toss a few more things and then go down before the pile down there gets too big."

"Sure." I had the tape measure on the floor and was trying to measure the width of the attic in small bits.

After a few minutes, she started down the ladder. "When you get over this way, why don't you open that wardrobe and throw me down some of the clothes that are in there?"

"Sure thing." As she descended, I studied the room more carefully. It looked as though the oldest items were in the far corners. I could see what looked like a treadle sewing machine and a couple of other dress forms, and a rusty shovel. Next to the shovel was a large rocker with the woven seat in tatters. *That would be hard to fix, but it would bring a pretty penny if you did.*

I made my way back to the trap door and looked down. Gracie had shoved most of what she had tossed down to one side. "Holler when you're ready."

"Any time." She looked up.

I opened the wardrobe and was surprised at how tightly packed it was. I pulled out about six inches of old wooden hangers and their contents on the far left, and immediately sneezed a bunch of times. My arms were full, so I leaned over and rubbed my nose on my shoulder. *Gross.*

I turned and threw the batch of clothes toward Gracie and reached into my pocket for a tissue. A couple of good blows and I turned back to the wardrobe. The next group of clothes was much heavier, maybe winter clothes, I thought, so I put half of them back in the wardrobe. As I gathered the clothes, the man's suit closest to me felt stiff, and I held it back to look at it.

My scream was instinctive and, Gracie said later, very loud. I had a good look at the head of the skeleton before it rolled onto the floor and I jumped back to topple through the open trap door.

CHAPTER THREE

I ONLY WENT TO THE HOSPITAL because Gracie insisted. She had grabbed my shoulders so my head didn't hit the floor very hard. It was my derrière that hurt, and I walked hunched over down the steps to the first floor.

I have to give Gracie credit. She was very calm until we actually got to the hospital. Then, with me in the capable hands of a nurse, she began to cry in deep gulps. "I thought you were going to end up dead."

I eased onto the gurney, with the nurse's help. "Somebody sure did."

This stopped her tears. "Do you suppose…did you ever hear the story?" Gracie started groping in her purse for a tissue.

"If you can't lie on your back, turn so you face me," the nurse was saying. "I need to take your blood pressure."

"Aunt Madge told me something about your grandmother's brother."

"Are you Madge Richards's niece?" the nurse asked. "You were in the paper again yesterday, weren't you?"

"Ouch. Yes." I tried to get comfortable, but it was a losing battle.

"Our tenth high school reunion," Gracie sniffed. "Who would have thought we'd find a skeleton in the attic?"

"Skeleton?" the nurse looked up sharply from trying to fasten the blood pressure cup to my arm. "Where?"

At this, I got the giggles. All I could think of was a skeleton in the closet.

Gracie sat up straighter. "It could have been murder, you know."

"Whose murder?" the nurse asked, aghast.

Gracie hesitated. "Well, one of my grandmother's brothers disappeared. This was a long time ago."

"Aunt Madge said 1929," I added.

"I'll need to call the police," the nurse said.

"Why?" Gracie and I asked.

"It's my responsibility." She left the room.

We looked at each other. "Does it really hurt?" Gracie asked.

"I'm sure it's just bruised." Seeing her worried expression, I added, "I'm too well padded to do any real damage to my buns."

She smiled weakly. "Should I call your aunt?"

"No need," Aunt Madge said, as she pulled the curtains aside and walked into the tiny examining room. "Sonya at the front desk knows me from the Red Cross."

"You know everyone." I wished that my activities were not so immediately known. Sometimes it feels like I live in a bubble.

Aunt Madge extended her hand to Gracie and they introduced themselves. "I knew your grandmother and mother, of course," Aunt Madge said.

"Of course," I said.

"Don't be sullen, Jolie. You aren't hurt that badly."

I, preferred sympathy to scolding "Maybe I broke my back"

She raised an eyebrow. "I suppose you should tell me what happened." She pulled up a chair and then looked at her watch.

Every afternoon, Aunt Madge makes homemade bread for her guests at the B&B, so I knew she would want to get back there within an hour.

We relayed the events at the Tillotson house, and I played down my fall from the attic. "Really, Gracie made such a good catch she's thinking of trying out for the Mets."

"Try the Yankees," she said, and even Aunt Madge smiled.

WHEN I HIT THE FLOOR, the sharp pain seemed to go from my butt to my toes, and then settled in my tailbone. It turned out I had cracked my tailbone. Obviously this would be easier to recover from than a cracked skull, but I'm not sure it's less painful. I had no idea that wiggling your toes could cause so much pain. And getting off the sofa in Aunt Madge's great room was like getting spanked with a paddle.

I had slept on the sofa so as not to have to walk up the flight of steps to the room I share with Jazz. Much as I love my cat, I was furious with her. The chipmunk was still in residence under the book case, and several times during the night Jazz had walked over and stuck her paw through the small oval opening at the bottom of the bookcase, which caused the chipmunk to chatter incessantly for almost a minute each time.

I relayed this to Aunt Madge when she came out to start the coffee pot for her guests. "At least you know where the darn little thing is." I had gotten off the sofa and was making my way to the powder room that adjoined the great room. This was harder than usual, as I was at a forty-five degree angle, staring at the floor as I walked.

"I've been keeping it in there by putting little bits of nuts and water under the bookcase." She opened the can of coffee and began measuring it into the coffee maker. "I don't want it strolling into the dining room."

I half straightened up, winced, and bent back over. "You're trying to domesticate it?"

"Don't be a twit. Next time I see Adam I'm going to ask him to move the bookcase. I'll have the door open and the poor thing can run out."

Because Scoobie has never corrected her use of his proper name, I recently asked him if he wanted me to use it. "Do I look like an 'Adam'?" he'd asked. *Case closed.*

It was just as well that I could not straighten up enough to look in the bathroom mirror. I knew my shoulder-length brown hair with its blonde highlights was hanging in clumps, and I had not taken off my eye make-up the night before. I likely would not be able to raise my arms enough to style my hair with the dryer, so I'd have to get used to looking like a drowned rat for a couple of days.

It was becoming apparent that I would have to break down and take another one of the pain pills the hospital doctor had given me. Since it's hard to think clearly on narcotics, I try to avoid them and had been taking only aspirin. *Bad idea.*

As I made my way back to the couch I heard Aunt Madge emit what could only be called a giggle. "What is it?" I asked.

She crossed the room and held back my covers so I could climb onto my makeshift bed. "It won't surprise you that the paper mentions you finding the body."

I groaned as I lifted my legs onto the sofa. "Skeleton. There's a big difference." I met her eyes and could tell she was suppressing a laugh. "What?"

"Your friend George Winters did not make the skeleton the prime focus of the article." She handed me the paper.

> While appraising the home of the late Mrs. Audrey Tillotson Fisher, Ocean Alley resident Jolie Gentil discovered a skeleton hidden in an attic wardrobe packed with clothes. There is speculation that it may be the remains of Richard Tillotson, Audrey Fisher's brother, who was reported missing in 1929.
>
> When asked if he suspected foul play, Ocean Alley Police Sgt. Morehouse said, "We will have to determine whether there was any reason for prior owners to have a skeleton such as those used in medical schools. At this point we've no reason to think so." When asked if he thought it could be Richard Tillotson's body, he merely said, "If so, and DNA tests might show this, it would certainly confirm that he did not leave his home in 1929 of his own accord."

I looked up at Aunt Madge. "Did not leave of his own accord?"
"It gets better." Aunt Madge said.

> Tillotson supposedly had an argument with his sister Audrey's husband, Peter Fisher, on the couple's wedding day, which was two days before he disappeared. Fisher believed that Tillotson may have deliberately stepped on the bride's wedding gown – nearly causing her to trip – as Richard Tillotson escorted his sister into the ceremony. Several older residents in town said they heard that Richard left because he was ashamed of his behavior the day of his sister's wedding.
>
> An upset Gracie Fisher Allen, Audrey's granddaughter, told the *Press* that she was never sure whether this story was true or something people made up after the fact to account for her grandmother's brother's disappearance. "I heard my great-grandmother didn't want to think that Richard deserted the family."
>
> Allen explained that Gentil had offered to throw some of the attic's many items down to Allen, who stood on the landing below. "I certainly didn't expect to find a skeleton, and I know Jolie was really surprised when the skull fell off at her feet. She lost her balance and fell through the trap door. I was just barely able to catch her head."
>
> A hospital staff member, speaking on condition of anonymity, said that Gentil had cracked her tailbone but did not stay overnight at the facility. Instead, the hospital provided her with painkillers and a foam donut, to make sitting more comfortable.

"What happened to all those privacy forms I signed?" I yelled, then winced.

Aunt Madge nodded. "That was very inappropriate." I could tell she was still trying not to smile. "Would you like one of those painkillers the article mentions?"

"No." I frowned at her and she raised an eyebrow. "No thank you. Well, maybe later."

News accounts of Richard Tillotson's 1929 disappearance contain a number of interviews with family members and friends, but provide little information. Several people remembered seeing Richard late the night of his sister's wedding. He was serenading the newlyweds under their hotel room window, with Fisher shouting from the window that Tillotson should go home. Tillotson ate dinner with his family the next night and said he was going back to the store after dinner. Staff of Bakery at the Shore, which Tillotson and Fisher operated together, said Tillotson was not in the store the next day, and they expected he was "hung over." He was reported missing later that day, when he did not go to the train station to bid the newlyweds goodbye as they left for their honeymoon.

I looked at Aunt Madge. "Somebody had to kill him."

She shrugged. "I suppose so. I can't imagine they'll find out now. That was so many years ago. Anyone with first-hand information is long since dead. Peter Fisher died more than twenty-five years ago."

THIS WAS EXACTLY Sergeant Morehouse's take on it a day later. "Listen, Jolie, any potential suspect is dead, there aren't any suspects, and there's plenty of current crimes to solve."

"You mean you're just going to let it alone?" I did my best to look reproachful, but this was difficult when I was slouched in a chair in his office, much as a senior citizen with an osteoporosis hump in her back.

He took on the parental tone he uses with me when I'm bugging him. "We aren't letting it alone. Before your friend Gracie went back to Connecticut she gave us a blood sample. We'll compare DNA from the skeleton to hers. That may tell us if she's related to the guy."

"You know it was a man?"

"The medical examiner says it was a man, yes. And," his voice rose a bit as he saw I was about to interrupt him again. "If the DNA test shows the two are related we can pretty well figure it's Richard Tillotson. Unless you have reason to think," he gave me a smug look, "there might have been other missing Tillotsons or Fishers."

I hate it when he patronizes me. He has said several times that he appreciated my help in solving Ruth Riordan's murder. I believe him, but I know he thinks I can be a busybody. I'm not. I'm just persistent, and I can't stand loose ends.

He held up his hands when he could tell I was about to ask another question. "Enough already. I've got current stuff to work on." He stood and gestured toward the door of his small office, then seemed to take pity on me as I stood up from my hunched-over position. "If Gracie says it's all right, I'll call you when we get the DNA test results." He shook his finger at me in a scolding gesture. "And it'll be a few weeks at least. It's not a high priority so we aren't paying for a quick-turnaround."

I nodded and called thanks as I walked into the hallway. The officer at the front counter buzzed me out of the office area into the small waiting room that leads to the street. My strategy with glass doors, which seem a lot heavier when your tailbone hurts, has become to wait by them and pretend to be looking for something in my purse. When someone whose tailbone isn't killing them comes along I let them open the door for me. I had rummaged for probably thirty seconds when I heard a polite cough behind me and looked up.

"Can I help you with that, ma'am?" I looked into the face of Lieutenant Tortino, and he had the nerve to laugh. "Sorry Jolie." He swung open the door and stepped out ahead of me. "The way you were standing I thought it was someone older."

I thanked him nicely, since he knows Aunt Madge pretty well, but his comment did not improve my mood as I drove toward Java Jolt, the boardwalk coffee house I frequent.

As I entered the shop, which has a lightweight wood door I could open myself, my eyes met those of Joe Regan, the affable owner. "Coffee's on the house Jolie, since you were in the paper today."

"Thanks, Joe, that's really nice of you." I pretended not to get his sarcasm, and set my purse and canvas tote bag that contained my foam donut on a chair and went over to serve myself. Java Jolt is one of the only boardwalk businesses open in the winter months, and its cozy atmosphere and free Internet access make it a popular place. Luckily it was not too busy now.

I could feel Joe's gaze on me as I added sugar and cream, and looked at him. He smirked. "Jeez, not you, too."

"You gotta admit that you get into some crazy situations. And you've only been back here what, two months?"

I regarded his Irish countenance and made a face at him. "Going on three, and it's not like I create my problems."

"Uh-uh." He turned to wipe the counter behind the large coffee thermoses.

I carried my coffee to the small table, and wished I had picked one further from the counter so my donut would not be so obvious. Lacking a reason to move to another seat in the nearly-empty shop, I pulled it from the tote bag, placed it on a seat, and sat down gingerly. As I winced I met Joe's eyes, which now looked concerned.

"Gee, kid, I didn't realize you were really hurt bad."

I sensed he felt a bit guilty for teasing me, and didn't mind a bit. "The doctor said it's almost as painful as crushed vertebrae." Seeing his increased concern I added, "But this might heal faster."

I hadn't been sitting there long when my mobile phone rang. Harry Steele asked how I was feeling. When I said a bit better, he said he had two appraisals to be done the next week. "If you aren't up to it, I can handle them, of course."

Both were cottages with few steps and I said I'd do them.

"Oh, and Reverend Jamison called. He said you've been considering running the food pantry over at the church." Harry's expression was questioning.

"Reverend Jamison is considering me doing it. I can't see how I could manage that."

"Hmm." He paused for several seconds, and I wasn't sure if he had hung up or was thinking. "You would have the skills, of course. Just a matter of whether it's something you think is worth doing."

"Are you trying to make me feel guilty if I say no?"

"Maybe just a little." I could hear the smile in his voice. He and Aunt Madge both go to First Presbyterian, which they and most of its other congregants affectionately call 'First Prez.'

I sighed. "I'm going to see what Scoobie thinks. He's gotten food from there." I took down the addresses of the houses and said I'd come to the office in a couple of days to get keys if I needed them.

The coffee seemed to have a bitter taste, and I almost said something to Joe when I realized it could be the pain medicine I had taken an hour earlier. Without it, I'd still be standing at a 45 degree angle. However, taking it meant I had to walk and drive very carefully. I could only imagine what George Winters would make of an arrest for being under the influence of narcotics.

My cell phone rang again and I was surprised to hear Gracie Allen's voice.

"I thought you left town."

"I had to come home because I'm the one who drives the kids to school, but I wanted to see how you are. I feel so bad."

I knew her sympathy was genuine, but as I was the one walking around with the pain in my butt, I wasn't inclined to let her totally off the hook. "I'm standing up straighter, but the doctor said it could be a couple of months before I'm pain-free."

"Will you be able to work?"

"Uh, if you mean can I finish your appraisal…"

"Goodness no. I don't even want to think about that house until you're really ready to do it." She was tripping over her tongue making sure I didn't think her unsympathetic. Maybe she was afraid I'd sue, or something.

"I just meant," she paused for a couple of seconds, "I know you're self-supporting. I wondered if I should offer to well, you know, give you some money. It was my grandmother's…"

I laughed. "Harry's already found two houses with no steps that I can do next week. It takes more than a sore tailbone to keep me home."

"That's good. I mean, that you can get out, and all. If you need anything, anything I can do from Connecticut, would you let me know?"

"Sure. You gave me six phone numbers, you know." She had. Two at her house, her mobile, numbers at her husband's office, plus his mobile.

"Listen," she went on, "I'm not sure when I can get down to Jersey again, and I don't like the idea of spending a lot of time in that attic…"

"It beats the floor below." When she didn't respond, I added, "I'm just kidding."

"Oh, right." She stopped, and I could hear her take a breath. "I wondered if, when you feel better, you would be interested in sorting through the attic. For money, I mean."

My initial inclination was to say no, and then I thought about Sgt. Morehouse's reluctance to investigate, even if it did appear to be murder. "Well…"

"We could pay you by the hour, or you can quote an overall amount. I just, I just don't want to go through that stuff. I can't imagine there's much up there I'd want. And now there's all this talk about Richard." Her voice trailed off.

"I don't mind, but you know I can't cart anything out of the attic." Idly I wonder if it would be hard to get things out of there. It's a wide trap door, but it would take at least two people to get some of that stuff down the ladder.

"What about Scoobie?" she asked. "Or when you get it organized I can pay movers or something."

Why hadn't I thought of Scoobie? "Scoobie probably wouldn't mind." The more I thought about it, the more I liked this idea. Scoobie and I would probably have fun.

We talked for several more minutes, discussing the kinds of things she would like to know about ("Mostly if it looks like some kind of heirloom, like the quilts. I don't give a tinker's damn if it's just an antique") and how much she would pay us. We left it that Scoobie and I would go back to look through the attic and work up an estimate for her. Harry still had a key.

As I hung up, my gaze met Joe's. "I could see you salivating," he said, not bothering to suppress a grin.

"I'm not that hard up for money." I tried to keep an edge out of my voice.

He laughed. "I meant about the chance to look around. You know you like getting into other people's knickers."

I tried to look affronted, but failed. "I just like things to add up. This doesn't."

He was still chuckling as he turned to greet a new customer. "If it isn't the king of Ocean Alley real estate."

Lester Argrow barely nodded at him. "Say, Jolie. Ramona told me you were going to try to get out today." Without invitation, he pulled out a chair, turned it backwards, straddled it, and looked at me like a puppy. "When do we start?"

"It'll be a couple of days until I can get back to the appraisal…"

He waved a hand dismissively. "I don't mean that. I mean the investigation."

At the counter, Joe turned his back, probably so I wouldn't see him laughing.

"Lester, you know that's up to the police. Sgt. Morehouse will really get into it."

"That old fart? He doesn't like to do anything extra. Beside," he eyed me with some suspicion, "he said he told you he figures there's not much to be done after all these years."

Caught in a lie of omission, I tried not to look as uncomfortable as I felt. As much as I like Lester's direct approach to the world, his level of tact is many degrees below mine. "I don't know what anyone can do at this point." I carefully did not say *we*.

"I was thinking," he continued, unrebuffed, "that we could probably poke around that attic. George Winters said the cops said it was full of old stuff. Maybe there's clues."

"That sounds like the perfect place to start," Joe said, leaning on the coffee bar.

I tried to remain unruffled, reminding myself that Joe's coffee shop was the only one open in the Ocean Alley off-season. "We'd need permission," I shot Joe a warning glance, "and I can't imagine that Gracie would want people poking through her family's things."

"I have a key. On account of she's going to ask me to list it."

"But if you enter for another purpose, that's trespassing, isn't it?"

He gave me another dismissive wave. "I could say we need to look around, since I'm trying to establish an asking price and you're the appraiser." He changed tacks seemingly without missing a beat. "You are going to appraise it for a good price, aren't you?"

Since I preferred this topic, I tried to be encouraging. "It's a beautiful house, and they've kept it in terrific condition. But," I needed to put on some brakes, or he'd be trying to convince Gracie to sell it for twice its worth, "It's almost unique in Ocean Alley. You know people don't like to buy the most expensive house in an area because they may not be able to recoup the price when they resell it."

We argued this point for a couple of minutes until Joe said, "Lester, I thought you did your real estate business over at Burger King."

"Yeah." He turned to Joe with a small frown. "But I'm startin' to think they're gettin' tired of it. I think it's since I started getting more popular. You know, bringing more customers there. Usually they only order coffee."

I saw the light bulb go off in Lester's mind, but Joe seemed to miss it.

"Hey, what if I brought them here?" He turned his chair to face Joe by bumping it along the floor. "That could be good for both of us, right?"

I stood, or stooped, at that point, excusing myself by saying I needed to go home to take a pain pill. I was tempted to stay and listen further as Joe tried to tactfully suggest that there was better parking at Burger King, but I didn't want Lester to push me more on the value of the Tillotson-Fisher house. Joe gave me a dirty look as I put on my coat.

CHAPTER FOUR

SINCE HE DOESN'T HAVE a phone, it took me awhile to find Scoobie. Librarian Daphne, another of our classmates, gave him my message when he stopped in for his evening session, as he calls his routine visits, and let him use her phone to call me.

He was enthused about the idea of doing the work together, but not as much about the money. "I have to be careful not to earn much, or I get kicked off of Social Security disability," he explained. "You see," he added, "There's this thing called New Jersey workforce investment, and this counselor, he's trying to help me get some training."

"Training for what?"

He warmed to the topic. "I think I could work in radiology. You know, x-rays." He paused. "Which you certainly know all about."

"Very funny. What, they pay for you to go to school?"

"Yep. If I can be trained in something that I could do without getting depressed or ticked off a lot, then I could go off disability."

"And doing x-rays fits that bill?" I was not sure how to phrase the question.

"It means I wouldn't have to work in a room with lots of people all day. I'm better off that way." He said it very matter-of-factly.

"I don't think of you as easily ticked off," I volunteered.

"That's because I don't find you to be a major source of frustration." I could hear the humor creep into his voice. "But," he continued, "I'm sure Sgt. Morehouse does."

AUNT MADGE HAD TWO of her muffins and a plate of scrambled eggs for Scoobie when he came over at nine o'clock the next day. "I'm concerned you don't get enough protein, Adam." Scoobie thanked her profusely.

She was also concerned that I not go up the attic ladder while I was still so "rickety," as she put it. I heartily agreed, as did Scoobie, who said he didn't want me getting injured on his watch. While Scoobie ate and I had another cup of coffee we agreed that I'd go up to the second floor and take notes as Scoobie yelled down a rough inventory from the attic.

Before we left, Aunt Madge opened her sliding glass door and Scoobie moved the bookcase away from the wall, working slowly so as not to squish the chipmunk. I was not too worried about the little rodent. I was tired of looking for it every time I took underwear out of a laundry basket. However, we were disappointed that he was not in residence. He had left a couple of small black dots, which I took to be chipmunk poop.

Scoobie looked at the plastic lid from a coffee can, in which Aunt Madge had placed two sunflower seeds and a little water. "I don't know why he'd move out with you providing free room and board."

"You're worse than Jolie." She stooped down to look under the sofa.

GETTING UP THE LONG FLIGHT of stairs from the first floor of the Fisher house was not made any easier by Scoobie telling me he'd watch my back side. By the time I finished laughing as we climbed the steps I needed a pain pill. Since I had to walk down the steps in an hour or two, I decided to forgo it until then.

I stood back as Scoobie pulled down the attic ladder and made sure it was fully extended. "So this would be about where your butt hit the floor?" He stamped lightly on a spot a couple of feet from the base of the ladder.

"Not something I care to think about. Get *your* butt up the ladder."

He saluted and climbed. "Good grief! This place is packed." He sneezed several times and I saw him rub his nose on the top of his sweatshirt. He peered down at me. "Do you have any ideas on where you want to start?"

"Not really. I guess start closest to you and work back."

I watched from below as he turned slowly, taking in the enormity of our project. "I guess I'll start right where I am and work back toward that really old trunk under the eaves. I bet that'll take us a couple of hours."

I groaned. "I should have thought about bringing a chair."

"Wait a minute." He strode across the floor above and I could hear him moving some heavier pieces out of the way. His face, with a cobweb descending from his chin, appeared at the top of the trap door. "Move back and I'll walk this little stool down."

The narrow stool had an oak seat and had metal rungs down each side. He blew dust off the seat as he placed in on the floor. "It goes to that old sewing machine in the back."

"Perfect. Thanks." I put my donut on the seat and sat down.

With another salute, he went back up.

He first hollered down the contents of the wardrobe that had contained "your friend Richard." He thought that most of the clothes were from the 1940s or 50s, which is what I remembered, too. "Are you some kind of fashion expert?" I called up.

His face appeared at the trap door. "Salvation Army sometimes has really old stuff around Halloween. You'd look good in one of those 1940s suits with the huge shoulder pads." He pulled back up as I pretended to be about to launch my pencil at him. "Oh boy. I think one of these little furs has a fox's head on it."

"That's because it was a fox. Anyone who wore that today would probably get paint thrown on them." I wondered idly if there was anyone I'd like to see this happen to. As I wrote down the number and types of items in the wardrobe it occurred to me that these were of much more recent vintage than the skeleton, assuming Richard Tillotson had been killed just after his sister's 1929 wedding. I hollered this up to Scoobie.

His voice drifted down. "We're taking inventory, not solving a murder. Do I need to remind you that the only reason you lived through your last attempt to meddle is because of me?" There was a sound of a metal latch being opened and Scoobie said, "Wow. You should see what's in this little chest!"

"What? What?" *A murder weapon?*

"It's all these old games and toys. Geez. This is a really early Monopoly game."

I chided myself for wanting something gory. "That'll be worth something on eBay."

I wrote down the number of wooden toys and listed the games – chess, checkers, and a cribbage board in addition to the Monopoly game.

Why was the skeleton in a wardrobe with clothes from the 1940s?

"Scoobie?" He sneezed in response and I continued. "Was there any dirt on the floor of that wardrobe?"

"What do you care? You aren't coming up to clean." He blew his nose loudly.

"Maybe they buried him and dug him up."

Scoobie's head appeared again. "Did anyone ever teach you to mind your own business?"

"No. You don't get to know about potential properties coming on the market if you mind your own business." When he looked puzzled, I added, "When I did real estate work in Lakewood."

He shrugged and disappeared and I heard him reopen the door to the wardrobe. "I don't see any dirt. But lots of people looked up here after you found your friend."

"What? Oh, police." Of course, I knew they had visited the attic during their cursory investigation. Sgt. Morehouse's words came back to me. *Any potential suspect is dead, there aren't any suspects, and there's lots of current crimes to solve.*

"What are you looking at now?" I stretched my neck, which was becoming sore after looking up at the attic opening for so long.

There was the sound of a something being opened, a metal trunk I thought.

"Wow," Scoobie said, "this is full of old photo albums. Like ten or fifteen of them."

"Gracie will want those. Why don't you start bringing them down?"

"Why?" he asked.

"Because they don't have their own legs and it's the only way to get them out of there."

"I don't have to do this, you know."

I knew he wasn't mad. His backside appeared at the top of the ladder, several photo albums in his right hand and his left reaching down to steady himself as he climbed down the ladder. Dust stuck to the cuff of his jeans and what I could see of the palm of his left hand was darkened with dirt.

"Where do you want these?" he asked as he neared the bottom of the ladder.

"My car, I guess. I'll look through them a little so I can tell Gracie what they are."

"Why don't we go get a drink and come back?" I started to say we'd never get done if we took a break every hour, and then Scoobie sneezed again. I realized he probably wanted a break from the dusty attic and agreed.

We went to Java Jolt where Joe looked less than thrilled to see Scoobie until, while Scoobie was in the men's room cleaning up a bit, I explained what we were doing.

"That's nice of you," Joe said as he poured Scoobie's requested large hot tea. "I was worried his red nose might mean he was drinking again."

"Not that I know of."

Joe gave me a look that seemed to say "Right," and handed me Scoobie's tea. I put it on a table, filled my coffee cup from the thermos on the counter, and dug in my purse for money to put in the sugar bowl next to the thermos. Joe puts us all on the honor system during the off-season.

As I sat on my foam donut, Scoobie came back in and bought two muffins, one chocolate chip and one blueberry. He grinned as I groaned.

"I don't need the calories. By the time I can move around well I'll have gained five pounds."

He shrugged as he took a bite of the blueberry muffin. "Skip dinner."

Since I can never resist chocolate, I took a bite of that muffin. "Did you look at any of the photos in those albums?"

"Nope. I figure you'll spend ten hours on it, so why should I?" He took a sip of tea. "Speaking of skipping dinner, what did you tell Reverend Jamison about the food pantry?"

"I'm avoiding it. Don't you think he'll get the hint?"

"Nope. He told me I'm supposed to help you. I think he scheduled some kind of meeting on it in a few days."

"Damn it." I stared into my coffee cup for a moment. I certainly could do it, but I definitely didn't want to. I knew I would be uncomfortable around people who are grateful for food, something I have always been able to assume will be available.

"How much?" I asked. When Scoobie only looked at me I added, "help. How much help will you give me?"

He shrugged. "I can tell you what I don't like about the way it's been done."

"What's not to like?"

"You can get a box of stuff six times a year. It's...."

"Why only six times?" I interrupted him.

"Because that's all the food they have to give." His look told me not to interrupt again. "I'd rather be able to go once a month and get smaller boxes. So would a lot of other people."

"There's got to be a reason they do it that way," I mused.

When I glanced back at him his look was unreadable, but I sensed he hadn't liked my comment. "What?" I asked.

"The people running things always like schedules the way they are. At the treatment center I went to in Newark there's hardly any staff there on weekends because they don't like to work weekends." He gestured with the remaining half of his muffin. "We didn't need any less counseling on Saturday and Sunday."

I nodded slowly. "I get your point. If I do it, I'll look at all of it. Just don't expect," I paused, not wanting to offend him, "Don't expect a lot of changes all at once. It'll take me some time to figure out how everything works."

He stood and began pulling on his jacket.

"Does this mean you're through with ideas?" I asked.

"Nope." He finished shrugging into his jacket. "But it probably makes sense to talk more about it after you get your feet wet. At least after you talk to Elmira Washington." He grinned.

Scoobie knows I'm not a fan of Elmira, who told everyone she knows in Ocean Alley that I left my husband Robby because he embezzled money to support his gambling habit. I groaned. "You mean she's on the Food Pantry Committee?"

"Unless you kick her off. Come on, pick up your little pillow and let's get back to work." He moved over to help me with my coat.

"You an expert on the food pantry, Scoobie?" said Joe Regan from the other side of the counter.

"Did you hear something?" Scoobie asked, looking at me intently.

"I think…" I began.

"Forget it," said Joe.

Scoobie walked out ahead of me, not looking at Joe. I glanced at Joe whose shrug in my direction seemed to be half apology and half 'go figure' expression.

It took me a few seconds to catch up with Scoobie, and only then because he slowed down enough to allow me to. "I, uh, don't think he meant to be rude."

Scoobie's expression was unreadable. "Then he should mind his own damn business."

"Right." We walked a few more steps in silence, and Scoobie stopped, so I did, too.

"I think I'm going to the library. I'll catch you later, Jolie." He turned and strode the other direction down the boardwalk.

I walked the short distance to my car wishing I'd said something different. When Scoobie and I were by ourselves it was easy to forget that he had "issues," as he put it. Maybe Scoobie thought I was sticking up for Joe. "Damn it!" I kicked at the lid of a soft drink cup, and then swore again. My tailbone was not up for kicking anything.

CHAPTER FIVE

AUNT MADGE HELPED ME CARRY IN the photo albums. She placed them on the large oak table in her kitchen/great room combo.

I moved toward the kitchen counter. "I'll get some damp paper towels and wipe off any dust."

"I'm not sure that's a good idea." She almost stroked the cloth binding on the top album.

"It's not sacred scripture, you know."

"I'm well aware of that. But they are part of someone's life, surely someone long gone. It almost feels as if we'll be trespassing to read them."

I smiled at her use of 'we' as I dampened a couple of towels. Aunt Madge prides herself on not gossiping, but I knew she was as eager to look at the albums as I was. For starters, I wanted to see Richard Tillotson's face in something other than a grainy old newspaper photograph.

The albums weren't that dusty, since they'd been in a trunk. What they were was falling apart. As Aunt Madge opened the top one – its velvet cover a deep red in all but a corner that had evidently been more exposed to light and was almost pink – there was the crackle of aged paper and the three photos slid sideways on the page.

"Do you suppose someone took them out at some point?" I asked.

"No. The glue just dried up, that's all." She moved the photos back to their original spots on the page and closed the book. "I have some of those little adhesive corners you use to put photos in albums. I don't think it would hurt anything to fasten these more securely. I'll help you after dinner."

AFTER I FINISHED DUSTING all the albums, I settled on Aunt Madge's couch and pulled one of them to me. I started with one that seemed close to the time of Richard Tillotson's disappearance. It was a challenge to figure out which photos went with which captions, and I was not sure I should refasten the ones that had come unglued. Eventually I figured if I didn't one of Gracie's kids would grab an album and scatter all the old photographs.

Richard was taller than most men in the 1920s, perhaps six feet. It made me realize that his skeleton must have been bent a little at the knees to stand up in the attic wardrobe. The pre-skeleton Richard had wavy dark hair and a broad smile. This was in contrast to his future brother-in-law.

Peter Fisher was almost a head shorter than Richard and his expression was usually somber.

There were several photos of a smiling Audrey Tillotson, and one of the captions said, "The day Peter proposed." Standing next to her, Peter Fisher almost cracked a smile. Two pages further there was a picture of Richard and a woman identified simply as Mary Doris. They had posed with the ocean in the background and were holding hands as they smiled at the camera. I jotted her name in my notebook. If she were still alive, she might know more about Richard's disappearance. Perhaps Aunt Madge would know who she was. I studied Mary Doris more, taking in the flapper girl's clothes and small hat and the long string of pearls that hung to just above her belly button. She and Richard looked as if they didn't have a care in the world.

Mary Doris was in several other photos, sometimes with Audrey and other young women of their age, which looked to be early twenties. This was clearly the Ocean Alley jet set of the times. I smiled at my mental choice of words. These women would never have heard of a jet airplane.

I couldn't take my eyes off their dresses. Did they always get so dressed up? The Tillotson family must have had a lot of money back then. My own has very few pictures of grandparents or aunts and uncles of the time.

When Aunt Madge came into the room a few minutes later I asked her about Mary Doris. "Mary Doris Milner," she said. "She lives at the nursing home on the edge of town. She must be, oh, in her mid-nineties."

"She's alive then? How do you think she'd react to a visit?"

Aunt Madge shook her head. "You need to leave her alone, Jolie. Uncle Gordon said Richard's disappearance struck her so hard that she went to stay with family in the Midwest for quite some time afterwards. She said she didn't want to see the ocean without Richard."

"She must have been embarrassed because she thought he left her."

Aunt Madge settled next to me on the couch and opened a copy of *Popular Science* magazine. "She got over him just fine, eventually. She got a teaching certificate and worked until she was well into her sixties."

"Did she ever marry?"

"No, but she was so close to her brother's family that her nephew and later his daughter would visit every summer for several weeks." Aunt Madge closed the magazine. "Her brother's granddaughter eventually moved here to stay with Mary Doris. What was her name?" She tilted her head back and closed her eyes, then opened them and looked at me. "She came her junior year of high school. She fought a lot with her mother, I think, but not Mary Doris."

After looking through another album that was after Richard's disappearance, I was done for the night. The albums had served their purpose. I had a lead in the form of Mary Doris Milner, and she was close at hand.

WHEN I WENT DOWN TO BREAKFAST the next morning Aunt Madge handed me a piece of paper with Reverend Jamison's name and phone numbers. "He won't give up, you know." She eyed me as she poured cream into a creamer. "He's at least as stubborn as you are."

"I prefer to think that I'm disciplined enough to follow through with things." I stuck the note into the pocket of my cotton slacks and helped myself to some orange juice.

Later that morning I called Reverend Jamison, who asked me to come to the vicarage to talk about the food pantry. "Feel free to bring Scoobie, if you want to."

I went alone, and listened patiently as he downplayed the time commitment, talking about how to get volunteers and which food banks donated to the church food pantry. He introduced me to the church secretary as we left his office to visit the pantry, which was adjacent to the church in its community room area.

"You're Madge's niece." She said this as if she thought I didn't know.

I took in her tight perm, slightly pursed lips, and the cardigan over her shoulders. She was probably about Aunt Madge's age, but dressed severely. I sensed disapproval oozing from every pore. "Yes, one of them. You might have also have met my sister Renée, she's the one who was more likely to go to church with Aunt Madge."

"I do remember the time you tried to take money out of the collection basket. For ice cream, I recall that you said."

"Chocolate." I followed Reverend Jamison out of the room.

He tossed a grin over his shoulder. "Mrs. Mackey doesn't think you are holy enough to work with our clients."

I appreciated his comment. "In my defense, I was three years old and didn't understand the concept of the collection plate. Besides, it's not like I'm supposed to make extra bread and fish appear from thin air."

"You may have to do a bit of that." His tone was more somber. "It gets harder to secure what we need. More people need help every year."

"Oh." The sinking feeling I'd had in my stomach dropped to my knees. *What am I getting myself into?*

He unlocked the door leading to the pantry and flipped on a light switch. The layout reminded me of a dry cleaner's shop. There was a no-nonsense counter at the front, but instead of rotating garment racks there were rows of shelves, none of which was full.

We walked through the approximately twenty-by-twenty room, and I noted that each shelf was labeled – canned fruit, tuna, vegetables, canned ham, and row upon row of pasta noodles. "Nothing fresh?" I asked.

"Rarely. We aren't set up to store it. We get some frozen turkeys before the holidays, but we pass them out the same day."

"So, if someone has kids..." I started.

"Some of the families have food stamps, some don't." He stopped to smooth a label that had come half unattached from its shelf. "If they get some non-perishable goods here it leaves them more for milk and eggs and such."

The door opened again and a young woman with a teenage girl came in. "Good morning Reverend. We're a little early, but I was able to get a ride instead of taking the bus."

"Megan, this is Jolie Gentil. I'm trying to get her to take the helm of the Food Pantry Committee." As I shook hands with Megan, he added, "Megan is one of our most regular volunteers. And," he glanced at the teenage girl, "her daughter Alicia comes with her sometimes."

Alicia nodded but said nothing. It appeared coming here was her mother's idea, not hers. As we left, Alicia was taking things from under the counter and setting them on top – a metal can with pens and pencils, a clipboard that appeared to be a sign-in sheet, and a large stack of paper bags.

We walked back to the vicarage without talking. I had my hands balled in the pockets of my hooded jacket, and was trying to imagine myself being in charge of the food pantry. I really didn't want to do it, but seeing Megan made me think there would be at least a few good volunteers.

"So," Reverend Jamison asked as we walked back to his office, "you want the keys and list of volunteers?" When I didn't answer immediately, he said, "At least give it a try. If it really isn't something you can do, you can always quit."

"The problem is I'm not much of a quitter. Even if I didn't want to do it, I'd let it eat me up rather than quit."

He nodded. "That's what I'm counting on."

I THREW THE KEYS INTO MY small jewelry box and set the two folders on the bed. One had a list of volunteers and the food pantry hours, the other food suppliers. Though the pantry is only open to the public three days each week, and Reverend Jamison stressed I did not have to be there every time it was open, I sensed that I'd spend a lot of time rounding up food. "Damn it, Jolie, how do you get yourself into these things?" Jazz meowed from her perch on my pillow, and I knew this was all the response I'd get.

Aunt Madge was out, so I went looking for Scoobie. I wanted to spend more time on the attic inventory so we could be done with it. I also intended to make him work as hard as I did at the food pantry.

Scoobie was in his usual spot at a table in the library, his notebook in front of him, probably working on some poetry. I placed my donut on the seat across from him and he raised his eyes to meet mine.

"I need to finish this." He bent over his writing again, and I sat still for almost three minutes. I knew it was that long because there is a big clock above the check-out desk.

Finally I stood and went to browse the magazine rack. Five minutes later Scoobie joined me. "What's up?"

Since he was holding the notebook in his hand I nodded toward it. Sometimes he shares his writing. "Can I see?"

He handed me the notebook and I read the few lines.

Midnight's here, the choice is ours
Lowered voices drift up the stair
We can choose to sleep and ignore the rest
Stay unconcerned, try not to care
Pay attention, they're about to decide
Watch the wall, better unaware

I never know what to say when I read Scoobie's poems. I met his eyes. "I thought you were writing something longer."

He reached for the notebook, not offended, but seeming to wish I'd said something different. "This is the first draft. Long is easy. Short takes more thought. Why are you here?"

"You want to go back to the old house again?" I asked. "We probably didn't even inventory ten percent." I tried to discern the mood he was in, but failed.

"I told Ramona she could come with us one of the times. She's really into antiques." He turned to walk back to the table that held his knapsack.

I liked this idea. "We can swing by the Purple Cow and pick her up." The Purple Cow is the local office supply store, and Ramona has worked there ever since she graduated from college. As close as I can figure, it gives her a salary but doesn't involve much use of her brain, which she likes to reserve for her art.

Every day, unless the winds are gale force, Ramona places a white board on a stand just outside the store and puts an inspirational saying on it. Occasionally someone erases it and substitutes a funny or rude message. I recently learned it's Scoobie, though Ramona doesn't know this yet. We pulled in front of the store, and I saw that today's message board read, "I believe that every single event in life happens as an opportunity to choose love over fear." Oprah Winfrey

"Hmm," Scoobie said. "Ramona's creeping into the modern age."

Rekindling Motives

We had called before we drove over to see if Ramona could leave early. She could and had her coat held over her arm as she showed a customer how to use the small photocopy machine.

We waited by the door and she joined us a minute later, her face flushed. "I am so excited about this. I bet there are lots of super things in that attic." She waved goodbye to Roland, the store owner, and thanked him for letting her leave an hour early.

"Did you see any dress forms?" she asked. "I make most of my own skirts and tops you know."

That explained how she had so many outfits that looked as if they were from the 1970s, a period she seemed quite fond of. "I think I saw one. But, um, you'd have to talk to Gracie about it. I had the impression she's going to have an auction or rummage sale."

"She'd let me buy it before then," Ramona said. "I used to help her write her English compositions in high school. She hated to write paragraphs and stuff."

I drove the short distance to the old house and as we got out of the car each of us stared at the top floor. "Hard to believe Gracie didn't know there was such a treasure trove up there," Ramona said.

"Or a dead person," said Scoobie.

I opened the car trunk and pulled out my donut. I planned to sit at the bottom of the ladder and take notes. I hoped Ramona's participation would let us move faster, but I thought it equally likely that she would stop to examine each item.

After an hour, the list of attic contents was growing, but so was the pain at the base of my spine. I was finding it hard to be interested in the whoops of laughter from Scoobie as Ramona tried on a broad-brimmed hat or draped a fox fur over her shoulders.

"Omigosh, this is awesome," Ramona yelled.

"What? What?" I called up to her.

"There's a bunch of really old dolls."

There was a clunk and Scoobie laughed. "And now there's a headless one."

The parts of me that didn't ache wished I were up there with them. "What kinds of dolls? Like Barbies?"

"Better," she said. "Did your mom have any of those dolls that wet themselves? They were my mom's favorites."

"Betsy or something, I think. My sister has it." I added it to the list.

"Damn, look at this train set." I could hear someone pulling a box across the floor toward the attic opening and Scoobie's head appeared. "Do you think Gracie would mind if I set this up at your aunt's to see if it runs?"

I shrugged. "I don't see why not. Then if she wants to sell it she'll know if it works."

He balanced the box on his shoulder and climbed carefully down the ladder. "I'll take it out and put it in your trunk." I tossed him my keys and he headed down to the main floor.

I jotted 'Lionel Trains' on my list. Gracie might have enough in that attic to pay for a couple of semesters of college books for her kids.

"Jolie, there a metal box in the back that's full of little..." Ramona sneezed several times.

"Bless you," I called up.

"Thanks." She sniffed mightily and continued, "Full of a bunch of what look like ledgers. Hmm." I could hear her flipping through pages. "Hard to figure out what they're about."

"Why don't you bring a few down and I'll take them home and look at them?" I couldn't imagine anything more boring, but it's not like I'm out on the town at night.

Scoobie's steps on the staircase were slow, and I figured the almost three hours we'd been here were a lot more tiring for him than Ramona and me, since he was the one who traipsed up and down the attic ladder the most. "You want to head home?" I asked.

"In a few minutes. I saw some old books in the back in a couple of boxes. I'll at least look in them to see what kinds they are." He steadied the bottom of the ladder as Ramona climbed down with an arm laden with the ledgers.

I had been thinking of the larger books with green pages that Uncle Gordon used to use for record-keeping, but these were smaller, maybe six by nine inches.

"Stop looking up my skirt," Ramona admonished.

"I'm not." He winked at me. "It's too long to get much of a view."

He climbed back up and Ramona sat on the floor next to me. "My nose is getting clogged from all that dust." She reached into the pocket of her skirt to pull out a handkerchief.

"We'll go as soon as Scoobie looks in those boxes of books he found." I leafed through the top ledger. They were leather-bound and had several thin pieces of ribbon affixed to the top of the binding. The ribbon was a light yellow at the top of the ledger, but when I turned to one of the pages a ribbon marked I could see the portions not exposed to light were brown. Though it had some pages with figures, more contained entries in sentences, and each entry was dated.

June 19, 1928. New mixer delivered. RT unpacked and read instructions. Painter finished in back room, carpenter did not come to put up shelves. Storm coming in, so left at two.

The writing was small and even, each letter written with precision. I scanned a few more pages. I assumed that RT was Richard Tillotson and that he and the writer were preparing for the opening of a store of some sort. Maybe it was Peter Fisher who referred to Richard as RT. The cramped writing made me think of Fisher's dour expression in several photographs.

More sneezing announced Scoobie as he came down the ladder. "Look at this! This might be a first edition of *All Quiet on the Western Front*, and there's a 1932 edition of *Tom Sawyer*."

I closed the ledger, placed a hand on each side of the sewing machine stool and stood, slowly. This was how I had figured to get up with the least pain, and it was hardly elegant. Undoubtedly Scoobie was only refraining from making cracks because I looked so sore.

"Did the doctor say when it would hurt less?" Ramona looked sympathetic as she held my coat for me.

"He said I'd start to feel a lot better after a week." I stretched, something that was already less painful than it had been a couple of days ago.

Scoobie carried the ledgers and his books out to the car, and I drove the three of us toward the Purple Cow, where Ramona wanted to be dropped off. Scoobie was absorbed in a book, and Ramona appeared lost in thought until she said, "You know, I keep thinking about that skeleton. When do we find out if it's Gracie's great uncle, or whatever he was to her?"

"Sergeant Morehouse more or less told me not to bug him about it because it would take some time. Something about not paying for a rush DNA analysis."

Scoobie snorted. "The skeleton's not in any rush."

"Hand me one of those ledgers, would you?" Ramona asked Scoobie.

"There aren't any empty pages for you to draw on." He passed one to the front seat.

We had arrived at the Purple Cow, and Ramona stuffed the ledger into her oversized handbag. "Sometimes numbers tell you a lot."

SCOOBIE JOINED AUNT MADGE and me for grilled cheese and clam chowder. Aunt Madge had moved a small table out of a corner near the sliding glass doors that lead to her narrow back yard. She ordered the dogs to stay a certain distance from the box of trains. Amazingly, to me, they sat about five feet away, occasionally looking at Aunt Madge and giving a short wag of a tail, as if they wanted to see if she had changed her mind.

Aunt Madge, who is always looking for ways to use her carpentry skills, was far more interested in the trains than the ledgers or albums and was soon on the floor with Scoobie going through the box to see which pieces of track went together to create the picture that was on the outside of the box.

When I pulled the third album from the coffee table to my perch on the couch I was pleased to see that it had pictures of the Tillotson house "the day we moved in." A photo taken inside the house also noted the date, which was in 1917. A young Audrey and Richard posed in front of a tea set and their parents in dressy attire as if they were going to a party. *You can bet they weren't unpacking the boxes.* The real estate appraiser in me took over and I marveled at the full wrap-around porch and shutters at every window. They were stout looking storm shutters and the lattice work around the base of the porch was intricate. The album ended with Richard holding a new baby and Audrey at about age ten standing next to him looking as if she were worried he would drop the little darling.

It wasn't until I looked at that photo that I realized that the fourth Tillotson child apparently wasn't born yet, and the two youngest children were enough younger than Richard and Audrey that they might still be alive. More people to talk to. I glanced toward the corner and was surprised to see Aunt Madge on her hands and knees, apparently trying to peer under a piece of track. Scoobie caught my eye and gave me an almost imperceptible shrug.

"I saw that." She straightened up.

"What are you looking for?" I asked.

"That piece of track is a little bent, and I want to see where I need to straighten it." She dislodged the piece from its connecting piece of track. Aunt Madge stood and walked toward her pantry where she keeps her indoor tool box, as she calls it.

"Having fun?" I asked Scoobie.

"I am, actually." He glanced towards Aunt Madge. "Learning a couple things, too. Did you know that the guy who invented Lionel trains tried to make the first one with a steam engine? It blew up."

"Nope. No brothers."

Aunt Madge made a harrumphing noise. "You don't have to be a boy to like trains." She had found a small pair of pliers and was walking back to sit on the floor next to Scoobie.

"True, but can you imagine my mother buying Renée or me something with tires other than a baby buggy?" My mother wanted her girls to be girls, as she put it. My sister is trying my mother's patience by letting her girls play soccer.

"Good point." She began to show Scoobie which part of the piece of track needed to be gently straightened.

I decided to wait to ask her about the youngest Tillotsons – she would only accuse me of trying to find more people to bother, and she would be right – and went instead to the stack of four old-fashioned leather books.

Just as I was trying to decipher the titles at the top of the columns on the first page Aunt Madge shouted, "Annie Milner. I knew I'd remember it."

"You mean the girl from our graduating class?" Scoobie asked.

"I most certainly do," Aunt Madge said.

I remembered Annie not from high school but because she worked in the county prosecuting attorney's office and had interviewed me when the windbag attorney was planning his case against yet another classmate. During the probable cause hearing she handed the prosecuting attorney notes a couple of times, leading me to think she was the one with the brains.

Scoobie said, "She got one of the mock awards that Jennifer passed out during the reunion, but I don't remember what for." He continued, looking at me. "She didn't come until the end of junior year. Really quiet, too. You wouldn't have known her."

"So, what about her?" I asked.

"She's Mary Doris Milner's grandniece." Aunt Madge looked as proud as if she'd finished replacing a board on the front porch.

CHAPTER SIX

I WAS HAVING A HARD TIME not calling Annie Milner. It made no sense to talk to her until we knew if the skeleton belonged to Richard Tillotson. I decided to annoy Sergeant Morehouse instead.

He made me wait twenty minutes before he came to the reception area to get me. "Thought maybe you'd get tired of waiting." He keyed digits into the security pad and opened the entry to the bull-pen of officers' desks and the tiny cubbyholes – they hardly qualified as offices – for sergeants and lieutenants.

"But you knew I'd be back, so why bother putting me off today?" I smiled at him and was half surprised when he smiled back.

He gestured to the one guest chair in his small, crowded office and plopped himself in his own. Sgt. Morehouse is about forty, and if he didn't wear polyester pants and inexpensive looking sports coats you might not think of him as a cop. Though he can be quite curt when he wants to be rid of me, his usual expression is halfway friendly.

"I told you we wouldn't get DNA evidence too quickly," he said.

I nodded. "I thought of a couple of other things, though." At his raised eyebrow, I continued, "Did you notice if the skeleton was dirty, or if there were specks of dirt on the wardrobe floor?"

"I'll tell you, Jolie, I don't know the criteria for a clean skeleton, and the floor of the wardrobe was damn dirty after who knows how many years. Why?"

"Because I wondered if it had been buried and dug up. I thought it might have soil on it." I met his eye as he gazed at me, unblinking.

He sighed. "It was dusty, mostly. But, the coroner's office did find some white powder in the back of the shoulder socket. Someone – whether it was a murderer or someone who had a deceased person exhumed for some other damn reason – did a good job cleaning the skeleton." He raised a finger to shake at me, "Like I told you…"

"I know, I know. You have lots of open cases to work on." I kept my tone pleasant. After all, he didn't have to tell me anything. "You may find this hard to believe, but I don't have skeletons jump out at me too often, so I'm naturally curious."

"There is nothing natural about your level of curiosity." His look was direct. "Why'd you ask that, anyway?"

"Because the clothes in that wardrobe were from the 1940s, according to Scoobie and Ramona. Seemed as if the skeleton was put in there long after 1929."

Morehouse made a note on a small pad in front of him and stood. "Gracie did say you could know the results of the DNA analysis. That'll still be at least a few weeks, probably." When I didn't stand immediately, he asked, "Doesn't Harry Steele have enough work for you?"

MY SEARCH FOR INFORMATION to use in appraising the Tillotson house was very frustrating. There were tax records on the property dating to the early 1900s, and I could see the steady rise in the tax bill as the value of the property rose, especially after the late 1950s. In 1918 it had been assessed at $2,600, a reflection of the family's wealth in times when many houses were worth far less.

The most recent assessment was for $380,000, but I couldn't use the tax assessor's value alone to come up with the appraisal amount. Anyway, there was no guarantee someone would pay as much as $380,000 for the house, which was in good condition for its age but would likely require a lot of updating in the kitchens and bathrooms, at least. On the other hand, get the right buyer and they might be willing to pay $425,000 or more. Especially if they were wealthy Manhattanites looking for a weekend place. What I needed were comparable recent sales, and there simply weren't any.

As I sat tapping my pencil on the binder in which the Miller County Registrar of Deeds kindly places information on recent house sales in each municipality in the county, George Winters walked in. "Fancy meeting you here." He sidled next to me at the Formica-topped counter.

"And you thought I was dying to see you?" I asked. "Maybe I wanted my picture taken again?"

"You left yourself wide open for that, Jolie." When I didn't respond he continued, "I heard you and Scoobie were going through the attic. Wondered if you found anything interesting."

"Scoobie really likes the Lionel trains." I put my pencil in my purse.

"You know what I mean, anything related to the skeleton." I turned toward the door and he continued, "Come on Jolie. I can't go in there to poke around."

I faced him squarely. "You promise not to write insulting stuff about me?"

He dropped my gaze.

"Ha! See, you can't promise."

A slow grin spread across his face. "It's just you give me so many opportunities." I pushed past him into the hallway.

"Okay, okay. Nothing insulting." He paused as I gave him a skeptical look. "For how long?"

"See," I, pushed the down button on the elevator, "You look for ways to needle me."

"Aw, Jolie. Come on. You're fun to cover."

We entered the elevator and the door closed. "I'm serious Winters, lay off for a while."

"Promise. Now, did you see anything interesting in the attic?"

As he opened the courthouse door to the street, I told him, "It's a treasure trove. Lots of old furniture, clothes, games. Ramona wants one of the dress forms. She's the only one I know thin enough to use it. But…" I considered whether to tell him the skeleton was in the cupboard with clothes from the 1940s and decided against it. "I can't say there was anything newsy."

His face fell. "Nuts. My editor keeps insisting there's a big story there. Solve that old murder somehow."

For a fleeting second I thought about discussing the clothes and photo albums. Of everyone in town, Winters might be my best brainstorming partner. Reporters were always trying to put pieces together. But, Gracie might not like the attention on her family, and she was paying Scoobie and me to look through the attic. Not that we had settled on a price. Instead, I said, "There might be a story there, but so far you don't even know if the body was Richard Tillotson's."

"How many other skeletons would be in that attic?"

WHEN I GOT BACK TO THE COZY CORNER B&B Aunt Madge had a message for me from Annie Milner. Though I'd seen her a couple of times other than the reunion I couldn't figure out why she'd call me.

"Jolie. Thanks for calling me back." Her voice was smooth as soft butter. "I wanted to run an idea by you, if you don't mind." When I said fine, she outlined her thoughts about running for the position of county prosecuting attorney in the spring primary. "I don't know if you were aware, but a lot of people thought Martin Small proceeded too quickly in accusing a suspect for Ruth Riordan's murder."

"I tended to agree with them," I said, dryly.

"I assumed you and your aunt did," she continued. "Rushing ahead is Small's general mode of operation. I would ask you not to repeat my opinion," she added hastily.

"Of course." I thought she was already talking like a politician.

"It's my opinion that the citizens of Miller County would be better represented by a more thoughtful approach to litigation. On top of the issue of basic fairness, there is the cost of pursuing a case too hastily."

Although I thought this was probably a carefully rehearsed speech, it also made sense. "So, what are you asking?" I didn't know much about a prosecuting attorney's job, and certainly knew nothing of local politics.

"I'd like you to get to know me well enough to endorse my candidacy."

"Me, why me?" My voice was almost a squeak.

"First, you are becoming well known in Ocean Alley, and this is the county seat."

I snorted and made a disparaging comment about George Winters, and she laughed. "Really, Jolie, it's the substance of your opinion I'm interested in. I've talked to Michael Riordan and his father."

My ears perked up. Michael and I had briefly considered what Aunt Madge would call a fling, but we pretty quickly realized our temperaments were too different. Or maybe too similar.

"Michael shares my views about the current prosecuting attorney," she continued, "but he doesn't want any more attention."

"Can you blame him?" I asked.

"Not a bit. You might not want to talk a lot about that case either, but your name on a published list of supporters would mean a lot." When I hesitated, she added, "You don't have to give money."

"I tell you what, Annie, I am willing to consider it." I paused, thinking about Mary Doris Milner. "Why don't we meet for coffee at Java Jolt this weekend?"

With her delight ringing in my ears, I replaced the phone and turned to see Aunt Madge making herself another cup of tea, probably her tenth for the day. "Did you get the gist of that?"

"Pretty much." She took her teabag out of the mug and setting it on a spoon rest. "I have heard she's very bright, but…"

"Young?" I asked.

"I hate to say that." She paused, then added, "Prosecuting attorney is a big job. Maybe one that requires more experience."

I shrugged. "I guess it depends on whether someone uses their experience well. I sure don't think Martin Small's any good."

"You've got a point there."

There was a scratching noise across the room and we both turned toward the sitting area near her TV in time to see the chipmunk run across the floor and dart under the bookcase again. Aunt Madge looked at me. "He's been climbing the curtains again."

"Great. Have you figured out if he can climb the steps to the bedrooms?"

"So far I haven't seen either of them up there."

THE NEXT DAY I CALLED GRACIE to ask about the whereabouts for the deed on her grandmother's property. Technically, that's more the business of the attorney who handles the closing when the property gets sold, but it occurred to me that since the house had been in the family so long it might require a hunt. Might as well give her a heads up. And, I was curious as to whose name was on it now.

"Deed?" she asked. "Oh dear, I never thought of that."

"Maybe your mom has it," I suggested.

She sighed. "My mom and I have a hard time talking about much more than how cute my kids are."

I could relate to that, except for the kids part. "This will give you some time to talk to her without having to force the conversation."

I hung up and called Harry to see about any new appraisal work. He didn't have anything for the rest of the week, and thought it might be just as well for my back, as he referred to my tailbone.

"It's getting better, mostly hurts when I get in and out of chairs."

"Then I don't feel too bad. You can stay home and rest."

I assured him I would and immediately called the library to see if Scoobie was there. Daphne said she thought he had gone to the diner for lunch but he usually got back just after one o'clock, so I made a sandwich and called up to Aunt Madge to see if she wanted one.

AFTER LUNCH I PICKED UP Scoobie at the library with the intention of heading back to the Tillotson-Fisher house. I let him know that when I talked to Gracie I had asked her to pay Scoobie for doing the lion's share of the work and we had settled on four fifty-dollar gift certificates to Wal-Mart, to be provided each month for four months; that way Scoobie would not earn too much in any one month and get thrown off his disability payments. I didn't mention that I had decided not to take anything. I'd get paid for the appraisal, and I sure wasn't helping Scoobie much at this point.

En route to the old Fisher house, Scoobie decided we should make a detour to Midway Market, the small, in-town grocery store, to introduce me to the manager as the new head honcho at the food pantry, as Scoobie put it.

"Why does he care?" I asked.

"Because when the pantry is really low and needs stuff right away the church passes the collection plate and the money goes to buy food at Midway. He sells it at forty% off the store price."

"How do you know all this?" I asked as we pulled into the small parking lot.

"Because when they need someone to carry it into the pantry sometimes Reverend Jamison finds me."

As we walked into the aging market the overcast sky began to dispense sleet.

"Maybe," Scoobie said as he held a hand out to feel the light pelting of frozen water, "we should get you straight home. I don't want to be around if you fall on your ass again."

"Look, we're here. We'll talk fast." We walked to the door and I stepped on the mat to let the automatic door open. "I wish every door in town were like this." In response to Scoobie's questioning look I added, "You have no idea how much opening a heavy door can make your tailbone hurt."

He nodded, but he was already scanning the aisles for the owner, whom he said was named Mr. Markle. We found him in the back of the store, near swinging doors that led into a warehouse area. Mr. Markle held a clipboard and had been making checkmarks on a list, apparently making sure the pile of boxes next to him held all the products he had ordered.

He regarded me over the top of his reading glasses and did not look at all friendly. "So, you'll be taking over the food pantry."

"With a lot of help." I didn't want to imply that I knew what I was doing.

"All right then." He turned slightly, "Hey Jimmy, get these diapers to the front. Mrs. Nodaway's coming in at two." He turned back to us. "Twins. She's in here every other day. Had to order extra."

He set the clipboard on one of the boxes. "Now, all I ask is if you need to buy give me as much notice as you can." As a clerk walked up, he pointed to a huge carton of diapers, and turned back to us. "See, there's a couple of distributors will give me a better deal if I'm selling direct to you, and I can pass the savings to you. You need stuff already on the shelves, I can't go as low 'cause I already paid more for it."

I nodded. "That's very generous of you."

"You aren't competition." He turned back to his clipboard.

"Not so friendly," Scoobie said in a low voice as we walked toward the exit, "but…"

"Scoobie," yelled Mr. Markle from behind us, "there's a box of dented cans back here."

Scoobie grinned at me, "Get a cart."

Scoobie loaded it and pushed the cart of cans across the now slippery parking lot and I held on to the edge of the cart and focused on keeping my balance.

"What I was going to say was he's kinda grouchy, but then he saves dented cans and stuff that's not selling well and sends over boxes of stuff.

For example," he pulled a can of black bean soup from the top of a box, "there's a ton of these in here. The fart club didn't buy enough, I guess."

I giggled as I popped my trunk and he loaded the first box. "The fart club?"

"Yeah, I think Sgt. Morehouse chairs it, he…" There was a ripping sound as the lightweight box he was loading into the trunk tore in the middle and cans cascaded across the parking lot. I stooped to grab one and Scoobie grabbed me by the elbow. "In the car. Your Aunt'll kill me if you fall."

I didn't argue. Telling myself I was doing us both a favor by getting the car warmed up, I slid into the driver's seat and flipped the heater knob as soon as the engine turned over. Two minutes later Scoobie opened the passenger door. "Dang." He brushed water off his coat. "I like the beach, but why the hell can't I like it as well in Florida?"

The weather had made it clear we should not be on the roads much, so we scratched the idea of going to do any more work in the attic, and I decided the food would sit in my trunk overnight. I invited Scoobie to come back to the B&B, but he said he was up to his 'people quota' for the day. I dropped him at the library before heading to the Cozy Corner.

I thought I'd take a pain pill and curl up on the couch and take a closer look through some of the photos or ledgers we had taken from the house. Since normal people don't usually end up with a skeleton in the attic, I hoped the ledgers or pictures would show some of the abnormalities in the Fisher family.

PETER FISHER'S LEDGERS contained ingredient lists, what seemed to be portions of recipes, and notations about prices, and places where he bought items. I had started with what I judged to be the oldest ledger, since it had been held together with twine and had a rotting cover. The first few pages were a hodgepodge of lists and numbers, but eventually he became more methodical. He seemed to buy large quantities of sugar, flour, molasses, yeast, cornmeal, rye, and lard, so I assumed his store was a bakery of some sort. Why hadn't I thought to look in some of the old city business directories when I was in the library?

Aunt Madge was leafing through a magazine about home repair, but she looked as if she could stand an interruption. "Do you know what kind of business Peter Fisher and Richard Tillotson had?"

She looked up and stared at a spot just above my head. "I saw something in the antique store just off the boardwalk that had their name on it. A child's rolling pin. Bakery at the Shore." When she saw my blank look she continued. "They must have sold a toy with their name on it. Why?" she asked, suddenly suspicious of my motive.

I stood and walked the few feet to where she was sitting and showed her the ledger. "I figured it had to do with food. They must have baked a lot of bread – look at all the yeast they bought." I pointed to the neatly inscribed list of ingredients, which included twenty pounds of yeast.

Aunt Madge laughed. "Yeast was also used to make whiskey you know."

"Oh, right. Prohibition." I looked at the ledger again. "A bakery would be a good cover, wouldn't it?"

"Sure." She picked up her magazine again. "Almost everything on there except the lard and molasses could go into hootch." She looked down at her magazine and then back at me. "And some rum recipes call for molasses."

As I settled back onto the couch I decided to forgo asking her how she knew what went into the recipe for hootch.

CHAPTER SEVEN

WHEN MY FANNY DONUT and I joined Scoobie in the library the next afternoon he was intrigued by the seemingly nonsensical lists of numbers on some of the back pages of the ledgers. I had given up on these, figuring that if they were income from an illegal moonshine business they would be deliberately obscure.

Scoobie's eyes lit up. "I'm going to play some of these."

"Play…"?

"The lottery." He pulled a small notebook from his knapsack and began writing down several lines of numbers.

I left him to his copying and went to the reference section to look at some of the business directories from the 1920s. I plopped them down on the table next to Scoobie and opened the directory from 1928. Bakery at the Shore was at 227 C Street. I thought for a minute. The 200 block was between Main Street and Seaside Avenue, but it seemed unlikely that the building was still there.

I placed the directories back on the shelves and, after saying goodbye to Scoobie, I drove slowly across C Street. The building at 227 C Street looked old enough to have been standing in the 1920s. It was vacant, and a sign had been covered in white paint. Still visible were the words "Little Mamas Café." Sitting in the window was a for sale sign for none other than Lester Argrow's real estate firm.

After parking in the Burger King lot I walked over to the First Bank building and climbed the side stairway to Lester's small office on the second floor. The last time I'd visited him there cigar smoke had wafted down the hallway. Given its absence, I figured he was out, but as I moved down the narrow hall I could see the light under his door. I knocked.

There was a very loud sneeze and he said, "Come in" as he concurrently blew his nose.

Charming.

I opened the door and he gestured me in. "Hey, Jolie! Good to see you." He moved a pile of newspapers off the client chair and pointed that I could sit down. "What's up?"

"I wondered about the building you have listed at 227 C. Is it…"

"Hey, you gonna break away from the geezer and set up your own shop? That'd be great. We could really go to town…"

"First, Harry is not a geezer." I took a breath, not wanting to antagonize Lester. I like getting business from him. "I wondered who owned it and if you knew the history of the building."

He studied me for a couple of seconds, then grinned. "You're investigating, ain't you?"

Coming here was a mistake. I had forgotten for a moment how painfully awkward Lester's amateur detective methods were. "Not investigating. Just interested in the Tillotson family since I seemed to have met one of its older members."

He barked his distinctive laugh. "You know Mary Doris Milner? She owns it."

Why did I know that name? Then I remembered this was the name of Richard Tillotson's seeming girlfriend. "I think Aunt Madge knows her."

"Funny broad." At my expression he added, "Mary Doris, not your aunt. After she retired from teaching she ran the bingo down at the Catholic Church. Here I am, a Jew, and I still donate to the Catholics." He blew his nose again. "Can't shake this cold."

My mind was going in circles. Why did Richard's girlfriend of so long ago own that building? Had he left it to her? I gave myself a mental slap to the head, reminding myself that Richard likely was murdered long before he thought to make a will, and he probably didn't own the building anyway. Why was I talking to Lester when I could go to the courthouse and trace the building's ownership? I stood, "Gee, I should leave you and your cold alone."

"Hey, you just got here." Lester stood, all 5 feet seven inches of him. I noticed he had trimmed the hair in the mole on the side of his face.

"Really, you're busy," I almost stammered. "I told Aunt Madge I'd help fix dinner." I started out the door.

"Don't you even want to know what she's asking?" he called after me. I turned back toward him and he said, "Only $127,500. It's a steal."

That stopped me. "That is a steal. Why so low?"

He stood outside his office, hands in his pockets, jiggling his loose change. "I think her niece, the attorney, wants to buy it."

"Annie Milner? What could she want with a run-down building?"

He shrugged and turned to go back into his office. "That's what I heard is all."

I walked slowly down the steps and back toward my car. If Annie did want it, wouldn't Mary Doris sell it to her without a real estate agent? Then again, sometimes people put a house on the market just to see what it could bring before they sold it to a family member. Maybe that's what Mary Doris Milner was doing.

I STARED AT THE NOTES I'd made when reviewing the former bakery's ownership history at the courthouse. Peter Fisher sold the building in 1939. I assumed a true bakery did not bring in as much money as a bakery that was a front for liquor sales. During the 1940s, the building changed ownership several times, for less money each time. A couple of times I had a clue what it was used for because ownership was in a business name rather than an individual's. My personal favorite was The Teatotaler's Cup. This was in 1946. It sounded as if someone was sorry Prohibition ended. And maybe needed a spelling lesson.

It had the same owner from just after World War II and into the mid-1950s, a man named Joseph Sloan. Mary Doris Milner bought it from him in 1956 for $17,000. That was the last sale on record. A visit to the Assessor's Office showed 227 C Street was appraised at $171,000. The retired schoolteacher had it for sale at almost $50,000 under its assessed value. I was surprised Lester was letting her get away with this; it would lower his commission. "Why would she do that?" I mused to myself.

"What are you muttering about?" Aunt Madge called from her kitchen table where she writing in the notebook that serves as her accounting records.

"Mary Doris Milner has owned that building on C Street since 1956, and she has it for sale way less than the assessed value." I looked at Aunt Madge. "Why do you suppose she'd do that?"

"Maybe she just wants to be rid of it." Aunt Madge looked thoughtful. "I haven't seen her in some time. I don't know what her mental acuity is."

I DECIDED TO CHECK MARY DORIS MILNER'S mental acuity myself. She lived in the senior living center that I had first visited a couple of months ago. One wing is assisted living, another more a nursing home, and a third is for people with dementia. The small foyer had the same smell of disinfectant, but it was now festooned with Christmas decorations. I signed in at the front desk and got directions to Mary Doris' room from a bored-looking volunteer. She was in the nursing home wing. I knocked gently, not sure what to expect from a 94-year old woman.

"Come in if you've got chocolate," came a much stronger voice than I expected.

"I don't have any today, but I could bring you some tomorrow." What I had brought was a canning jar with some carnations from the grocery store, which I had clipped to fit into the jar. I took in her small room, which had a hospital-style bed and wheeled table but also a large flat-screen TV that sat on an antique bureau, and a tall set of shelves that was crammed with books, photo albums, and several boxes of various kinds of chocolate candy.

Her gaze was direct and not altogether friendly. Mary Doris was sitting in a recliner, and she muted the TV as she spoke. "I don't believe I know you, miss." She looked me up and down, and her eyes met mine when she was done. Though she looked too frail to do much walking, unlike the loose-fitting housecoats most other female residents wore she had on a sweater of deep purple, slacks with an elastic waistband, and a pair of tennis shoes, giving the impression that she was about to go out.

"You don't, but I know your niece Annie Milner." I sat the jar of flowers on a small table next to her bed. My name is Jolie Gentil, and Madge Richards is…"

"Your aunt. I haven't seen her for ages. You're the appraiser who found Ruth Riordan's body." She leaned forward, and I realized that she had a cataract in each eye and probably could not see me very well.

I pulled a small card-table chair close to her and sat. "Yes, that was me."

"I," she said. When I gave her a puzzled look she added, "Not 'that was me.' It's 'that was I'"

I smiled. "Aunt Madge said you taught for many years. I take it your subject was English."

She nodded. "I've been retired more than thirty years, longer than I taught. I don't believe Ocean Alley High has had a decent English teacher since. I base my judgment on the conversations I hear around here." She smiled as she spoke. "Of course, if I correct them they tell me I'm old-fashioned."

I was not sure how to broach the Tillotson family. After all, the photos of her and Richard made it pretty clear they were boyfriend and girlfriend in her younger days. "Right now I'm doing an appraisal of the old Tillotson house."

At my words she sat up straighter and glanced out the window at a bird feeder that was placed close to it.

I continued, "Gracie Fisher, she's Gracie Allen now, inherited it from her grandmother, and she's putting it on the market." I paused, taking in her now-pursed lips.

She turned to face me again. "Why are you coming to me?"

"I don't know if you read about it, but when I was in the attic I opened an old wardrobe and…"

"You found Richard." She said this in a matter-of-fact tone.

"The police aren't certain, they're doing some tests."

"They may not be certain, but I am." Her eyes filled with tears. "He would never have left me." Her voice was almost a whisper. "Never!"

I reached over and touched her arm. "I'm sorry to upset you."

She cleared her throat. "It was a long time ago, but I still think of him often." She regarded me intently. "I supposed Madge has told you what happened?"

"She did, and I read a couple of the newspaper articles. They're on microfilm at the library." I paused, uncertain how to approach the photo albums. "There were also some photo albums in the attic, and there were some pictures of you and…"

Her face lit up like the Christmas tree in the foyer. "Audrey Fisher's albums?" I haven't seen those in, well, I don't know when. Since before the war, I suppose." She looked toward the bird feeder again, and for a few seconds we both looked at the small sparrow pecking at the bits of dried corn sitting on the birdhouse rim.

"Do you have them? The albums?" she asked.

"Not with me, but I'd be happy to bring a couple of them over for you to look at."

"She gave a firm nod, and pointed toward her bookcase." The only photo I have of the two of us is just over there." As I rose to find it among several on the shelves she continued. "The Tillotsons had a fair bit of money, so they were always taking pictures."

I retrieved the frame and studied it as I sat down next to her again. It was one of the pictures commercial photographers took of tourists on the old Ocean Alley boardwalk. Back then, prior to the Great Atlantic Hurricane of 1944, the boardwalk was much wider and a pier extended into the ocean. A smiling Mary Doris and Richard Tillotson had their backs to the pier and the old wooden Ferris wheel was visible behind them. Richard's arm was around her shoulder and her head was tilted slightly toward his shoulder.

I could feel her stare and looked up. "Looks as if that was a happy day."

"It was. That was only about two months before he disappeared. I used to say "before he died," but it upset Audrey. Of course, she's long gone." She sighed. "You should promise yourself you won't outlive all your friends."

I set the framed photo back on her shelf and turned to face her. "So you were pretty sure he didn't just leave."

"Positive." Her strident tone seemed to surprise her as much as me. "Aside from the fact that we were talking about getting married, he and Peter Fisher were fighting like all get-out." She paused.

"I never told Audrey, but I talked to the police about that at the time. But Peter Fisher was an established man of business, and Richard was known more for tinkering with his old Model T and being a bit tipsy. People said he only had a job at the bakery because Peter dated his sister."

Rekindling Motives

She frowned. "The police thought I was just a girl who'd been jilted and didn't want to believe he'd simply left."

"I thought Richard and Peter were in business together."

"In a manner of speaking, yes." She studied me critically. "You're not writing some book or something, are you?"

"No ma'am. I feel…" I thought for a moment. "I feel as if finding him, assuming it was him, makes me responsible for learning more about him. I know it's too late to find out what actually happened." I stopped and looked at her. "You probably think I'm just being nosy."

She shrugged. "Doesn't really matter what I think. You say you'll bring those albums?"

"Sure. Tomorrow, if you like." I glanced around her room. "They aren't in very good shape, you couldn't hold them on your lap."

"I'll ask the staff to put up a card table in here for a couple of days. Now, fair's fair. I'll tell you a bit about Richard." She leaned back in her recliner and closed her eyes. If Aunt Madge were with me, she'd say we should let her rest and come back tomorrow. I didn't want to wait until tomorrow.

She opened her eyes again and smiled, more to herself than to me. "I used to sell taffy in the shop on the boardwalk. They made it there, and people would look through the glass at that noisy machine. It was real taffy, not this dry stuff they sell now. Anyway, Richard came in almost every day to buy a couple of pieces."

"I was so dumb, I thought he really just wanted taffy." Her expression brightened. "He finally got up the nerve to ask me if I wanted to go for ice cream with him. He was a bit older than I was, so my parents weren't too crazy about him at first. But, once they got to know him they liked him a lot."

I studied her for a few seconds as she paused, a dreamy look on her face.

"We'd go riding in that silly car of his," she continued. "Every time we went outside of town he got a flat." She stopped and I sensed she was trying to compose herself.

"There were some old ledgers in the attic too. It looked as if they had a pretty busy bakery."

She laughed aloud. "They had a bakery and tea shop, but that was just the public part of the business. What they really did was sell whiskey."

"Whiskey?" I asked, pretending not to know.

Mary Doris laughed. "Your Aunt Madge's husband knew them well. What was his name?"

"Uncle Gordon. Gordon Richards. Aunt Madge told me he helped his uncle bring in bootlegged whiskey and rum from just offshore. My father calls him Rumrunner Gordon."

"That's true. I suppose you could say they were competitors, but your uncle brought in hootch for the speakeasy in the hotel, and Peter and Richard mostly sold to individuals. Folks would come in to buy bread and they'd leave with a pint wrapped in the thick paper with it."

"And they never got caught?" I asked.

"There were some close calls, but a couple of guys in the police department bought from them, so mostly they were OK. When the revenuers from Treasury came snooping they would let local police know, so Richard and Peter had a bit of warning."

She laughed. "They had a large mirror along a side wall, and another on the closet where they hid the whiskey. Of course, customers didn't know it was a closet, the mirror hid the opening. Richard said a couple of times they saw a Treasury guy in the mirror before he actually got in the bakery." She chuckled. "Richard was such a kidder. One day when Peter was in the closet Richard shut him in and put a couple of crates of flour in front of the mirror."

I didn't say anything to this. Mary Doris might think it was funny, but if Peter Fisher was as stiff as his photographs, then I doubted he found any humor in the situation.

"Did they make it in the storage area?" I asked.

"Goodness no. People would have smelled it. Some they bought, some they made up in that very attic you fell out of. Audrey and Richard's mother wasn't too bright. Richard told her it was his 'bachelor pad." Mary Doris thought for a moment. "The hard part was getting glass bottles to sell it in. Mostly they used canning jars. The regulars would bring their own bottles or decanters."

"Were you at Audrey's wedding to Peter Fisher?"

"Oh yes." "Her look darkened. "Richard most definitely did not step on her dress on purpose. Audrey felt very bad later, that she'd accused him of that. She really missed him too." There was a catch in her voice. "She and Richard were a good bit older than the younger two children, and their mother had a 'weak constitution,' as they called it back then. I guess now we'd say she was depressed. Anyway, Audrey and Richard were very good to the youngest two."

"Are they still around?"

She gave me a puzzled look.

"The younger two children."

"Oh, Sophie and Robert. He died young. Well, he was fifty, I consider that very young. After high school she went to some school for girls in the city and then she married during the war, and they moved away, Chicago." Mary Doris' expression brightened. "She rarely came home and I had lost touch with her. But she actually came by the day after...the day after..." She teared up and reached for a tissue, which I pulled from the tissue holder and handed to her.

"I'm sorry, I shouldn't have asked." It was one of my rare moments of feeling guilty.

"I don't mind." She dabbed at her eyes. "That's been the one nice thing about the publicity about Richard being found. Other than me knowing with absolute certainty, I mean." She tossed the tissue into a trash can a few feet away and grinned at me. "Should have gone out for the Knicks."

"You would have been a crowd pleaser." I wanted her to continue, but recognized that I couldn't rush her.

"Someone called Sophie to tell her about you and Gracie finding the skeleton, and darned if Sophie didn't have her grandson drive her to see me the next morning."

"From Chicago?" I almost said "at her age" but caught myself.

"She lives in Cape May now. She's been a widow for a long time. In her late seventies but looks 15 years younger. Said she walks two miles every day."

I mentally filed that bit of information. "Richard was the big love of your life, wasn't he?"

"Oh yes." She sighed. "I never did meet anyone else I cared that much about. But," she noted my look of sympathy, "I enjoyed teaching, and I was very close to my brother and his family." Mary Doris glanced at the bird feeder again, and I wondered what fascination it held.

"You said that he would never have left you. Did you think he'd had an accident or…"

"Nonsense," she said, briskly. "I firmly believe Peter killed him. They were having some kind of running fight about their business, but Richard never said exactly what." She shrugged, "Probably over money. Peter put more money into their business than Richard did, but Richard thought he did a lot more of the work. He felt that Peter treated him more like a lowly employee than a partner."

She leaned her head back and her expression was drained. I realized I had probably stayed too long, and decided to try to talk more tomorrow. Maybe I could work in a discussion of the building she had for sale. Or, the photo albums might bring more memories to light. I stood to leave, and as I did so she grasped my hand very tightly with both of hers. "Do you believe me?"

"Of course." I paused. "The photos of the two of you show a couple very much in love."

"Yes, yes. We really were." She dabbed at her eyes again.

"I'm sorry if I upset you."

She dismissed my apology with a wave of the hand. "It's been a long time." She smiled up at me. "I'm really looking forward to seeing those pictures."

I WALKED TOWARD the lobby so deep in thought that I did not pay attention to the person coming toward me in the hallway. When she called my name I came to a quick stop and looked into Annie Milner's eyes.

"Jolie, you look…" she paused, "Is your aunt here?"

"No, in fact, I was visiting your Aunt Mary Doris." Was it my imagination or did she look shocked?

"I didn't realize you knew her." She shifted a shopping bag from one arm to another.

I thought fast. I didn't want her to think I was bothering her aunt. "I don't, but I saw her photo in the albums, the albums from the Tillotson's attic," I explained, at her puzzled expression. "I thought she might like to know of them. I told her I would bring them back tomorrow." I nodded at her bags. "Looks as if you're getting ready to move in."

She smiled, tightly. "Aunt Mary Doris is allergic to fragrances, so I take her nightgowns home to launder."

"That's really good of you." I made a mental note to see if Aunt Madge was allergic to anything. I couldn't remember her talking about any allergies.

"She and I have been close all my life. It's no trouble." We looked at each other awkwardly. "I'll see you." She continued down the hall.

I looked at her back for a few seconds. She's quite a bit taller than my five feet two inches and has very erect posture, almost like a model. I watched her neck-length dark brown hair bounce up and down with a couple of steps and then turned toward the automatic door.

What is she uptight about? It seemed to me that Annie Milner doing her aunt's laundry was the kind of thing that would give her a few points with voters, at least the ones Aunt Madge's age.

SCOOBIE WAS READY TO BE DONE with inventorying the attic. "You aren't up there sneezing your brains out," were his exact words when I met him for coffee at Java Jolt the next day.

I nodded slowly as I sipped my coffee. "That's true. What if…"

"You're going to say what if you did some of the work upstairs, and the answer is still no."

I pointed at the book he had sitting in front of him, the first edition of All Quiet on the Western Front. "You sure you don't want to find any more treasures like that one?"

"I should probably find something less depressing to read." He nodded at two younger men as they came in the door, apparently fresh from a stroll on the cold beach, and turned his attention back to me. "I know what you're doing. You want to guilt me into it."

Scoobie knows me too well. "Guilt, no. I guess the whole thing has my…"

"Dander up?" he asked, not concealing his smile. "Hard-headed nature in full gear?"

I ignored his jibe. "I was going to say it has my interest. It isn't every day you find so many old things so well preserved."

He almost snorted. "You don't give a flying fig. You want to know how that skeleton got in there."

"And you don't?"

He shrugged. "When we didn't know he was there we didn't care. I still don't." He reached in a pocket of his well worn pea jacket and extracted a folded piece of paper. "Read this." He shoved it across the small table.

homesick dreams
fly with angels
where they were born
they'll never die

sometimes lonesome
souls forget
future memory
truth becomes lie

not quite a dream
not near awake
reality of illusion
surreal and sublime

wonderful mystery
eyesight to blind
transcend your karma
in this life time

I sat staring at the paper for a moment. Sometimes I could understand Scoobie's poetry, sometimes not. This seemed to be the latter. I looked at him. "Did you just write this?"

"Yep, can't you see why?"

He had the intent look he often wore when he talked about his poetry. I never failed to feel like an uneducated buffoon, sensing there was so much I didn't understand. "You talk about..." I looked at the paper again, "Truth becoming lies. Are you talking about me wanting to find out how Richard got there?"

"So," he took the paper back and refolded it. "You're on a first name basis with a skeleton?"

Sensing his strong disappointment, I talked fast. "I'm sorry if I don't understand it. You know I'm not, not literary like you are."

At this, he grinned widely. "What you aren't is very introspective. But that's OK." He opened the paper. "Seeing that attic, what they thought of as junk, I figure they had a lot of stuff, and they seemed to like their lives. I mean, they took all those pictures." He paused for several seconds and folded the poem again, "But all that's left is beat-up belongings, ledger books, and of course the dead guy. What difference does it make?"

I didn't like his thought process, and tried to think of a positive spin to put on his poetry. I was also trying to remember the poem. "You talked about homesick, and, uh, souls and flying with angels. They, um, they're all dead, I guess."

At this he laughed so loudly that the few other people in Java Jolt glanced at us. "You're ok, kiddo." He swallowed the last of his decaf coffee. "I'll help you finish the attic, but I've got some stuff to write just now." He stood and bent to kiss me on the cheek, an unusual gesture for him. "I'll meet you here tomorrow morning and we'll head over to Richard's former home." He slung his knapsack over his shoulder and was gone.

I knew he wasn't mad that I didn't get his poem, but I figured he wished I did. I looked over toward Joe, whose eyes had followed Scoobie out the door. He glanced at me and half shrugged. "You're the one who likes him so much. And you don't get him."

Whenever Joe talked about Scoobie it made me want to defend him. "He's just..." I was going to say something lofty, like that he was deeper or smarter than me, but Joe interjected.

"Different." He grinned again. "You're good for him. Used to be he'd come buy coffee and just sit outside. Now he actually socializes."

As Joe went back to arranging a stack of mugs on the tall table that was the self-serve area for the winter crowd I turned back to my own coffee. I was sorry I had not kept in touch with Scoobie. He'd made me laugh a lot during a tough time in my life, and I forgot about him almost as soon as my parents finished 'working things out' and I returned to my cozy life in Lakewood. I stopped as I stood to collect my purse and put on my coat. I didn't even know where Scoobie had gone after high school. *What kind of friend are you?*

AUNT MADGE WAS NOT PLEASED that I had visited Mary Doris Milner and assumed I was taking the photo album to the nursing home for my benefit and not Mary Doris'. She was right, to a point. "At first I went because I wanted to know what she knows. Now, I like her."

Aunt Madge turned from the fridge, where she was placing leftover muffins from the morning's breakfast. "So what if you do? Those pictures might upset her. She's old."

"Actually," I chose my words carefully, "She reminds me of you. She's, uh, spunky."

"I hate that word," Aunt Madge snapped, closing the fridge harder than usual. "You wouldn't call a career woman spunky."

My eyes actually widened. She almost never snapped at me. "I meant it as a compliment. You've both lost men you loved and you didn't let it stop you."

Perhaps sensing he should put in his two cents, Mr. Rogers chose that moment to sit up from his prone position and give a huge stretch, complete with a high-pitched sort of mutter.

"See," I seized the diversion, "He agrees."

She looked from me to Mr. Rogers and back to me, her expression softening somewhat. "I just don't want her hurt again. She had a lonely life, despite all those kids she taught."

I started to say Mary Doris had her niece, but changed my mind. "Why don't you come to the nursing home with me?"

She shook her head. "I'm having lunch with Harry." She bent to pat Miss Piggy on the head. The two dogs had come up to her expectantly, as if assuming her attention meant they were getting a treat.

"Why?"

"Why do you have coffee with Scoobie?" she asked, as she turned to get the plastic bowl of treats from the cupboard.

"He's my friend..." I began.

She turned and pointed a finger at me. "Bingo."

I WAS HAVING INTERESTING conversations with people, but I wasn't making money doing appraisals and I didn't know much more about Richard Tillotson than I had guessed before I met Mary Doris. As I drove toward her nursing home I went a block out of my way so I could look at the ocean. The wind was fairly steady at about twenty miles per hour, and I wanted to see the whitecaps. The ocean looks so much darker on a cool, half-cloudy day and the tips of the waves stand out even more. I like that.

Some parts of the boardwalk are a few steps up off the street, but as it swings northwest it's lower, so you get a clear look of the ocean from your car. No one was walking on that stretch of beach today, too cool and windy. I turned left and drove the block to the senior home and snagged a space near the front door. I was glad; my tailbone was a bit better, but the photo album was heavy.

It wasn't until I was halfway down the corridor that led to Mary Doris' room that I saw a man in a suit talking to a nurse, and as her eyes met mine she raised a hand and pointed toward me. The man looked, too, and I didn't think Sgt. Morehouse looked at all glad to see me.

CHAPTER EIGHT

"WHAT ARE YOU DOING HERE?" he asked, sharply.

I nodded toward her room, "Visiting Mary Doris Milner."

Morehouse and the nurse exchanged looks and he said, more quietly, "I'm sorry to tell you she died early this morning."

I can't say I was 100 percent surprised. She was old, but she didn't look sick. *And I probably did upset her*. I tried to hide my consternation by saying, "I'm sorry to hear that."

He looked at me intently.

"So what are you doing here?" I asked.

Morehouse gave me one of his I-wish-I-never-met-you looks. "It was not expected." He turned to the nurse, "Thanks for your time. Jolie and I are just leaving."

There was no reason for me to stay. I wasn't family, so no one would discuss anything with me. I turned slowly and walked behind Morehouse, whose brisk pace was too much for my derriere. As if remembering my injury, he turned and slowed. "Want me to carry that?"

"That would be great. I'd been looking forward to setting it down." We exchanged the photo album and walked out side by side. When we got to the foyer he asked me to come down to his office, and I agreed. The C3PO character from *Star Wars* flashed into my mind and I could hear him say, "I have a really bad feeling about this."

I followed Morehouse's older Ford through town to the police station and he waited for me at the door, opening it for me. *He must really want something, to be this nice.*

When we were settled in his office, I on my donut across from his desk, he asked, "Why were you visiting her last night?"

Pointing to the photo album on his desk, I relayed how we had found it in the attic and Aunt Madge had identified Mary Doris in the photos. "I thought she might like to see the album, but I didn't know what her health was, so I stopped by to visit first. We talked, and..."

"About what?"

I stared at him, uncertain how much of her lost love life Mary Doris would want spread all over town. "She had a lot of fond memories of Richard Tillotson. She said she would love to see the albums."

He wagged a finger at me across the desk. "I'm not going to go so far as to say I know how your mind works, but I do know you can't leave stuff alone. Why did you go there?"

His look was so intense I smiled. "Not to injure her in any way." Seeing that he was about to scold me more, I added, "Yes, I did wonder if she could shed any light on Richard. You don't dance with a skeleton, fall down a ladder and forget about it." I shrugged. "She was nice. I told her I know her niece, Annie, and I think that made her comfortable talking to me."

"Did you talk about Richard Tillotson and Peter Fisher?" he asked, almost accusingly.

"A bit. She didn't like him, Peter I mean." I nodded slightly, remembering. "She said Richard locked him in the storage closet that was hidden behind a mirror, where they stored the bootlegged whiskey."

As Morehouse flipped open a small notebook and reached for a pen, I asked, "Why does this matter, anyway?"

"We got the DNA results just yesterday afternoon. That was Richard Tillotson you found in the attic. Now…"

"What difference does it make? And how did you get the results so fast? I thought you told me not to bug you for ages about it."

Morehouse hesitated, and then said, "Since I know you won't blab to your reporter friend..."

I made a face and he ignored it.

"I'll tell you the results were very much expedited because Mary Doris Milner paid for the cost of a private lab to do the analysis." He seemed to enjoy the look of surprise on my face.

Though I could see why she would want to know, I was surprised the police would accept the results of a private lab, and said so.

He shrugged. "It's not really a case. We aren't likely to be able to show he was murdered. His skull has a crack, but that could have happened before or after he died." He held up a hand, as if expecting me to ask if Richard walked into the wardrobe, "and if he was, anyone who did it died many years ago."

I could feel my temper creeping to the surface. "So, it matters to me, but not to you?"

He leaned back in his chair, annoyed with me. "I didn't say that. But it's not a solvable crime with someone to punish. There's nothing to investigate, and you know it."

I nodded slowly. "I get that. But, you're talking to me now because you want something. Usually what you want is for me not to bug you."

He actually smiled, but it faded before he spoke. "Mary Doris Milner did not have an easy death. She became very ill, vomited so profusely that she was dead before the ambulance arrived. That would seem…unusual for someone who appeared to be in what for her was very good health earlier in the evening."

"Poor woman." I could feel myself tearing up and took a breath. "She was really looking forward to seeing those pictures. She only had one of her and Richard, and there are lots in there." I nodded toward the album.

He opened the cover, and I told him to go to the page I had marked with a tissue. For almost a minute he turned the several pages that had the couple's photos, then closed the album and shoved it across the table, almost in frustration. "Can't imagine these pictures having anything to do with her death."

"What did Annie say?" I asked, realizing I should have thought of her earlier. "She was on her way in last night as I was leaving. Did she think Mary Doris looked sick?"

"Haven't talked to her yet. She's over at the funeral home."

"When I talked to Mary Doris she mentioned Richard still had a sister living. Sophie, I think her name is. She lives in Cape May. They hadn't been in touch for years, but she came to visit after, you know, the skeleton."

He wrote the name in his notebook, and was irritated that I couldn't give him a last name for Sophie.

"Maybe she got married here. Her name will be in the courthouse marriage license files."

"Annie will likely know." He strummed his fingers on the desk, and then said, "You can go."

As I rose and reached for the album, I winced. "Tell Annie she can call me if she wants to." I was halfway out the door when he reminded me to take my donut.

I HAD SCHEDULED a meeting of food pantry volunteers at four-thirty and even though I felt very out of sorts over Mary Doris' death I had no reason to cancel it. I got there a few minutes early and stopped by Reverend Jamison's small office, hoping against hope that he would say someone had volunteered to take the lead at the pantry. He was putting on his coat as I entered.

"You aren't coming?"

He smiled, perhaps hearing the desperation in my voice. "If I go everyone in the room will look to me. They need to see you in charge." He handed me keys to the side door of the church that led through the community room to the pantry. "Don't label these, ok? If you were to get your purse stolen I don't want someone to know what the key goes to."

I figured that was all the advice he was good for today, so I murmured goodbye and walked toward the small conference room near the community room. I could hear muffled voices, which obviously meant at least a couple of people had showed up. I had invited Scoobie, since he had gotten food there and I planned to rope him into helping me. Aunt Madge said she would come to the first meeting, since she was the member of First Prez, not me. "I'll introduce you and get a feel for who's there so I can let you know which ones will really do what they say," she had told me that morning.

When I walked in conversation stopped. I didn't recognize anyone, but held my hand out to a short man who was standing by the door. "I'm Jolie Gentil," I emphasized the soft J and G and stressed the long 'e' sound at the end of my last name. *Always good to get people to pronounce my name right.*

"Doctor Welby. I'm a church member and retired physician." In response to the smile he saw about to crease my face he added, "And I've heard every joke about the TV show, so don't go there."

"Promise." I thought he even looked a bit like the fictional Dr. Marcus Welby.

Dr. Welby seemed to think he was in charge of introductions, which was fine with me. "Lance Wilson, he's a deacon and he's been treasurer of the Food Pantry Committee for many years."

Lance looked to be close to ninety, which made him a good twenty or so years older than Doctor Welby. Lance had light brown hair with only a few strands of grey. He had a gray cardigan that looked as if he wore it a lot.

"Monica Martin. She's pretty good about badgering Mr. Markle at the grocery store about donations." Monica's handshake was soft, and nothing about her buttoned navy blue blazer or round face gave the impression of an ability to badger.

"Sylvia Parrett. She's our newest recruit, started last year." Sylvia's ramrod straight posture barely bent as she reached across the small table to shake hands. Her silver grey hair was in a severe bun, which made me think she was either a retired teacher or had been a drill instructor.

"And last but not least, Aretha Brown. She's great about rounding up a crew when we need extra volunteers around the holidays."

Aretha's broad smile in her dark brown face was friendly, and she was the only one to speak. "You're younger than my daughter. It's about time we had some young blood on the committee."

I could like her. "Thanks. I'm going to try to learn a lot fast." She wasn't so old herself, maybe fifty-five.

As we were taking our seats there was a bang as the door to the outside shut with the wind, and Scoobie's voice drifted down the hall. "I bet they're only just starting."

I recognized the brisk footsteps as Aunt Madge's. She hates to be late, so I figured she must have picked up Scoobie and been sidetracked somehow. The two of them entered the room, faces pink with cold, and there were calls of "Hi, Madge," and a couple of nods to Scoobie.

"Sorry to be late," Aunt Madge said as she sat and shrugged her coat off her shoulders. "We ran into Elmira at the library and she wouldn't let us go." She nodded at the others. "In part, she wanted to make it clear she was not going to serve on the Food Pantry Committee anymore."

"Praise the Lord!" Aretha slapped her hand over her mouth in the second that followed, then removed it and smiled, half sheepishly. "Sorry, my Southern Baptist ways lead to loud praise."

No one said anything, but there were polite nods and Lance Wilson almost cracked a smile. I figured Elmira's gossiping ways had probably made everyone wary of talking too much when she was in the room.

Dr. Welby spoke as he moved his chair to make room for Scoobie who was pulling up one of the chairs that sat around the wall. "I assume she heard about Mary Doris Milner."

There was a small chorus of "what-do-you-means" and "what-about-Mary-Doris?" The only one besides Dr. Welby who didn't seem surprised was Lance Wilson.

"She died during the night." Aunt Madge said simply.

Scoobie caught my eye and added, "Elmira wants to know why the county medical examiner took the body when Mrs. Milner had been ill for a long time."

I listened to the expressions of sympathy for Annie Milner and a couple of comments about what a good teacher Mary Doris had been. I would have let the conversation go on longer, but it didn't seem they were going to talk about anything I didn't know, and I was determined that this meeting would end in less than an hour. When there was a two-second lag in the talk, I sauntered into the conversation. "Annie will have some free time now that she is not visiting her aunt, maybe we can invite her to help."

The term "silence is deafening" took on new meaning for me. "I meant," I almost stammered," she might like to have something to do."

Their expressions softened a bit, and I continued. "Reverend Jamison mentioned one reason he asked me to take the lead was that he thought I would continue to meet new people through my work as an appraiser, and..."

"Did he say none of us was willing to do it?" asked Dr. Welby?

My sense was he saw himself as the leader of this group, or at least a person of influence. "No. Did you, uh, want to be in charge?"

He shook his head firmly. "We're all booked pretty tight. As soon as you retire everyone from the Chamber of Commerce to the Lions Club to the animal shelter asks you to volunteer."

"Yeah, but Rev Jamison is the most persuasive," Scoobie said with a grin.

"I'll say." My tone was glum.

Aunt Madge shot me a look.

I continued. "Ok, I went through notes of some meetings to get a sense of how things work. But, that doesn't tell me the nitty gritty. I wonder if each of you could tell me something about what you do, and then maybe we can go around the room a second time and you can tell me what you think needs to change."

Aunt Madge and I had talked about a format for the meeting. She had not been to the Food Pantry Committee meetings, but she is on the church's Social Services Committee. Aunt Madge's sense was that the former food pantry chair ran roughshod over any group she chaired, and this group would appreciate a participative style. Since I was looking for others to do more of the work than I planned to do, I wanted active involvement from the people here.

I listened as Lance Wilson talked about accounting rules for about 5 minutes, and finally said what I was waiting to hear, which was that we had a balance of $2,042.16 in the food pantry account. It did not sound like much to me.

Monica Martin had been on the committee the longest, seven years. In a soft voice she said she had taken the notes at most of the meetings she attended, and offered to continue to do this. I nodded, glad not to have to ask someone to do what I regarded as an onerous job.

Sylvia Parrett spoke in clipped sentences. She had spent the last year trying to drum up additional donation sources and said she had urged, with no success, that they do food drives rather than working with just the main food bank in Lakewood or a couple of local grocery stores. "I guess I should have held that comment for when we talk about suggestions."

I thanked her, and smiled at Aretha Brown as she began to talk. "Reverend Jamison asked me to serve on the committee about two years ago. I came into the pantry and said I wanted to know the hours so I could put up signs in laundry mats. That's where a lot of poor people go, you know. I guess he figured I'd bring another perspective." She smiled almost grimly at Sylvia Parrett. I didn't know what that was about, but figured their perspectives must differ. *What have I gotten myself into?*

At this point, Scoobie hijacked the meeting. "I have some suggestions for change," he began.

I had not thought Sylvia Parrett's back could get any straighter, but I was wrong.

"I think," he continued, "that it would be good if we went to Mr. Markle's store and the big store on the highway and asked if we could set up a donation truck sometimes. Maybe have a big box in the stores all the time. We get the store to give people a discount to people who buy food for us. And we have a list of what we want at the stores. And if it could include Coco Puffs that would be great."

I could tell by the sidelong glance he threw my way that he added the last part in hopes of irritating Sylvia. It scares me that I know how Scoobie's mind works.

Scoobie continued. "We don't have a lot of money, I know, but I have some ideas for raising some. That way we could maybe buy more turkeys and stuff at Thanksgiving. My best idea," he looked up from his list and grinned at each person individually, "is to have a dunk tank at St. Anthony's Spring Carnival. Get a lot of people, including all of us and every big shot in town, to let people donate money to see if they can dunk us in a big tub."

To say the meeting went downhill from there would be a massive understatement. If Aunt Madge had not been sitting next to Sylvia so she could put a hand on her arm Sylvia would have left. Aretha laughed so loud at the dunk tank idea that even Scoobie looked surprised. I think I was the only one who heard Monica Martin say, "I don't even own a bathing suit," as she hugged herself.

To his credit, Doctor Welby got us back on track. "Brainstorming, that's what we're doing," he boomed. "We used to do it at the state Medical Society meetings to develop ideas to offer to the government to improve Medicare."

"Didn't work, did it?" Lance Wilson asked. He started to offer a comment about the government not balancing its books, but by that time I had taken courage from Doctor Welby and asked the others to continue with their suggestions to improve the food pantry.

Soon I had a list of fifteen suggestions, including several on how to recruit more volunteers. Those were my favorites.

Though I did not expect to like her ideas (something Aunt Madge would chastise me for even thinking), in a way Sylvia had the best one. "We need a name. Something catchy. Something that will let people know what we do without making it sound as if there is a stigma attached to coming here."

"We could have a contest," Doctor Welby said.

I managed to catch Scoobie's eye to keep him from offering an immediate idea. I wasn't sure the group could take it.

CHAPTER NINE

MY TAILBONE WAS KILLING ME from being tense for so long during the meeting, so I let Aunt Madge cook supper and did not even set the table. Scoobie did that while I lay on the sofa with two pillows under my knees. It seemed natural that he drove back to the B&B with Aunt Madge. I wanted to talk to Scoobie about Mary Doris' death and the fact that she had paid for the DNA tests on the skeleton we now knew belonged to Richard Tillotson. I had not decided whether to tell Aunt Madge this, and finally decided she'd find out anyway, which is my primary criterion for bringing up topics that might encourage her to tell me to stop poking my nose into what she perceives as not my business.

For the first time in my life, something I said made Aunt Madge stop in her tracks. "Mary Doris paid for the DNA test. And then she didn't get to know," she finally said.

I glanced at Scoobie. "I think she knew. She just wanted everybody else to know." I sat up on the couch, wincing. "She thinks, thought, that Peter Fisher killed him."

"You told me you talked about the photographs!" Aunt Madge looked angrier than I'd seen her since the day I spit chocolate ice cream on Renée as my sister tried to make me sit on the porch swing instead of the front steps.

"I didn't bring it up. She did." *OK, I encouraged her, but I didn't ask.* I got up gingerly and moved toward the kitchen area. I intended to give her a hug, but Aunt Madge's posture was not encouraging.

"Why would she do that?" Aunt Madge snapped as she took biscuits out of the oven.

"Too late to ask her," Scoobie said. I think he regretted the words as soon as they were out of his mouth, because he turned and went over to the train set on the floor.

"I think," I said to Aunt Madge's back as she scooped the biscuits into a basket, "that she wanted to talk about him. She said he would never have left her, and she hoped finding him would prove that."

I could see Aunt Madge's shoulders relax. I hated to have her mad at me. All she said was, "You can get the butter out of the fridge, Jolie."

Scoobie's eyes met mine and he wiped his hand briefly over his forehead in a 'whew' gesture.

AFTER DINNER SCOOBIE and I looked at a couple of the ledgers while Aunt Madge watched a detective show on TV and, I thought, deliberately ignored us. After twenty minutes of staring at pages of Peter Fisher's apparent shorthand, I hadn't learned anything except the price of baking ingredients in the late 1920s and that Peter was uncertain of how to spell yeast. He alternated between 'ea' and 'ee.'

"Does your book have any figures about how much they made?" Scoobie asked, as he gently moved Jazz from her spot on his lap to the floor.

I flipped through pages, seeing only the usual routine information on quantities ordered, prices, and delivery dates. "Nope."

Scoobie moved his ledger in front of me. "See, this one is for late 1928. At the end of it," he flipped to a page that started approximately the last third of the book, "you start to see figures about how much money comes in each day."

It took me a couple of minutes, but I finally understood that the numbers represented money taken in. At the top of a page was the date, and at bottom of the far right column a figure that seemed to represent a day's total. In between were sales. Sometimes there were names of customers next to amounts, sometimes product names, such as molasses cookies or tea cakes. Usually there were scratch outs by the day's total, as if the person adding the numbers wasn't very good at it.

"The first part of the ledger," Scoobie flipped back to earlier pages, "shows the ingredients they bought. What's funny," he flipped back and forth between pages at the beginning and end of the ledger, "is that it seems that they were buying more yeast and sugar and stuff, but they didn't seem to have more money coming in."

I could see what he meant and studied it for a minute. "That could make sense if the income is only for the baked good and such, the legal sales. Maybe they recorded the liquor sales in another ledger."

"I suppose so." Scoobie closed his ledger almost defiantly. "There were lots of other ledgers up there, but I gotta tell you Jolie, I'm not too keen about going through them."

I lowered my voice, "You know who's good with numbers," I began, thinking of Lance Wilson.

"You better be talking about Ramona," came Aunt Madge's voice from the recliner she sat in as she watched TV. At the sound of her voice, Mr. Rogers poked his head up from where he had been resting it on his paws. Not seeing any indication that anyone was about to pet him or provide a treat, he resumed his lethargic position.

Scoobie grinned at me. "Ramona is very good at numbers."

I rolled my eyes at him as I shut the ledger I had been studying. "That's exactly who I meant." Which was a lie. The one class I had with Ramona had been geometry, and she spent half the time drawing in the margins of the text book.

THE NEXT DAY'S *Ocean Alley Press* had Mary Doris Milner's obituary, with a notation that "services would be announced at a later date." As Aunt Madge refilled coffee cups for the B&B customers in the breakfast area that adjoins her living area I read every word of the obit, noting that Annie was the first survivor mentioned. I thought it odd that her name appeared before her father's – Annie was the grandniece, her father the closer relative – but figured it was because she had lived with Mary Doris in high school and visited her aunt so often in the senior home.

As the last B&B guest left the breakfast area Aunt Madge dumped coffee cups in the sink and sat next to me at her oak table, nursing a cup of tea. "Why do you suppose they don't announce the date of the service?" she mused, looking again at the obituary.

I hesitated, figuring she would accuse me of making too much of my conversation with Sgt. Morehouse yesterday. In as offhand a way as I could manage I mentioned his concern that she had not been ill until just before her death, and that he found that odd.

Aunt Madge shook her head. "Poor Annie. She shouldn't have to worry about that. Mary Doris was ancient. She probably had a stomach flu and her body couldn't handle it."

Foul play seemed about as likely as a pale-skinned lifeguard in July, but I didn't think Sgt. Morehouse would let the idea drop until he was sure Mary Doris died of a virus or something equally benign. "I think I'll give Annie a call."

Aunt Madge shot me a look. "To see if she's OK. She was really close to her aunt." I started upstairs to shower and dress before calling her. I had my foot on the bottom stair leading up to my room when Jazz flew across the floor in pursuit of a chipmunk, which darted under an antique washstand that sat in the hallway.

"Damn!" I jerked back and the pain shot from my tailbone to knees. Fortunately, Mr. Rogers and Miss Piggy were outside. I looked at Jazz, poised in front of the washstand, ready to pounce. "I can't believe that little thing can outrun you."

Aunt Madge walked over and stood looking down at Jazz. "I'd really prefer that Adam get the thing out of here. Cats play with their captives, and it comes down to torture."

I waited a beat before responding. "Maybe you should ask Scoobie to sleep on the sofa one night."

"Don't be silly. Harry said he'd get me a small live animal trap. Then I can catch it and release it in someone else's yard."

"Didn't you say there were two?"

All Aunt Madge said was, "Hmmm."

ANNIE'S HOME NUMBER was unlisted, so I called her office to see if I could talk them into giving it to me. I was surprised when the secretary put me through to her. "Annie. I didn't think, I mean…"

She politely cut me off. "Prosecutor Small said I didn't have to be here, but it's easier than sitting at home."

"That makes sense. "I was just calling to see if you were okay. She was," I paused, "your aunt was the liveliest ninety-four year old I ever expect to meet."

Annie gave a small chuckle. "She was so excited about the photos you were going to show her she had me go out and buy a couple of small frames. She was going to ask you to make her copies of a couple of them."

Anxious to overcome the lump in my throat, I told her I would be happy to make copies of a few pictures Annie picked out. I doubted Gracie would mind. There was a pause of several seconds before Annie said, "I don't think so, Jolie. I have a lot of pictures of Mary Doris, and I want to remember her the way I knew her."

Though I was surprised, I figured she was entitled to her thoughts. I remembered that Mary Doris had said she had few photos from the time she spent with Richard Tillotson, having characterized photography as a hobby of the rich in the 1920s. "Would your mom or dad like any, do you think?"

Annie's laugh bordered on harsh. "They rarely spoke the last 15 years." As if sensing the tone of her response, she added, "I'll let them know you offered. Listen, Jolie, I have to get ready for a deposition." She hung up.

Aunt Madge, sitting next to me nursing a cup of tea, said, "If Gracie doesn't want those albums, the historical society here would likely love to have them."

The phone rang, a loud tone since the portable receiver was sitting on Aunt Madge's oak table. It took me a few seconds to decipher Scoobie's excited voice. "Remember I told you I was going to play some of those numbers?"

"Uh, play…" I stuttered.

"The lottery, some of the strings of numbers from the ledgers. I just won fifty dollars." His excited voice was loud, and Aunt Madge looked interested.

My brain clunked into gear and I remembered Scoobie talking about the lottery one day in the library. "That's great. You going to spend it all in one place?"

"I'm taking you to lunch today. Where do you want to go? Any place but Java Jolt is OK with me."

Aunt Madge gave me an amused look as she stood to carry her tea mug to the sink. I thought for a couple of seconds. "What about Newhart's? Aunt Madge got me hooked on that."

"Great. I'm at the library. Darlene's letting me use her phone. You can pick me up any time after noon." He didn't wait for me to agree before he hung up.

"So," Aunt Madge said, "Scoobie's flush." She started toward the stairs, likely to check the room of her one guest to see if they had used all their towels or left a note saying clean sheets were needed.

After apologizing for the tenth time that my tailbone and I could not help, I pulled the file of food pantry folders to me. Sylvia Parrett was managing the name contest, with suggestion boxes in several churches and the library. That was a big help, but I still had to figure out what we needed to order from the food bank in Lakewood. *This food pantry gig is old already.*

NEWHART'S IS A CASUAL place that is popular with summer tourists and year-round residents as well. Arnie Newhart gives large servings and the blue plate specials he serves in the off-season are always a bargain. Mostly it's fun to look at all the local photos and memorabilia that line the walls. A couple of years ago Arnie inherited a bit of money from his mother and he replaced the Formica tables and wobbly metal chairs with booths around the walls and wood tables with Windsor-style chairs that look as if they were built to last a long time.

As we ate crab cakes and clam chowder Scoobie enlightened me on how he had picked the winning combination of numbers. "This one page had so many erase marks it caught my eye. Looked as if they couldn't figure what their take was for that week. Anyway, I needed six numbers, so I took their final daily sales tally from each day – because they were closed Sunday. Everything cost so much less back then that all the numbers were under fifty."

He bit into the second half of his crab cake and I pointed at him with my soup spoon. "If I'd known it was that easy I'd have waited 'til you won a bigger pot and we could go into New York to see a show."

"Ish too much." He swallowed a bite. "I can't make too much in a month or I lose my benefits, and I haven't figured out how to live life without meds yet." He grinned at me. "And anyone who knew me before I got clean and sober and went on meds would be sure to tell you I need them."

"Right." Since I had not seen Scoobie in this phase of his life, I had a hard time envisioning him drunk or seriously stoned. "You still thinking about becoming a radiology tech?"

Before he could answer, someone near the door said, "Hey Scoobie. Heard you came into some money." It was Ramona's boss, Roland, and his smile was friendly.

Scoobie grinned back. "Yeah, it's a lot to me." Roland gave a thumb up gesture and moved to a table on the other side of the small eatery.

Scoobie pulled one of the small ledgers from a pocket of his coat and opened it to a page marked with one of the several ribbons that extended from the top of the binding. "See, today I'm going to use the numbers at the bottom of this page."

I feigned interest. Since Robby's arrest I have little desire to talk about any form of wagering.

Scoobie was onto his third marked page when he looked up and seemed to catch my lack of enthusiasm. "Jeez, I'm sorry Jolie, I should have thought..." his voice trailed off.

I didn't want to be a killjoy. "I'm really glad you won, especially since I got lunch out of the deal. And," I hesitated before continuing, "you're not going to pour all your money into lottery tickets or slots. Most people just have fun." Part of me wondered if my former marijuana smoking friend would be easily addicted to the possibility of winning regularly.

He nodded slowly. "Yeah, when I tell them about this at AA at least five of the guys will tell me to watch out for that." His eyes grew brighter as he picked up his mug of decaf coffee. "I'll offer to give them some of my picks, that'll shake 'em up."

We added some of Arnie's chocolate pie to our meals and then I dropped Scoobie at the library and headed over to the Purple Cow to check Ramona's schedule for helping with the attic inventory. Despite their antics as they rooted through old clothes and such, the team of Ramona and Scoobie worked a lot faster than if Scoobie was searching by himself and hollering down to me.

Ramona's white board was inside the store today as the wind had picked up over night. Today it read, "The journey of a thousand miles begins with a flat tire." The first part was in Ramona's handwriting, the second in someone else's, meaning Scoobie must have stopped by to tell her about his good fortune and taken advantage of her inattention while Ramona helped a customer. Since the board was angled toward the entry, she hadn't seen the editing.

"Hello Jolie," came Ramona's lilting voice from the counter near the cash register. She had on a skirt in deep purple that came to mid-calf and a lavender top with deep purple trim around the V-neck. Only Ramona could pull off that outfit, and for the twentieth time since returning to Ocean Alley in October I was conscious of her strong sense of style and my feeling of ineptness around her. No one would call my brown corduroys and gold turtleneck ugly, but no one would take a second look, either.

"Did you talk to Scoobie?" she asked, as she stooped to pick up a pen.

"Yes, and I figured he'd been in." Before she could ask why I added, "We saw Roland at Newhart's and Mr. Purple Cow congratulated Scoobie."

Ramona nodded, but her expression looked more concerned than happy for Scoobie. "I'm worried that a lot of people will hear him talking about what all's in the attic." When I gave her a puzzled look she continued, "There's no security system at the house, at least not that I saw, and there are a lot of antiques in that attic."

"Ah, I get your drift." I watched Ramona wipe a smudge off the countertop with glass cleaner and a paper towel. "Don't you think it would be tough for someone to sneak in and out of there with a load of stuff?"

"Yes, but they don't know that until they're in there."

With this cheery thought rattling around in my brain I set up a couple of times to go look through the attic some more and then trekked over to the Food Pantry. Megan was going to train a new volunteer on how to manage the front counter, and I figured I needed to know how the place worked.

CHAPTER TEN

AS I DRANK ORANGE juice the next morning I stared unhappily at a short *Ocean Alley Press* article about Scoobie's good luck. Winning fifty dollars was hardly a big news story, but I knew George Winters was looking for anything to write about the Fisher-Tillotson house and its skeleton discovery. At least the story didn't mention the kind of business the ledgers dealt with. I was pretty sure Gracie did not want her family's moonshine roots noted on the front page of the paper.

Scoobie and I picked up Ramona at three o'clock at the Purple Cow and we headed to the Fisher-Tillotson house to continue our inventory. We hadn't been at it long when my cell phone rang. "Where you at?" asked Sgt. Morehouse without so much as a hello.

"At the old Fisher house," I tried to keep irritation out of my tone. I wasn't obliged to tell him what I was up to.

"What the hell are you doing over there?" he bellowed. I dropped the phone, but it didn't keep me from hearing him as the phone skidded across the hardwood floor, stopping just at the edge of the stairs that lead down to the first floor. Words such as "crime scene" and "don't touch anything" drifted up to me.

I leaned down painfully and picked up the phone and held it a few inches from my ear. "We're doing an inventory of the attic for Gracie. What do you mean 'crime scene'?" I looked up to see Ramona's and Scoobie's heads looking down through the trap door.

"I'm on my way over there." Morehouse hung up and Scoobie came down the attic ladder faster than I would have thought possible.

"What are you…?" I began.

"He doesn't like me, and he isn't first on my Christmas card list either," said Scoobie as he started down the stairs.

"Jeez, Scoobie, we're supposed to be here."

He paused and gave me a look that said "that won't make any difference."

"I mean, go if you want, but we aren't doing anything wrong," I added, feeling kind of naive as he looked at me.

Ramona was making her way carefully down the attic ladder. She had to gather her wide skirt in her hand so it didn't catch on a ladder hinge, so she was holding onto the ladder with only one hand. Scoobie walked the few steps back to the ladder and steadied it. "Don't you own a pair of jeans?" he asked as she stepped onto the hallway floor.

"One, but I don't know where it is." She fixed a stern gaze on Scoobie. "You're acting like you've done something wrong. You aren't sitting here smoking a joint."

The slamming of a car door at the front of the house told me the discussion was moot. Morehouse must have been on his mobile phone when he called. "I'll let him in," Ramona said as she walked down the steps.

MOREHOUSE SEEMED TO have calmed down a bit since his bombastic phone call. As he and Ramona walked up the steps together he asked her if she still volunteered as an art instructor at the local Boys and Girls Club. Her answer did not carry up the steps. When he saw me his expression grew harsh. "Have you moved much up there?"

I met his gaze directly. "Of course we have. We're doing an inventory and Gracie didn't say you had asked her not to touch anything."

His posture sagged a bit and he ran his hand through his hair. "We just got the autopsy report from the medical examiner. Mary Doris Milner did not die of natural causes."

Uncertain I could keep standing, I sat back on the sewing machine stool and adjusted my donut. Scoobie leaned against the ladder and Ramona sat on the top step of the stairs that lead to the first floor. Scoobie spoke first. "I liked her. She used to see me working on poetry in the library and sometimes she'd read some of it."

Morehouse gave him a barely perceptible nod and turned his attention to me, but before he could say anything I asked, "How did she die?"

For a few seconds he seemed to have some sort of an internal debate with himself, then he said, "Methyl alcohol poisoning."

"But, but...you mean she drank herself to death?" I couldn't imagine how she had gotten enough alcohol for that. Or whether she would even be able to drink that much.

Before Morehouse could answer, Scoobie said, "It's not the kind of alcohol that's in what you drink. It's made from wood, not grains." He folded his arms across his chest and looked directly at Morehouse. "During Prohibition a lot of moonshiners made whiskey using it and a lot of people died. People would drink anything." He glanced at me.

Ramona's sob brought me back to the present. She bent from her waist and put her head in her lap. Scoobie was sitting next to her and had an arm around her shoulder before I could think about getting off my donut. "Why?" Ramona wailed. "Everybody loved her!"

Scoobie gave her shoulder a hug. "Unless she flunked them."

"Stop it! It's not a joke." Ramona pulled a handkerchief from the pocket of her skirt. Even with Mary Doris' death I couldn't help but wonder how many people our age carried a handkerchief instead of tissues.

"I know," Scoobie said.

She blew her nose. "I'm sorry, I just..."

"It's hard for everybody," Morehouse said, more kindly than I'd ever heard him. He turned to me and changed tacks in a second. "The thing is, only you and Annie Milner saw her in the hours before she died, and I have a hard time pointing a finger at either of you." He leaned against the railing that overlooked the foyer on the first floor. "But," he seemed to rally, "you're nosing into her business and Annie, well Annie will be a rich woman now. Everyone in town knows that."

Except me, of course, but it didn't make sense that Annie would murder her aunt. "Annie told me she's thinking about running for county prosecuting attorney. A murder investigation doesn't strike me as a vote getter."

Morehouse glared at me. "You sure you didn't give her anything to drink, or see her drink anything?"

I shook my head slowly. "I didn't bring her anything except some flowers in a jar, and I doubt she drank the water." I thought for a moment. "I don't remember seeing even a mug of tea in the room. But, I wasn't really focused on drinks."

"There was a cup of water. We took it to the lab, but it was just the usual crap that's in our city water. I'm just..." he looked over the railing to the floor below.

"Looking for someone to blame," Scoobie said.

Morehouse fired up. "Yes, damn it, I am." He paused for a moment. "I liked her. She was my mother's English teacher forty years ago. It's always harder when you know 'em."

I empathized a bit, but still did not appreciate his overall attitude. "Can we do anything else for you?" I asked, I hoped coolly.

He looked toward the attic. "You found those photo albums. Anybody know what you were doing up there?"

I looked at Scoobie and Ramona. "Us, Aunt Madge, umm, I told Annie when she saw me with the albums..."

"Roland," Ramona said. "He let me leave early a couple of times to come over here. I didn't ask him to keep it a secret."

"Joe at the Java Jolt," Scoobie said. "And he could have told anyone. Plus, the paper sort of implied it. Anyway, how could cleaning out the attic matter?" Scoobie asked.

Morehouse pulled away from the railing and nodded at each of us as he started down the stairs. "Hearing that you found the albums was the only thing in Mary Doris' life that was different in the last few days. I doubt there's anything in that attic that relates to her death, but if you see something, you tell me." He glanced back up at me as he descended. "And I don't mean a week after you find it."

NEWS ABOUT MARY DORIS' MURDER took the fun out of the afternoon, and without discussing it we began to pack up. For me all that meant was standing up with my donut, but Scoobie and Ramona had to collect a couple of books and ledgers they wanted to take and close the attic ladder.

In the car I asked Scoobie how he knew so much about methyl alcohol. He turned his body rather than just his head, but I didn't want to take my eyes off the road so I couldn't see his expression. "You know where I hang out, right?"

I had to smile. "OK, there are lots of books in the library. How did you happen to read all about methyl alcohol and Prohibition?"

He shrugged. "I just go where the books take me." He paused for a second. "It was right after I got clean and sober and I was reading a lot about alcohol and pot. Maybe there was an article about Prohibition and Ocean Alley or something."

I thought for a moment. "But even if people made that stuff back then, who would have it now?"

"Maybe it's not that hard to make. I'll look it up."

In a brisker tone than I'd ever heard her use, Ramona interjected. "Enough on Prohibition. Let's get back to business here." She tapped me on the back of the head with one of the small ledgers she had brought with her. "They're funny little sets of business records. These two are earlier than the one I took before -- there are dates on the first page."

"How so funny?" asked Scoobie.

"Maybe they wrote them to be hard to follow, but I think the other one I looked at shows they're buying more ingredients but not bringing in any more money." She flipped through a few pages of the ledger on her lap. "I want to see what some earlier ledgers say."

First Scoobie and now Ramona had certainly given me something to think about. If numbers didn't add up, Peter and Richard may have both been trying to hide something from anyone who saw their ledgers. But, what if one of them was cooking the books instead of just bread or whiskey?

CHAPTER ELEVEN

I WASN'T REALLY IN THE MOOD for food pantry work, but having Scoobie around was a reminder that more people depend on the pantry than I would have thought. I had asked Lance Wilson if he would meet me to go over the books for a few minutes and he'd asked that I come to his house. I had a second goal, which was to show him a couple of the ledgers to see what he thought about them, and I pushed them deep into my purse, so Aunt Madge would not glare at me about minding police business.

Lance's tiny house two blocks from the ocean had often caught my eye, though I didn't know it was his until now. Heck, I didn't know him. I figured it likely to be the smallest single family home in Ocean Alley, maybe no more than 600 square feet. The appraiser in my head took in its neat lot – part sand and part grass, all of it neatly landscaped – and the newer vinyl siding and roof. Given that he looked close to ninety and could have had the house paid for long ago, Lance could be sitting on the beach real estate version of a gold mine.

Lance let me in with a brief nod, not saying anything, and I walked down the hall to the tiny living room. However, instead of the older person's sitting room I had been expecting it was outfitted with a large screen TV and a couple of leather recliners, with a large collection of DVDs on a set of shelves along one wall. The hardwood floors were polished to a high sheen and there was a deep burgundy area rug in the middle of the room. There was barely room to turn around, but it was modern and functional.

As he came up behind me I turned to face Lance and took in his impish grin. "Not what you were expecting is it?"

I shook my head.

"People think I'll have shag carpet and easy chairs with doilies, but you don't have to be twenty-five to enjoy a good New York Giants game."

I grinned at him and nodded to the DVDs. "Or watch a good movie."

"Yep." He gestured to a small table and chairs near the doorway, and I noticed a couple of file folders and a small ledger not unlike the ones from the Fisher-Tillotson attic. "Let's get started."

Lance had records going back fourteen years, when he became treasurer. "Don't know anything about before that. The minister at the time kind of ran the pantry out of his hip pocket and on a wing and a prayer. More power to him," he added.

He flipped to the back of a ledger. "I don't record the value of all the food items that come in. Meagan gives me a summary of each week's donations, and she notes where they come from. What I pay most attention to are the cash donations and how we spend that. And I do a list of who gives cash or major food donations so we can do a thank-you letter. Aretha does those once a month, which is swell."

Swell. That's a word you don't hear a lot these days. I smiled to myself as I glanced at the last few pages of the ledger. "It looks as if we get anywhere from $300 to more than $1,000 in cash each month." I could see the pattern; more came in around the holidays.

He nodded. "We use the cash especially for stuff kids like. The Food Bank in Lakewood is never going to send us enough jelly, chicken noodle soup, mac and cheese, or sandwich cookies. Not," he glanced up at me, "that we buy a lot of junk food, but kids can't eat just green beans. And twice a month Mr. Markle orders about thirty pounds of apples for us and we give those out the same week. Don't have a place to store them."

"Scoobie took me in to meet him a couple of weeks ago."

"He can be abrupt, but he's really good about letting us order in bulk and charging us hardly more than he pays for the stuff." Lance shut the ledger. "You have any ideas for raising more money?"

I took a deeper breath. "I liked a few of Scoobie's ideas."

Lance raised an eyebrow.

"I don't mean we should all go in the dunk tank," I said quickly, "but maybe a bunch of kids from the high school would do it."

He nodded, seemingly relieved. "I know the churches do special collections for us every month, but do we go to the service clubs, like Lions or Rotary?"

"Hmmm. Hadn't thought about going to them. Kiwanis send us a check for fifty dollars every December."

"I wondered, I mean we don't have a huge volunteer base," I didn't want to seem to be criticizing someone who had given a lot of time to the pantry.

Lance chuckled, "And it's not too spry."

"True, nor am I now." I gestured to the donut I was sitting on. "I thought maybe some of the groups would do some kind of fundraiser for us. You know, fun stuff that would raise some money and get people to know us better."

"You mean, like a bake sale?" he asked.

"Well...more like a silent auction or pancake breakfast. I don't know." The idea of asking service clubs for help seemed good, but maybe it was lame.

He surprised me by slapping his palm on the table. "By golly, you're right. I didn't think of either of those things. They can be in charge of thinking of what to do. Now let's see," his smile faded a bit. "Course, everyone I knew in Lions is either dead or up at the nursing home."

"You don't need to know them, just ask if you can come to a meeting to make a presentation. People came to my Rotary Club in Lakewood all the time to ask for money for their charities."

Lance thought about this. "I'll talk to Doctor Welby and Sylvia about it."

My instinct was to say we didn't need their permission, but I remembered my goal to make this a participative committee. "Great, thanks."

There was a short pause and he added, almost gruffly, "We'll be coming into a little money, of course."

I'm sure my expression was blank, because he continued, "From Mary Doris Milner."

"Oh!" Memories of her death came flooding back, and I felt my eyes prickle with tears.

"Good friend of mine she was." He cleared his throat. "She was several years older than me. When you're kids that seems like half a lifetime, but we got close as we got older. Got so we were the only two from our generation at those annual high school alumni dinners. When she went in the home I quit going."

I sensed he was close to tears and might not want to cry in front of me. "It was very generous of her to leave us something." *Us, I'm calling the food pantry group us.* "Do you, uh, know about how much it is?"

He cleared his throat more loudly and pulled one of the manila folders toward him and opened it. "The initial donation is $40,000, to let us heavy up the electric and add some refrigeration cases so we can get milk and eggs. That was her specific intent." He looked down at the legal-looking forms. "Then she's set up an endowment of $200,000, but it can only spend the interest each year."

I sat back in my chair, thunderstruck, as Uncle Gordon would have said. I had not fully grasped the positive aspects of that term, having most recently associated it with learning of Robby's gambling debts. "Kept that little secret, did you?"

He looked up at me sharply, and then seemed to relax as he didn't see sarcasm or anger on my face. "I only just learned of it yesterday. When you called to see about getting together I figured you'd seen the lawyer's letter, too." He pointed to my name as one of the three people getting the letter, the others being Reverend Jamison and him.

I shook my head slowly. "Maybe they sent it to the church." I was silent for what seemed like quite awhile to me. "This is great, but," I didn't want to sound ungrateful, "it really doesn't change our financial picture much, does it?"

He nodded. "She was smart, Mary Doris. Getting those refrigerators is really important, but my guess is she didn't want to just give us a lot of money we'd spend and then have to put our hands out again."

"Yes, but her gift will call a lot of attention to us. Maybe someone else will think of us for their will."

"Preferably earlier," he said, dryly.

I laughed. "Right. Goodness," my thoughts were swirling and my laugh died. "We'll have to do a press release. We should do a brochure so other people can have something to look at if they're thinking of giving. And, and..."

He was grinning broadly. "You're really going to tackle this. I figured Reverend Jamison must know you better than that guy at the newspaper."

WHEN I WOKE UP the next day I lay still and watched Jazz's breathing as she slept on my stomach. I'd given up trying to convince her to sleep on a towel at the foot of the bed and finally went to sleep each night with an empty pillow case on my stomach so she didn't get the comforter dirty.

I was so astonished at Mary Doris' gift to the food pantry that I had forgotten to show Lance the small ledgers. This thought morphed into a fast mental list of what I needed to do at the food pantry. *What did you get yourself into?* My unspoken question issued in the form of an internal yell.

I shifted to my side and Jazz slid off onto the comforter and gave me a sleepy look. Then she walked over and put a paw on my nose to see if I was going to get up to feed her. When that did not look promising she settled into a ball near the crook of my neck.

I stared at the small bookshelf I had recently bought to store notebooks and files in addition to a few books. I had drafted a brief press release sitting in Aunt Madge's kitchen and she had added a paragraph on the food pantry's history. Who could I get to take charge of "heavying up" the electric, as Lance had referred to it, and buying refrigerated cases? Doctor Welby's face floated through my mind.

I sat straight up in bed and Jazz swatted me. "Wait a minute." How could I have not thought of this? Lance Wilson said he had known Mary Doris Milner well. *I could ask Lance about Mary Doris and Richard Tillotson.* Smiling I slid my legs out of the bed and reached for the packet of cat treats on the bedside table.

WHEN ANNIE MILNER CALLED later that morning her frosty tone caught me off guard. I was in Harry's office going over a couple of appraisal prospects to see which ones were one-story homes. "Aunt Mary Doris' attorney just sent me the information on her bequests. It looks as if you'll be handling the donation to the food pantry."

"Yes, we're really grate…" I began.

"It was one of her last bequests. I wasn't aware of it until this morning."

Did she expect me to feel guilty? I kept silent, no longer sure what direction the conversation would take.

"I suppose you'll want to know when the funds will go to the pantry?" she asked, in an I'm-an-attorney-and-I-know-what-I'm-talking-about tone.

"Ultimately, yes, but I don't want you to have to deal with this now. It must be…"

She interrupted again. "I'm just looking down the road. I'd like to get all the estate stuff as wrapped up as possible before I begin my campaign in earnest."

Stress can do funny things to people, I acknowledged to myself, and Annie had seemed very close to her great aunt. Still, I didn't like her attitude. "I know the others on the board would say we want to make this as easy for you as possible." *Bitch.* "Lance Wilson said he'd known your aunt nearly all his life."

It was as if a wave had washed over her and Annie had come out of the roil as a different person. "You must think I'm uncaring. I just want to stop thinking of Aunt Mary Doris in terms of an estate to be settled and get back to my memories of her."

How could I have called this woman a bitch? "Makes perfect sense to me. I can contact her lawyer directly to make the arrangements." I could, or maybe Doctor Welby would do it for me.

There was a brief silence, and I broached the topic that was serving as the elephant in the room. "I'm truly sorry your aunt's death was, well, that it does not seem to have been a natural one."

She seemed to brush that off as easily as if I'd said 'please accept my sympathy,' and frost was back in her tone. "I don't believe the police. They must have read some report wrong."

Even I, a master at ignore-it-and- it-will-go-away, thought her logic was as likely to hold true as a crab surviving long on a hot beach. "I hope you're right." I wasn't about to ask her who she thought would kill her aunt.

As I hung up the phone Harry looked at me questioningly. He spent a lot of time in Ocean Alley as a kid, this house he was remodeling having been his grandparents'. But he didn't live here full-time until after he retired, so he had not known Mary Doris or her background. I talked to him a bit after we found the photo albums in the attic, but he had apparently had a longer conversation with Aunt Madge more recently. "She's not taking her aunt's death well, I take it?" he asked.

"I guess not. I mean, who would?" I paused. "She's just a lot more focused on her work and her aunt's estate than I would be a couple of days after Aunt Madge died."

"May that be a long time away." He turned on his computer.

I keep waiting for Harry and Aunt Madge to become an item, as she would say, but they don't give any indication that they are more than good friends. *Too bad.*

"I'm heading out to check that bungalow on F Street." I picked up the folder of information and headed for the door.

"Look out for George Winters if you go to the courthouse." He smiled as he caught my eye. "He calls here almost every day. Maybe he's getting sweet on you."

I almost snorted at Harry.

DUCKING GEORGE WINTERS IS never easy, and I can't avoid the courthouse, since that's where I look up the information on prior home sales that I use to reach an opinion on the value of whatever house I'm appraising. I was in the Registrar of Deeds Office looking at some older sales records for bungalows near the one I was appraising when he came in with a pleased-as-punch expression on his face. He nodded at one of the women at a desk near the door and as I glanced at her she blushed. *He's got her tipping him off when I'm in here.*

He sidled up next to me at the counter and I finally looked to the right and saw his wide grin. George Winters is not much older than I am, but he dresses like a high school kid, except he wears khakis instead of cut-offs. I eyed his long shirt for a second – an expensive pullover that was a cross between a dark green t-shirt and a sports jersey – and then went back to the home sale information in front of me.

"C'mon Jolie. If you don't see me for a couple of days you miss me."

"As much as I miss stepping on sand crabs on the beach." I didn't look up.

He drummed his fingers on the counter for a second. "Did you get a look at any of those old ledgers Scoobie has? Do they have information about Peter Fisher's business?"

I turned to face him. "There is nothing up there that relates to the skeleton. I told you before, the attic has some antiques and old furniture, and…"

"What about those photo albums you were taking to Mary Doris Milner the day she died?" The look on George's face had gone from that of a person bantering with a buddy to that of reporter on the prowl – very intense.

I sat my pencil on the counter. "How old do you think Mary Doris is…was?"

"Ninety-four, I wrote her obit. Outlived almost everyone she knew."

"Right. So of all the Fisher and Tillotson friends who were in those old albums, how many do you think are alive?" I was thinking fast here.

"Could be zip. What's your point?"

"So, when Aunt Madge and I looked at them, she spotted Mary Doris in a picture and suggested Mary Doris might like to see it." I rubbed my nose, sure it was getting longer. "Like half the town, Mary Doris was her teacher."

He eyed me for two or three seconds. "Uh uh, Jolie. You and your sore tailbone wouldn't lug those old albums over there ASAP. You wanted her to tell you what she knew."

"It so happens," I closed the folder I was looking at, "that I'm nicer than you think I am. Unless," I sat the folder in the tray for refiling, "I'm talking to you of course." I gave him my sweetest smile and hitched my purse back on my shoulder.

I had planned to look at a couple of other recent sales, but he would probably just stand there and talk to me. Winters trailed me as I walked out. In the hallway, I stopped. "Look George, I'm tired of you coming up to me about the attic."

"Don't you mean about the skeleton?" He grinned.

"Whatever. It's Sgt. Morehouse you should be talking to, not me."

It suddenly occurred to me that he must not know that Mary Doris' death had been a murder, and I realized there had been no news stories about that. *What is Sgt. Morehouse up to?*

"You know something," he said.

I must have shown the realization on my face. "I know a lot of stuff. See you later George."

He didn't follow me out. I had just beeped open my car door when I realized he was putting a lot of time into the late Richard Tillotson's demise. He had someone in the Registrar of Deed's Office watching for me and he'd talked to enough people at the nursing home to know that I'd taken photo albums over there. I gave a mental shrug. *What do I care?*

A LOT, IT TURNED OUT, when I read the next day's paper. Winters was giving Ocean Alley readers an update of the "decades old murder," as he put it. He had done more digging and learned that Gracie's grandmother and mother had a long-standing "cold relationship" with Mary Doris, though no one seemed to know why. Though he did not say so, this fact seemed to be what had gotten his interest. At least that's how I read between the lines of his article. He had talked to Gracie, who had told him she'd never met Mary Doris, and then her mother who had told him she'd "forgotten more than she remembered" about the "tragic nature" of her uncle's disappearance. I didn't know George well, but I would bet Scoobie's lottery winnings that it was that comment that had fueled George's interest.

My mobile phone rang as I pulled into the small parking area at the B&B, but I didn't recognize the number so I didn't pick up. Remembering that Scoobie might have called from any phone, I listened to the message as I poured a glass of water.

"Jolie, its Annie Milner. We never did get to Java Jolt for that coffee, and I wanted to get a few friends together to talk about my options."

Now I'm her friend?

"I thought it might be fun to meet in the building I'm going to use as my campaign headquarters."

Sounded as if she figured out her best option on her own.

"Are you free Saturday afternoon about two o'clock? We'll meet at 227 C Street. Call me." She rattled off her number.

I sat on Aunt Madge's sofa holding my glass of water out of Jazz's reach as I thought about the invitation to Annie's campaign meeting. I didn't especially like her, but I didn't dislike her and I thought she'd be a much better prosecuting attorney than the current one. Who I had liked was her Aunt Mary Doris. *You barely knew her.*

"Wait a minute." I said, aloud.

"What minute?" asked Aunt Madge as she came into the great room through the swinging door that leads to the guests' breakfast room. She was carrying a small sack of groceries and opened the fridge to put some cream and butter in it.

"Annie called me to see if I would meet with her and some others to talk about her campaign, or whether she should run, or something." I began. Then I decided to be honest. Aunt Madge would find out anyway. "The building we'd meet in is one that I guess she will inherit from Mary Doris, 227 C Street."

Aunt Madge looked at me and raised an eyebrow.

"The building that used to be Peter Fisher and Richard Tillotson's bakery."

Aunt Madge filled her electric tea kettle. "Why does the building make a difference to you?"

I shrugged. "I guess it doesn't. She just seems to be," I paused.

"To be moving kind of fast after her aunt's death." Aunt Madge finished for me. "Which of course you would not do."

CHAPTER TWELVE

I LEFT ANNIE A VOICE MAIL saying I would meet her the next day. It was late afternoon and I still had two of the small ledgers crammed into my handbag. I decided to pay Lance Wilson an unannounced visit, and told Aunt Madge I was going down to the library to look for Scoobie. As I got to the front door I saw the two chipmunks sitting on the landing that was two steps up from the hallway. Each had a sunflower seed. I stopped to stare at them, then proceeded more slowly toward the door. *Maybe they want me to open it and let them out.* As I got closer they jumped down the two steps and ran under the washstand.

Great, they've learned to climb steps.

If Lance was surprised to see me on his porch he didn't show it. "I wondered if you could look at these ledgers for me." I held them up for him to see more closely.

He opened the door and motioned that I should precede him down the hall. I sat them on his small table and he picked one up and flipped through the pages without saying anything. Slowly he sat down and kept reading, still not saying anything.

I and my donut sat down.

After several minutes he raised his eyes to look at me. "I'd say they bought a lot of yeast, even for a bakery."

"Aunt Madge said most people knew they brewed and sold some kind of alcohol."

He nodded. "Mary Doris talked to me about that quite a bit the last couple of years. I guess," he stared down at the open page and then looked back at me, "she knew she wasn't going to be around forever, and she wanted to talk to someone about Richard." I stayed quiet, which was a struggle.

He continued, "She really believed that Peter killed Richard but, as far as I could tell, it was just a strong belief, she hadn't seen them quarrel, though she said that Peter thought Richard was cooking the books; I think that was her expression."

"She sort of implied that to me the other night." His eyebrow shot up, and I told him that I had gone to talk to her and had come back the next day with a photo album, but she had already died.

Hearing this, his mood seemed to visibly lift. "Well now, that's nice to know. She was looking forward to something when she died."

I let him think about this for a few moments, and then broached what I really wanted to know. "Is there anything in those ledgers that makes you think one of the two men was shorting the other?"

He shook his head. "Can't tell. You see all these erasure marks and it makes you wonder." He flipped through a few pages. "Maybe someone, for our purposes let's say Richard, took some money out of the till. You can see that the handwriting is different sometimes. One person wrote the original numbers and a couple of lines below it looks like some numbers were erased and others written in."

He slid the ledger to me and I looked again. The handwriting had not looked that different, all the numbers were written with the kind of old-fashioned penmanship that looked very neat to me, as if each letter were formed with care. The sevens had a line across the stem of the number. Looking more closely, I could see that there were differences in the writing styles, but they were not great. I slid it back to him. "It almost looks as if the second person was trying to write like the first person."

He shrugged, "Could be. If you don't mind me asking, why is this important?"

Before I could answer, there was a loud knock on the door and Lance stood up. "I haven't had two people stop by to visit me at the same time in years."

As soon as he opened the door I knew I was in trouble. I heard Sgt. Morehouse politely asked if he could come in for a few minutes. I quickly stuffed the ledgers in my purse. Deep into my purse. When he walked into the small living room I knew Morehouse would have hollered at me if he wasn't in Lance's house. "You! What are you doing here Jolie?"

"Ms. Gentil is the new chair of the committee for the food pantry," Lance said, having glanced at the table and noted that I had picked up the ledgers. "Did you hear about our good fortune?" he asked, gesturing that Morehouse should sit in one of the leather chairs.

I watched Morehouse deflate as he sat down. "Good fortune?"

"Yes. My good friend Mary Doris Milner left the pantry a substantial sum of money. A good bit of it will help us modernize the facility and add some refrigerators." Lance smiled.

"That's terrific." Morehouse paused. "I'm here to talk about Mary Doris, in fact." He glanced at me.

"Would you like me to leave?" I asked, trying to be courteous and hoping he'd let me stay.

"All right with you if Jolie stays?" Morehouse asked Lance.

"Fine by me," he said, appearing puzzled by Morehouse's visit.

"I have some...uncomfortable news. It'll be in the paper tomorrow." Morehouse drew out the small notebook I'd seen him use when he interviewed people. "I know you were good friends. Partially I didn't want you to be surprised by it, and in part I hope you can help me."

"Help you?" Lance asked.

Morehouse took a breath. "I'm afraid Mary Doris did not die of natural causes. She was poisoned with methyl alcohol."

Morehouse and I both jumped to Lance's chair as he leaned forward, almost falling out of the chair. Morehouse kept a hand on Lance's elbow. Which was good, because jumping had not helped my tailbone and I don't think I would have been much help to anybody.

"Steady there. I'll get you some water." I walked down the short hallway into the kitchen and grabbed a coffee mug from the small dish drainer and filled it with water.

When I got back to the living room Lance was sitting back in the recliner, his eyes closed. My own met Morehouse's, and for once he did not look angry at me. He took the mug. "Ready for a small sip?"

Lance waved him away. "It was just the shock. I'm okay." He opened his eyes. "Are you going to find the bastard who did this?"

Morehouse sat back down, placing the mug on the floor and picking up his notebook from where it had dropped at his feet. "I'm going to do that, yes. That's what I meant about you helping."

Lance sat up straighter. When he spoke, his voice was clear and strong. "What do you want to know?"

Morehouse went over the events of the day before her death, including my visit, and the suddenness with which her stomach flu seemed to arise. "That's why we did the toxicology tests at the police lab. The nurse who was on that night insisted that Mary Doris had been healthy as can be. She actually," here a small smile appeared and vanished, "thought Jolie here might have given Mary Doris something that didn't sit well with her."

Lance glanced at me. "Jolie didn't know about the money for the Food Pantry. None of us did."

Great, give Morehouse a motive for me.

"I can't think of anything to arrest Jolie for other than being a pain in the ass." He did smile at Lance then.

"Hey." Then took Morehouse's look in my direction to be a command to shut up.

Lance shook his head slowly. "I can't think of a soul who didn't like her."

"I can't either," Morehouse said. "It just seems like too much of a coincidence that Richard's skeleton is found and then Mary Doris is murdered."

Lance opened his mouth to speak, shut it, and then spoke. "She did have a secret."

Rekindling Motives

I sat up straighter in my hardback chair. "A secret?"

Morehouse didn't even look at me, he kept looking straight into Lance's eyes. "What kind of a secret?"

Lance looked from me to his big screen TV and back at Morehouse. "After Richard disappeared, Mary Doris left Ocean Alley. She said, I heard this later of course, that she couldn't stand to look at the ocean when Richard wasn't with her."

This registered with me. I thought Aunt Madge had told me the same thing.

"The thing is," Lance's eyes filled with tears, "she only told me this a few years ago, and she asked me not to repeat it."

"I don't think anything can hurt her now," Morehouse said, quietly.

"She left because she was carrying Richard's baby. They planned to elope the weekend after his sister Audrey and Peter Fisher got married." He cleared his throat. "They didn't want to take away from that wedding."

Mary Doris' firm assertion that Richard would never have left her made more sense now. "What happened to the baby?" I asked, and was surprised to hear that I was almost whispering.

Lance wiped a tear from the corner of one eye. "She said she gave it up for adoption; she never even said if it was a boy or girl. I don't know why I'm even telling you this, but it's likely the only thing you wouldn't find out any other way." He pulled a tissue from his pocket and blew his nose. "I can't imagine it matters."

Morehouse made a note. "Yeah, hard to imagine it would." He looked at Lance. "How old would that person be now?"

"More than seventy," Lance said, "possibly not even alive."

Morehouse nodded. "A lot more adoptions were private back then. Likely the records are gone, even if we knew where to look."

Lance nodded. "She never did say where she went. I think that was deliberate. She always liked Chicago though. Took a couple of trips to the art museum there."

Morehouse stood. "If you think of anything else…"

"Do you have to write that in a report or something?" Lance asked.

Morehouse hesitated. "I'll mention it to the captain, so two of us know. I won't write it down unless it's important later."

Lance saw him to the door, and I remained rooted to my donut. When he came back into the room we just looked at each other. "Thank you for not telling about the ledgers."

Lance nodded, unsmiling. "I figured you wouldn't have picked them up if you wanted him to see them." He sat down in the chair opposite me at the table and put his head in his hands. "Murdered. It's impossible."

"Would you like me to stay or go?" I asked, quietly.

"Nothing you can do here." When I stood, he looked up, "Could I borrow that album that has some pictures of Mary Doris?"

"I'll drop it by this evening." I let myself out.

CHAPTER THIRTEEN

SURE ENOUGH, THE NEXT day's Ocean Alley paper had a huge heading: *Retired School Marm Murdered*.

"Marm?" Aunt Madge said in disgust as she ran water in the sink to wash her guests' morning dishes. "No one has used that term in years and years. It's stupid."

I glanced at the headline. If they'd used teacher it wouldn't have fit on one line. I held my tongue.

"And," she turned from the sink to face me, soap bubbles dripping from her latex gloves onto the floor, "that business about the methyl alcohol is ridiculous. It would taste terrible. She would never drink enough to kill herself."

I hesitated, and then said, "Scoobie said if you put methyl alcohol with a strong-tasting drink it might not taste so bad."

"And what does Scoobie know about that?" Aunt Madge asked, furious.

I knew she wasn't mad at Scoobie, just mad. "He says he read about it in the library."

She seemed to sag onto the kitchen sink. "I just can't stand to think of her dying like that."

I walked over and gave her a hug. "Me either." Then inspiration struck me. "That's why we need to keep thinking about Richard's death. They must be connected."

Aunt Madge raised her head from my hug. "Nothing doing."

For once I gave as good a steely glint in the eye as she did. I had no intention of telling Aunt Madge or anyone else that Mary Doris Milner had had Richard Tillotson's baby. That was her business. But, I couldn't help but think a spurned adult child might have found her. "I liked Mary Doris. I want to figure out how Richard got in that attic."

Aunt Madge looked at me for a couple of seconds and then turned back to the sink. "Just don't get shot at this time."

I DECIDED TO WALK to Java Jolt. My back wasn't feeling a lot better, but some, and I felt as if my whole body needed to stretch. As I left Aunt Madge told me to call her if I needed a ride back. Sounded as if she wasn't going to hold it against me that I wanted to learn more about Richard's death.

Which was ridiculous, when you stopped to think about it. It was more than seventy years since the murder. The thing that nagged at me was that the skeleton was clean and stored with clothes from the 1940s. That meant that long after his death – assuming he died when he disappeared – someone knew where to find his body, could get to it to clean it, and could put it in the old wardrobe. That person had to be pretty unfeeling, and downright kinky.

I tried to envision what the murderer had done. He couldn't have buried Richard in Ocean Alley. Beach towns don't have cemeteries. I know this because Aunt Madge visits Uncle Gordon's grave on Memorial Day weekend; I went with her often until I was in high school. When I was about ten I asked her why he was so far from Ocean Alley, and she said you can't bury someone near the ocean; the soil is too sandy and moist. She said that in New Orleans the cemeteries host mausoleums rather than graves. That was certainly obvious after Hurricane Katrina.

I felt a pang of guilt. I hadn't gone to the cemetery with her in years.

My mind went back to Richard Tillotson and his murder. Whoever did it couldn't bury Richard nearby – assuming he was killed in Ocean Alley – and not everyone had cars back then. Even if the murderer did have a car, where do you drive with a dead body in the trunk? And do you just wander into a cemetery and try to sneak in an extra body?

I glanced toward the ocean and decided to climb up the few steps to get onto the boardwalk so I could walk the last couple of blocks toward Java Jolt without a row of houses between me and the water. The sun was bright and I shielded my eyes as I looked toward the water, watching waves roll onto the deserted beach and recede. A lot of years had passed since Richard and Mary Doris had looked at the ocean together.

All this time Mary Doris had kept a pretty important secret. Or had she? Maybe she had told someone. Perhaps, as an adult, that baby had even found its birth mother. But what would that matter? If the adoptive parents had been less than perfect that would not have been Mary Doris' fault. Anyway, if there had been a reunion it could have been decades ago.

I gave my head a shake as I walked along. I could not see any way a long ago adoption played a role in a poisoning death now. A sharp gust of wind made me pull up my collar and then thrust my hands into the pockets of my jacket. I felt the notebook I planned to use as I sat in Java Jolt to think and make a list.

I like lists. Even when things around me seem ridiculously busy, a list of what I need to do instills some order. At least in my mind. After a quick hello to Joe and pouring coffee from his self-serve thermos I plopped my donut and derrière in a chair at the back of the shop.

What I Know
1) Someone killed Richard Tillotson, whom MD loved very much.
2) The killer (or someone else) put the body somewhere for a time. (Attic would have stunk if in there.)
3) RT and Peter Fisher did not seem to get along.
4) RT and PF ran a bakery and were moonshiners.

What I Don't Know
1) When did RT's skeleton get put in the wardrobe in the attic?
2) Who put it there? Duh
3) Did MD know something important about who killed RT?
4) Who benefits most by MD being dead?

My cell phone rang and Gracie Allen's name was on Caller ID. "I can't find it anywhere!" She sounded as if she'd been crying. "And I want to get rid of that house."

It took a couple of seconds before it registered that she may have been talking about the deed to her grandmother's house. "It's not the end of the world, Gracie." There was a loud sniff on the other end of the phone. "You'll likely pay more for the title search and an attorney can draw up a new deed, so it'll be…"

Now she was sobbing. I couldn't imagine why she was so upset. "Really, Gracie, it'll be okay." *What do you say to a Connecticut-stay-at-home mom who is bawling into the phone?*

She calmed a bit and blew her nose. "That's only part of it. First you get hurt and the paper has articles about Richard's disappearance, then poor Mary Doris Milner is killed, and, and…Oh, and the skeleton. I forgot the skeleton!" She was taking up right where she left off.

"Gracie, Gracie, get a grip." I wasn't sure what to say. "It'll get worked out somehow."

"But it's all my fault. My husband wanted to keep the house and I thought it would be a lot more fun to have a place on Cape Cod." She stopped because I had started to laugh. I couldn't help it.

That probably wasn't good either. I tried to keep the humor out of my voice. "Listen, none of this is your fault. You think poor Richard appeared in that wardrobe because you wanted a place in Cape Cod instead of Ocean Alley? Can you imagine if you kept the house and one of your kids found him? They'd be scarred for life." I was hoping to make her see how absurd she was being, and for a minute it worked.

"I know, Jeremy says that, too."

Jeremy, who's Jeremy? Oh, her husband.

She started up again. "Poor Mary Doris Milner," she wailed. At this point I realized the four other customers and Joe were staring at me. I grimaced at Joe and shrugged. He pointed to a door behind the counter and I walked back there as I listened. "And she was Annie Milner's aunt!"

I walked into the tiny room behind the coffee bar and sat on a stool. "This stuff happened in spite of you, not because of you. Is anyone home with you?"

The response was akin to the local foghorn, followed by words. "You must think I'm an idiot."

"No of course not." *Well, maybe a little, it's not as if you knew Richard or Mary Doris.* "All of this is upsetting." I glanced around the small room. It had shelves from floor to ceiling along the back wall and they were lined with small plastic tubs, each with a five-pound bag of sugar, dry coffee creamer, or sugar substitute, all carefully labeled. When the tubs ended there were shelves of napkins and disposable cups.

"The thing is," I continued, "it will be over pretty soon, and you'll have your life back. Plus a place on Cape Cod."

It took about five more minutes before I thought she was calm enough for me to tell her I had an appointment for an appraisal and had to get going. I walked back into the shop, which now was empty except for Joe and me. "Jeez, did I scare away your customers?"

"Nah. They were here long enough to have two refills." He looked up from pouring beans into a grinder. "Gracie okay?"

"She will be." I moved back to my table, happy to sink onto the donut and review my list. I sat with my chin resting on my fists as I concentrated. It didn't make sense that Peter Fisher would kill Richard. He could be an obvious suspect, and it would mean he and his new bride would have to move in with her mother and siblings, or at least watch out for them. Of course, it could have been an accident.

I glanced at my watch. It was time to go over to C Street to meet Annie. Joe walked over and picked up my coffee mug as I stood to leave. "Thanks. Anything that saves a couple of steps is good now."

"I wanted to steal a look at what you were writing," he said, with an unabashed grin. "Bet it was about your newest murder mystery."

"If you're so smart, you could solve it," I said, with more good humor than I felt.

THERE WERE FIVE PEOPLE in the former Bakery at the Shore when I got there. You could tell Annie, or someone, had worked hard to clean the place. A recent owner had installed a long bar that looked mahogany. It was clean and had a couple of small stacks of paper sitting on it. Long-dried wallpaper still curled around the mirror behind the bar but the rest of it had been pulled down except for the long wall that included a door that might have led to a former kitchen.

The only person I knew was Jennifer Stenner. She looked as surprised to see me as I was to see her. I've warmed up to her, but not a lot. She was one of the cool girls when we were in eleventh grade and I was miserable, wanting to get back to my high school in Lakewood. While my being in Ocean Alley that year was not her fault, she and her friends had been targets of my fantasies to have cheerleading banned, or maybe have all cheerleaders forced to shave their heads. They just looked so damn happy.

One of the three men seated around the table must have just complimented Annie on her work to clean up the place, as she said, "Yes, I've been in here several times. The wallpaper is hard to get down, but it will eventually all come together."

"Hey Jennifer." I sat next to her. "You did a great job on the reunion."

While she had regarded me with what seemed to be a forced smile, she now gave me a broad one. "I'm so glad you liked it. We worked really hard to be sure everyone had fun."

"The only problem is that Scoobie made off with my Sherlock Holmes bubble pipe."

"He actually brought it into Stenner Appraisals with a bottle of bubbles. Didn't he tell you?"

I could tell her question was a hidden one. She wanted to know if Scoobie and I dated. "Luckily he doesn't tell me everything he does."

"That does sound lucky," Annie said as she sat down on the other side of Jennifer and began introducing attendees to one another.

I felt myself redden, annoyed that Annie was putting Scoobie down. I supposed I had given her the ammunition for her comment.

"And this is Hardin Grooms, from City Council," she was saying. As she introduced each person she was giving them a stick-on name badge, already lettered. "I thought I'd make it easy for us to remember each others' names this first time we meet."

It was no wonder I didn't know the other two men, they were attorneys from other towns in the county. I had half forgotten that she was running for a countywide office. Jeff Markham looked to be about thirty-five and was exceptionally fit, while Sam Jefferson, the only African-American, could be fifty or thereabouts. His skin had almost no wrinkles, but the graying hair told more about his age than his face did.

While Annie talked I looked at the papers she had passed out that had her summary bio and a full resume. She had done a lot since high school – finished undergrad in three years, law school, one year in private practice and three with the prosecuting attorney's office. When she didn't work, she tutored children with low reading skills and she had been president of the Ocean Alley Rotary Club. *All this and she did her aunt's laundry.*

I turned my attention back to Annie as she finished talking about why she wanted to run for prosecuting attorney. "I think the current prosecuting attorney's priorities are skewed. He takes cases to court that could easily be settled, and he lets drug dealers plea bargain to probation." She paused. "I'm not going to prosecute based on public opinion, but I do think citizens are letting us know they want fewer burglaries and car thefts, and the only way to get that in check is to prosecute the people the police arrest instead of putting them back on the street so they can steal laptop computers to support their drug habit. People have a right to feel safe."

She looked at each of us in turn. I sensed she had expected applause.

Hardin Grooms cleared his throat. "I know several of us on City Council would love to cut the police budget, and if crime goes down we could do that." He paused for a moment, then continued. "As one who has run for office several times, I can tell you it's not cheap. And you'd have to run a campaign throughout the county, not just in Ocean Alley."

Annie studied the old mirror for a moment before meeting his eye. "I was dreading doing that kind of fundraising. However, my dear aunt looks after me even after death." She seemed to weigh her words carefully. "I'll have much of what I think I'll need. I'll raise funds of course. People expect it. It's just that I won't have to spend half my time doing it, and I won't have to take money from people who might expect favors later."

I'm no political expert, but that last part sounded pretty naive to me. Jennifer chimed in that she would be happy to host a "meet and greet" at her townhouse, and I looked around the room itself. There appeared to have been a hodge podge of renovations, but the tin ceiling tiles were still in place, which was more than you could say for a lot of buildings this old. The door at the back of this large room probably led to the kitchen where Peter and Richard had produced the goods for what I thought of as their cover business. No sign of a closet in which Richard Tillotson might have locked Peter Fisher. The wall that had the kitchen door still had wallpaper, which looked bumpy. I figured the paper covered some architectural sins.

"...do you think the same time would work next week?" Annie was asking. Jennifer and the three men pulled out pocket calendars or smart phones and I watched them agree on a time for the following weekend. I watched without committing to the second meeting and picked up the bio info she had provided and stuffed it into my purse.

As I made my way back to the B&B I thought about the meeting. It seemed odd that the only time Annie mentioned Mary Doris' death was when she was talking about money, but perhaps they had talked about her before I arrived.

CHAPTER FOURTEEN

THE *OCEAN ALLEY PRESS* RAN an article on Annie and the other two primary candidates. A man named John Abernathy had joined Annie and current Prosecuting Attorney Martin Small in the race. The primary was not until June, but because all three had declared their intention to run the paper was covering their announcements. Given the salary –$120,000 – I thought it odd several attorneys wanted the position. I would clean the meat out of crabs for six months to make that right now, but I thought lawyers could make more money in private practice.

There were two photos of each, a mug shot and one with family members. Looking at the photo of Annie and her parents I was surprised to see how much older they were than my parents. They looked as if they could be her grandparents. I vaguely remembered that Aunt Madge had said Annie and her mother did not get along well, which was why she had moved to Ocean Alley to live with Mary Doris during high school.

Because Annie was running I read the short pieces on each candidate. The two men had much more experience as lawyers, but Annie appeared to be the only one who had come up with a slogan – "Upholding our laws with a fresh perspective."

AFTER LUNCH I PICKED UP SCOOBIE and listened as he outlined his plan to look through the last couple of notebooks in the attic to see if there were any strings of numbers that struck him as worth playing in the lottery. I was tempted to ask him if he thought that he was focusing a bit much on the lottery, but I didn't. I wasn't in charge of his life.

I unlocked the door of the Fisher house and knew there was something wrong as soon as we walked inside. There wasn't usually a breeze coming from the kitchen.

Without talking about it we walked to the back of the house and stopped at the edge of the kitchen to stare at the broken glass in the exterior door. The door had six small panes of glass in the top half, and someone had apparently broken one and reached in to unlock the door. There was no burglar alarm and in winter months there would likely have been no one out at night to see anyone breaking in.

"Come on," Scoobie said, "outside."

I followed him. "You think someone would still be in the house?"

"No idea. And don't intend to find out the hard way." He nodded toward my purse. "Call your buddy Morehouse and ask him to look. He gets paid to check out stuff like this."

I made sure the police knew we didn't have a reason to think that anyone was in the house and then we sat on the front porch to wait. It was warm for December, almost fifty degrees. "I guess the articles about me falling out of the attic and you playing those lottery numbers let people know the house was vacant."

Scoobie shrugged. "Yeah, but it's been vacant for a while. Could just be somebody wanting in out of the cold."

I regarded him. "When you were drinking or whatever did you live on the streets a lot?"

"Not much. Mostly I was here and I knew people, so there'd at least be a porch I could crash on." He stood up as a patrol car pulled to the curb. "Remind me to tell you about my carny days sometime."

"What's that?" I asked, assuming I'd misunderstood him.

"Carny, carnival. I got a wild hair five or six years ago and hooked up with the carnival that comes to Saint Anthony's every year for the Italian festival and signed on to do site clean-up for a few months."

I stared at him for a few seconds and then extended a hand to the police officer who had been at Ruth Riordan's house the day I found her body. I glanced at her name badge – Corporal Dana Johnson. I would not have been able to come up with it on my own. She let us describe the broken glass and then said she would walk through the house.

She was back out in five minutes. "No one there now. I looked in the closets and behind doors. Didn't pull the rope down for the attic. If that's the only place that has stuff you can look at it with me to see if it looks like anything is missing."

We walked up the staircase in silence and Scoobie pulled down the ladder. "Police coming up," she shouted as she stood on the bottom rung. We watched as her torso leaned into the attic and she shone a long flashlight beam around the space. "Clear," she said. Then she placed her hands flat on the attic floor and nimbly leaned left, raised her torso by leaning on her hands, and then raised her legs in a quick bend-and-straighten motion until they were on the floor. By that time she had flipped her hands forward. She gave a push and came to a standing position and looked down at us.

I know my mouth was open, and Scoobie's must have been because she grinned at us. "Gymnastics when I was a kid." She gestured, "Come on up."

"Jolie's into tumbling," Scoobie said, steadying the ladder for me.

"You just can't let go of anything."

"Listen." He scrambled up behind me. "The time I caught you coming down the stairs was one thing, but if you keep falling without me at the bottom you're going to crack your skull."

Officer Johnson chuckled as I got to the top of the ladder. "Grab on." She extended her hand.

I did and was surprised at her strength as she basically pulled me up onto the floor. I winced at the pull in my back and saw the concern on her face. "No problem." I wished there weren't. "It's just this is my first time in the attic…"

"Since she fell out of it," Scoobie said, hauling himself up.

We did what all women do when they don't like a comment and ignored him. "Can you tell if anything is missing?" she asked.

Since Ramona and Scoobie had worked up here several times as I sat below on my donut it looked very different. "It seemed a lot more crowded last time I was up here,"

"Ramona took the dress form, and I've got the train set," Scoobie said, but I could hear the distraction in his voice. "Hey, though, look at the trunks in the back. We didn't leave them open."

I watched as he peered into them, then turned shaking his head. "Looks as if the books are still in that trunk, but those last few ledgers or diaries in the other trunk are gone."

Dana Johnson's expression went from half amusement to all business. "OK, down we go."

"But…" I began, half irritated by her words.

"No buts. Just go down, please." Her tone was firm, and she held out a hand. "Steady yourself on me as you go down the first couple of steps.

Scoobie was next to us in a flash. "Me first, for the obvious reason." He began to back down the ladder and called to me to start down.

When all three of us were on the second floor Officer Johnson took the radio off her belt and called for a fingerprint technician because of a break-in and gave the address. She ended her transmission and met our gazes. "If you'd said some antiques were gone I'd be concerned but not so much. I heard Ramona tell someone in the Purple Cow that those ledgers had business records and such. Richard Tillotson's body may have been there for decades, but someone who knows something about his death may still be around and wanting to know what you guys are finding."

NATURALLY, TWO POLICE cars in front of the house attracted more attention than one, and Scoobie and I were soon joined on the porch steps by George Winters. He was in worn blue jeans and a New Jersey Knicks sweatshirt and he looked as disgruntled as I felt. "You two could give it a rest on my weekend off."

"Or you could keep doing what you were doing on your time off," I said.

The porch steps were wide and he sat next to me. "I told my editor to call me on anything to do with this house. And you." He gave me a quick grin as he pulled his thin reporter's notebook from his back pocket. A stub of a pencil was in the spiral rings and he pushed on it with his pinkie until he could pull it out.

Scoobie seemed less irritated than I. "We found a pane out of the back door when we went in, so we called the cops. There was an article in the paper that let everybody know the house is vacant."

"You gotta love sarcasm," Winters said as he jotted notes. "So, anything missing?"

"Nothing we want in the paper," Johnson said as she sat on the other side of Scoobie. "Damn fine day, isn't it?"

Winters leaned around me and looked at her. "Come on Dana, off the record."

"Since you always keep your word on that, I'll tell you a couple of those notebooks you wrote about are gone. That seems to be all." She leaned around Scoobie to look at Winters. "You know anything more than you printed?"

"No." He jabbed his pencil back in the spiral ring and stood up. "I'll just print there was some broken glass and it was hard to tell if anything is missing since the attic's a mess."

"How do you know it's a mess?" Dana asked, a sharp edge to her voice.

"Gracie told me that you guys moved stuff when you went up there after Jolie fell on her ass." He walked down the steps and gave a small wave over his shoulder as he headed back to his car.

When he shut his car door and started the engine Dana looked at Scoobie and me. "He's a pain in the ass, but sometimes we learn as much from him as he does from us, and if he says it's off the record he means it." She stood and stretched. "I gotta get ol' Chuck out of the attic. He collects antique tools and stuff and he'll be up there all day."

When she was back in the house, Scoobie said, "I don't think they watch CSI enough."

I giggled in spite of myself.

We went by the hardware store to buy a piece of glass, some putty and – thanks to the clerk's suggestion – some tiny metal fasteners to keep the glass in place until the putty dried.

I didn't want to be the one to call Gracie so I made Scoobie use my cell phone to call her. "Just tell her I have a sore throat." Seeing his expression I added, "She'll either talk or cry for ten minutes if I call her. I'm not up for it."

With an eye roll worthy of my mother Scoobie placed the call and pushed the speaker phone button as the phone rang. It was answered by a surprisingly mellow-sounding Gracie. "Jolie?" she asked.

Scoobie started to hand the phone to me, but I backed up a step and mouthed, "Caller ID."

"Hey, Gracie, it's Scoobie. I just borrowed Jolie's phone for a minute."

"That was nishe of her," she slurred.

Scoobie tilted his head back and with his free hand mimed holding a bottle of beer that he was chugging into his mouth. "You sound like you're having a good day."

She giggled. "Can you tell? The doctor gave me these, umm, prescription something." She paused. "My husband calls them my happy pills."

Scoobie's expression softened and I felt guilty as hell. "Sorry you needed them. Listen, Gracie, I just wanted to let you know that everything's fine, but…"

"Jolie didn't fall out of the attic again, did she?"

I would characterize her laugh as maniacal.

"No, nothing like that. Jolie's fine, well as fine as you can be sitting on a donut all day." He grinned at me. "I just wanted you to know some jerk strolled into your grandma's house. Broke a pane on the back door, but we already got that fixed."

"Oh dear," she said, and it sounded as if she was clouding over.

"Think happy pills," Scoobie said.

She gave a calmer laugh. "Yes. Thasht a good idea."

"Doesn't look as if they did any damage. I just wanted you to know."

"And Jolie's OK? Why do you have her phone?"

"She, uh, went into the bathroom at Newhart's. We stopped by for lunch." He grinned at me. "She's treating."

"Oh, well, your lucky day. Say," I could almost see her sit up straighter. "I heard you won some money playing numbers from those little, watchyacallits, books."

"Yep. You want a cut?"

"No silly. Well, I need to go lie down for a few minutes before the kids get home from school."

Scoobie told her he thought that was a great idea and hung up.

"You left out the part about them taking some of those little watchyacallits," I said, dryly.

"Why upset her?"

CHAPTER FIFTEEN

WHEN HARRY STEELE called Monday morning I could almost hear the chuckle in his voice. "You'll be glad to hear even the county prosecuting attorney's staff is not above the law."

"You mean Annie Milner?" I asked.

"I do indeed. Seems she was getting ready to move stuff into the old storefront Mary Doris left her when the executor told her it has to be appraised to determine its value for the estate. He wants it done before she makes any changes to the place."

"And she wants you to appraise it?" I asked.

"Specifically, you. She said you were on her campaign committee."

"She, I never…All I did was go to a meeting with her and a couple of other people over the weekend." If Annie was going to go around telling people I was on her campaign committee I'd have to put a stop to that.

"You have to watch politicians," Harry said, but his tone was light. "I take it you'll do the work."

I thought about it for a moment. "You may need to review my comps. I only did residential appraisals in college."

"Sure. She wants it done pretty quickly, so stop by this morning and get the key. I'll square it with the attorney who's executor."

I sat stirring the pulp around in my juice for a minute and thought about Annie and her run for county prosecuting attorney. I was more than mildly annoyed that she was throwing my name around, on the other hand, the chance to snoop in Peter Fisher and Richard Tillotson's former Bakery at the Shore was way too good to pass up.

I was giving myself a head slap when Aunt Madge entered the kitchen. "Good heavens, Jolie. What's that all about?"

I explained Harry's call. "And I just remembered that Lester Argrow is the real estate agent. Or has been anyway. You know how he is."

Aunt Madge smiled. "I think he's easier on you than he is on Harry." She walked over to the electric kettle and turned up the heat, about to have what would likely be her third or fourth cup of tea, even though it was only about nine o'clock. "Besides, Lester likes you."

THE LOCK ON THE door to Mary Doris Milner's building was surely not the original one, but it was close. I finally figured out that if I pulled the door toward me and jiggled the key I could get in. The smell of must and age was more pungent than during Annie's campaign meeting; she must have aired the place for a good hour before we got there. I hated to close the door, but I've learned the hard way to lock myself in when I work in a vacant building.

I finally located the light switch in the back of the room, not far from the old bar, and made a mental note that the electrical system was woefully out of date. It had been awhile since I'd been in a building with push-button light switches. Dollars to donuts if she were buying the building a mortgage company would require a lot of upgrading before they would underwrite a loan. Maybe Mary Doris left her enough money to do some remodeling.

With light from two overhead single bulbs I stood in the center of the room and turned slowly. The mahogany bar was the only item that kept the room – the entire building, really – from being a true dive. The mirror behind it had been there for decades and had deep scratches in a couple of places. The floor must have been constructed with very hard wood, as it bore few marks. It had been painted white at some point in the past, so it was hard to tell what kind it was. Oak if I had to guess. The exception was a spot near the door that I assumed had led to a former kitchen. That piece of the floor had been replaced with pine and had a couple of deep gouges in it.

Reminding myself that there would be nothing worth finding so long after Peter and Richard had owned the bakery I pulled out my tape measure and got to work. By the time I finished measuring the main room, two small offices behind it, and the old kitchen, which still had a rusty iron wood-burning stove in it, I could not understand why Annie wanted this building. It was a dump. The windows had single pane glass that would surely let in more heat and cold than they kept out, and every surface was likely covered in lead-based paint.

I took more photos than usual. With a building this old I thought we might need more photos in the appraisal documents. I also wanted help from Harry, and I thought the pictures might help him work with me. I dropped the camera in my purse and stood with my back to the kitchen door and surveyed the main room from that vantage point. It was easy to envision glass bakery cases stocked with fresh bread and cookies, perhaps with a hollow area underneath to store bottles of illicit booze. When I was very young, my sister Renée took me to a candy store that would have been near this building, and I could imagine children running in and out of Bakery at the Shore as we had done at the old candy store.

My lower back was sore and I wished I had thought to bring one of Aunt Madge's lightweight lawn chairs. I leaned against the door jamb and pressed the small of my back into it. I sniffed. It smelled like some kind of heavy duty glue, sort of like the old rubber cement Uncle Gordon used to keep in his boat house. I was turning to look at the wallpaper behind me when there was a loud pounding on the front door.

I dropped my notebook and tape measure and jumped, then cursed up a storm at the pain this brought to my back. At the door was Annie Milner, who had the good grace to look chagrined for scaring the crap out of me. I walked over and unlocked the door to let her in.

"I'm sorry, Jolie. I didn't mean to scare you."

"No big deal." Why are you lying? Your heart is still pounding.

Her gaze went around the room and she said nothing for several seconds. "Looks as if I have a lot to do, doesn't it?"

"To be honest, this building's in such bad shape it's hard to imagine why you want it." I pointed to the molding at the top of the room, which had separated from the ceiling by at least an inch. "It's settled quite a bit. If it did that twenty-five years ago and not since, then it's not such a big deal, but my guess is it is more recent."

"Why?" she asked, following my pointing finger.

"It doesn't look as if there was ever a lowered ceiling put in, so anyone who looked up would see that spot. It would only take a ladder and a couple of minutes to move the molding up a bit and hammer in a couple of nails."

She sighed. "I get it. I wish I hadn't promised…" she chewed her bottom lip.

"Promised your aunt you'd keep it?"

She nodded slowly. "I don't know why she liked this old building. She owned two houses in town, used to live in one and rent the other, until she went into the nursing home. She didn't care if those were sold."

I thought for a couple of seconds before replying. "Aunt Madge might have some idea," I began.

She gave a small, dismissive wave. "If you mean that story about Mary Doris dating Richard Tillotson and him having a bakery here, I can't imagine she'd be that impractical."

I took that, and the pain in my tailbone, as my cues to leave. "I'll work up the appraisal tomorrow, I hope." When she glanced at me, I added, "It may take some creative thinking. There haven't been a lot of similar buildings sold lately."

She nodded. "This whole thing is ridiculous. Except for some specific bequests her entire estate comes to me. It seems silly to have this appraised before I move in and do some improvements."

I couldn't resist. "You know how lawyers are."

HARRY HAD GIVEN ME A KEY to the side door nearest his large home office, and I made myself at home there early the next morning. I wanted to start work on the appraisal package before I went to the food pantry to do some paperwork. If I didn't get an order to the main food bank by this afternoon we'd miss our monthly shipment of nonperishable goods.

It was too early to get into the courthouse to look at other commercial sales, so I spent half an hour entering data into the appraisal software program and was heading back out when Harry came downstairs.

"You're up early." He raised his mug of coffee to offer me a cup.

"No thanks. Have to go over to First Prez to place a food order and then I'll swing by the courthouse."

"Have at it." He turned on his computer.

I like Harry a lot, but find it hard to imagine why anyone would want to retire to Ocean Alley and fix up an old Victorian house. None of his kids live within an easy drive. I reminded myself that I live sufficiently far from my parents so they can't drop in; maybe he did the same.

CHAPTER SIXTEEN

SCOOBIE WAS WAITING BY THE entrance that led to the food pantry, collar pulled up and hands in his pockets. "Scoobie! If you had called I wouldn't have gone to Harry's first."

"I've only been here a couple of minutes." He stamped his feet to warm them as we walked down the short hallway to the counter where volunteers distributed food.

I scanned the area, which was as neat as it had been every time I'd been in there. I'd only met a few of the volunteers who distributed the food and I made a mental note to thank them. I walked toward the file cabinet just inside the food storage area and pulled a file from the top drawer. "This is what I'd really like you to look at." I handed Scoobie the master list of items we could order from the Lakewood Food Bank and a copy of our food pantry's last order. "I want to order things people are used to seeing, but there may be some things you think should have been on the shelves but weren't."

"Mac and cheese," he said, before looking at the list.

"That's a staple for little kids." I looked over his shoulder. "Is it one of the choices?"

Scoobie turned his head halfway to look me in the eye with an expression I can only call intense. I held my hands up in submission. "I'll leave you to look." I wandered to the shelves which were organized similarly to a grocery store—canned fruits and vegetables together, crackers and soup next to each other, and so on. I wasn't sure if all the empty spots were because it was time for an order or if there were always blank spots for sugar and cooking oil.

"Got a pen?" Scoobie asked, still looking at the list.

I took one from the empty can-turned-pen-holder on the counter and he began making small tick marks next to items.

After a minute he handed me the list. "What they ordered before is okay, I just added a few things."

He had checked mac and cheese, tuna helper, and canned pineapple as things to add. At the bottom he had written "Coco Puffs."

I looked up and saw the sparkle in his eyes. "Because, you know, I'm koo koo for Coco Puffs."

"I think I can only order what's on the list, but I can ask Aunt Madge to keep some Coco Puffs on hand for you."

"You'll be getting a lot of local donations in the next couple of weeks." At my blank expression he added, "Christmas. The one time of the year, the second time each year, that people think to give a lot." Scoobie took a piece of paper off the counter and began tearing it into small pieces.

"What are you doing?" I asked as I pulled the order form from the folder.

"What you need – hey maybe it could be a fundraiser – is a contest, you know, like guess the number of jelly beans in a jar. Only this would be to guess how many cans of sweet potatoes would be left over on December twenty-sixth."

I won't say it went downhill from there, but Scoobie had been his most helpful when he was telling me items he thought people wished were available. Coco Puffs aside.

I DROPPED HIM AT THE LIBRARY and went back to Harry's to pick up my folder on the old bakery building. I felt better knowing the order was completed. Rev. Jamison's secretary would fax it to the food bank for me; grudgingly, I assumed, since she did not think me holy enough for the job as food pantry head honcho.

I had a pleasant surprise when researching the Bakery at the Shore building at the courthouse. There were few good comps, which I expected, but in the Registrar of Deeds' folder that held information on all the past sales were several drawings of the earliest floor plan. Usually the Registrar of Deeds would not keep such a drawing, since the original plan and major structural modifications are in the assessor's office. I could see why these were kept. They were precision drawings on heavy paper stock, with notations on the side as to the purpose of each room. It was the kind of old-fashioned document you would expect to see on display in a local historical society.

It was a minute or two before I realized that the handwriting was Peter Fisher's. I would probably have recognized his tiny, perfectly formed letters, but the initials "PF" at the bottom corner and the date – May 6, 1928 – were a giveaway.

The layout was similar to today's, with the kitchen of that day also parallel to the main room. However, the old kitchen had a window that looked onto the street. The window and entry door were separated by only a couple of feet. That surprised me, as I would have thought the two booze sellers wanted as little visibility as possible. But, it had been the custom in the early beach businesses to let people see candy makers, bakers, and others at work. It would likely have seemed odd if they did not have a view into the kitchen.

I looked for the closet Mary Doris said Richard had locked Peter in, and decided it could have been next to the kitchen door. The closet must have been boarded over long ago. I frowned. The hallway was in the same place, and ran back from the main room, starting directly next to where the former closet door could have been. With no office on that side of the small hallway it meant there would be a lot of empty space behind that wall. That was odd. I'd have to ask Harry if that large former closet should be on my drawings.

Harry and I talked at length about the appraisal. The building was assessed at $171,000, so Mary Doris's taxes were based on that. However, there was no way it was worth that now. Aunt Madge thought it had been vacant for three or four years. Mary Doris had kept the utilities on, so the interior had not had to endure wide temperature swings, but it had probably been careworn when Little Mama's Café stopped doing business and looked worse now. If I owned it I'd tear it down, and said so to Harry.

He shrugged. "My kids would have torn this house down, and look at it now."

I glanced around the refinished floors and other woodwork and fresh paint. I knew he'd been doing a lot more than curb appeal type repairs, and figured he had sunk tens of thousands into his grandparents' old house.

"Maybe Mary Doris and Annie had a vision for revitalizing the building," he said.

I held my tongue, always an effort. I almost said that if that was their goal they should have started a decade or more ago. What mattered was what the evidence said the place was worth. We settled on $152,000, and I thought that was generous. "Annie should like it," I said. "Should bring down taxes, at least until she gets it fixed up."

LANCE WILSON'S CALL surprised me. His urgent tone told me he wanted to see me for more than a discussion of food pantry finances. He offered me tea as I came in and poured a mug from a thermos on his small living room table.

"Mary Doris' lawyer called this morning," he began. He struggled to compose himself. "In addition to the large donation to the food pantry, she had a small bequest for me." He smiled. "She knew I'd always wanted to see the Grand Canyon, and left me a couple thousand for the trip."

I grew a quick lump in my throat. "You must have been very good friends," I stammered.

He nodded. "That wasn't the big surprise, though," he paused. "You remember what we talked about."

I nodded. Who would forget hearing that Mary Doris had had Richard Tillotson's baby?

He continued, "As far as I know I'm the only one she told about the baby. I guess she wanted someone to know more about that child." He pulled a small envelope from his pocket and opened the letter. "I'm not going to read you the parts about our friendship."

"That's private," I said, quietly.

"And the rest of it should be, too. But since we know she was murdered..." He cleared his throat and began to read her words. *"I appreciated you letting me tell you about my little boy. And even more that you never brought him up again."*

Lance looked at me. "I don't remember her telling me it was a boy."

I nodded and he continued reading. "I don't know why I need to let you know who he is. It just seems right that one person in town know. Of course, if you die before I do, my attorney will tear up this letter, and no one will know. Maybe that would be better (except for you dying, of course)." He smiled at me. "She was a real kidder, Mary Doris."

His slow pace was maddening. I wanted to scream that he should hurry up. "I told you I gave the baby up for adoption. I didn't tell you that my brother John and his wife took him. They named him Brian, after our father. He never knew I was his mother, that was part of our agreement. As far as I know, John and his wife never told him he was adopted. Secrets were easier to keep back then."

My head was spinning. "Wait. Was Brian Milner Annie's grandfather?"

Lance nodded and continued. "So, Brian thought I was his aunt, and his son Matt called me, as you know, "Grammy" because my brother John's wife died when Matt was an infant and I filled the grandmother role for him. Matt was such a sweet child." Lance looked up. "Matt spent every summer here. Mary Doris taught you know, so she was off and Matt's mom worked. I know Matt brought Mary Doris a lot of joy."

He went back to the letter. "I never really understood why Matt and his wife – Jill, you remember? – had such a hard time with Annie as she got older. When I offered to have her come here to high school in her junior year I didn't expect them to say yes, but it didn't take them an hour to decide. Matt told me that later. Anyway, Annie has been as much a treasure to me as her father and grandfather. I never told her I was really her great grandmother, of course."

Lance folded the letter. "She talks a bit more about Annie, but you've heard the salient points."

I realized I'd been holding my breath and let it out slowly. "Wow."

Lance shrugged. "It doesn't change anything. Knowing how good Annie has been to her, it didn't surprise anyone that Mary Doris left her most of her estate. Turns out she was leaving it to a direct descendant." He folded the letter and put it back in his pocket. "I probably shouldn't have told you. Mary Doris placed great trust in me, to tell me all this."

"Yes, she did. I won't mention it to anyone, not even Aunt Madge."

"Or Scoobie," he smiled.

I could feel a blush coming. "Oh, we aren't…we're good friends, like you and Mary Doris."

"You're lucky there." He reached for a handkerchief.

IT DIDN'T CHANGE ANYTHING, of course. Still, it was hard to believe that Mary Doris had never told Annie that she and Mary Doris were great grandmother and granddaughter rather than great aunt and niece. It hit me that I knew more about Annie Milner's family history than she did.

I was sitting in my car outside the former Bakery at the Shore. I wanted to be sure where the closet had been and wished I knew why it had been covered up. If it hadn't been such a cold December day I'd have peered in the window, but for some reason the cold made my tailbone hurt more.

Even looking through the large window in the main room – which Annie had cleaned completely – I could see that there were about five feet separating the door to the kitchen and the hallway entrance. No closet door, just wall space with some old wallpaper. I closed my eyes, remembering how it looked today. When you walked into the kitchen you made a sharp turn, as it was parallel to the larger room, not behind it. Behind what I was pretty sure had been a closet was the uni-sex bathroom, clearly put there so that the plumbing could run straight back from the kitchen. The two small offices were on the opposite side of the hallway from the bathroom. Why waste all that space? They could have made a bigger bathroom, or had separate potties for girls and boys.

Really, it made no difference. *Or did it?*

CHAPTER SEVENTEEN

WHEN I STOPPED AT THE library the next day to get Scoobie, Daphne beamed at me. She pointed to a large mason jar on the counter, then raised it so I could see it had a lot of pieces of paper in it.

For a second or two I didn't get it. Then it hit me. "The food pantry naming contest. People really gave us names?

Daphne laughed. "It was on the radio last week. That DJ who was a couple years behind us in school."

I gave her a blank stare.

"Right, you were only there one year. I think he calls himself The Hot Nuts Man." Daphne dumped the suggestions on the counter.

"Jeez. Hey," I looked around. "Where's Scoobie?"

"Not sure." She was preoccupied with the proposed names, now spread on the counter.

Food for Thought
The Lord's Pantry
Nuggets for Nourishment
Helping Hands (and Feet)
Ocean Alley Food Cupboard
What the Lord Doesn't Provide, We Do
Sharing the Harvest

"You can bet names like some of these aren't going to be in the submissions from the different churches." I separated them into two groups and glanced at Daphne.

"Yep," she nodded. "Those would be Scoobie's." We had agreed that Scoobie's were: Nuggets for Nourishment, Helping Hands (and Feet), and What the Lord Doesn't Provide, We Do.

The door opened and Scoobie strode in, face pink from the cold. He had a Christmas wreath on one arm and a grin on his face. "Heard these came in at the hardware store. They run out fast." He took a deep sniff of the pine and said, "Better than a lot of stuff I've sniffed."

"Scoobie!" Daphne said in a whisper.

Undaunted, he looked at me. "Thought Aunt Madge might like this."

"She will." I nodded towards our small pile of name suggestions as I picked them up and stowed them in a side pocket of my purse. "We were guessing which ones were yours."

"My personal favorite is Nuggets for Nourishment." He placed the wreath on the counter as he took off his gloves.

"Don't get comfortable. I want you to help me with something."

With an exaggerated sigh he looked to Daphne. "No rest for the weary."

"You taking your stuff?" she asked, with a nod towards Scoobie's favorite table, which had his knapsack and a couple of pens.

"Am I?" he asked me.

"Why don't you? If we get done early you can always come back."

When we were settled in the car, he asked, "Are we getting Ramona?"

"She couldn't take off today. And why did you assume we were going back to the attic?" I asked.

He rubbed a gloved hand over the passenger side window so I could see out the side mirror. "Because you're not so good at asking for help, and that's the only thing you've asked me to help you with."

"Very observant. But," I turned the defroster on a higher setting, "I want you to look at something first."

"Etchings?" he asked.

That almost gave me a physical start. Scoobie and I had become best buds again, but I didn't see us as a couple. "Nope. We're snooping."

"I would expect nothing less." As we drove the short distance I looked at the grey sky. It was not supposed to snow, but the clouds looked as if they had a different idea.

We pulled up in front of the old Bakery at the Shore. While we looked at it from the warmth of the car I told Scoobie I had done the appraisal and seen the old closet on an early drawing, and thought it was now covered over with wallpaper. "And Mary Doris told me once that Richard locked Peter Fisher in a closet," I finished.

He shrugged. "What difference does it make?"

"Maybe it was big enough to store a body."

"I don't think you could have enough lime to keep the smell down." He peered through the foggy window. "And I don't think the rotting body smell could be covered over by baking cookies either."

"Maybe not, but somebody knew where Richard's corpse was and brought it into that attic a long time after he died."

"True, but if you would accept that you will never know who did that there would be more serenity it your life.

I nodded, knowing he was referring to the Serenity Prayer – God grant me the serenity to accept the things I cannot change, the courage to change the things I can, and the wisdom to know the difference.

"Most of the time I don't feel very serene."

He glanced at me and turned to stare at the storefront again. "I know. It takes work."

I started the car. "OK, let's see if anyone else broke in at the Fisher house."

AN HOUR LATER I WISHED someone had gotten into the attic and removed all its contents. I had climbed up to the attic for the second time since falling out of it and had been sitting on a small wooden rocker whose caned seat was half shredded. I had to continually rebalance my tailbone on the foam donut to keep from falling through to the floor. However, we were getting close to having a list of all the attic's items. Several times I had been tempted to tell Scoobie Mary Doris' secret, but I held my tongue.

"Look at this," Scoobie said, staring at a small framed photo. He had taken it from the last trunk we were going through, which contained a hodge podge of metal kitchen utensils, a bunch of bronzed children's shoes, and a couple of table clothes that were so rotted they literally fell apart in Scoobie's hands. He had quickly tossed them on the floor. The photo, however, held his attention.

"This kind of looks like some of those pictures of Mary Doris from the old albums." He walked across the room and showed me the picture, which was a headshot of a woman and small boy, taken by someone standing above them, as if the woman had been kneeling next to the child. Mary Doris was smiling slightly and the little boy had the wide grin of a child who had just been told to smile for the camera. *Mary Doris and Brian?*

"Could be." I stared at the photo some more and looked up at Scoobie, unsure what to say.

"Cute kid," was all he said, and headed down the ladder to get a plastic garbage bag from my trunk. Without saying anything about it we had known the old tablecloths were not going on the inventory.

I breathed more easily. The photo meant something to me, but would have no meaning for Scoobie, so I didn't need to worry about lying either directly or by omission. Did this mean Mary Doris had introduced Brian as her son, quietly perhaps? If some of the Tillotsons or Fishers didn't want to acknowledge Mary Doris' and Richard's child, why even keep the photo? "Ridiculous," I said aloud. "You'll never know." Somehow, I still did not feel more serene.

SCOOBIE AGAIN STAYED for what Aunt Madge called a light supper, and she had cajoled him to help her find the chipmunks, which she thought were in the coat closet in the entry hallway. "Every time I let them out of the kitchen, Jazz and the dogs sit by the closet door."

Mostly the dogs stay in her downstairs living area. They are not supposed to go to any areas the guests use, but occasionally they follow Aunt Madge to the front door when she checks on the mail. As a cat, Jazz goes wherever she wants.

Despite his assurance that he was happy to "catch the little buggers," Scoobie did not look too eager to find them. Aunt Madge gave him a pair of her gardening gloves, and I was trying not to laugh as Scoobie stood with pink-gloved hands on his hips as he methodically looked at the closet floor. He knelt down to sort through the boots, umbrellas and other items that were as neatly arranged as the items on Aunt Madge's pantry shelves.

Aunt Madge walked back into the hallway carrying a very small pet carrier. "You're going to keep them as pets?" I almost shrieked.

"Don't be ridiculous. Harry will take them." She looked at me as if she thought her thought process should be obvious. "The dogs brought them in before the ground was so frozen. I don't want to let them out in this yard when it's so cold. They couldn't make a winter nest now."

"Tell Harry to charge rent," Scoobie said, as he gingerly removed a couple of umbrellas.

"We're going to let them out under his porch. It's got lattice work on the sides so nothing can get them again, and the ground close to his house isn't frozen." She stooped and opened the door to the tiny cage as she set it on the floor.

I stared at her. "They don't just burrow in the leaves, you know. They chew wood and stuff."

She shrugged. "Harry says they may not live through the winter, but at least they'll have a chance."

"Holy shit!" Scoobie had just picked up a boot and a chipmunk hopped on his hand, jumped on the floor and scurried back under the hall washstand. "Damn those little jerks are fast."

All three of our gazes shifted to the floor by the washstand where there had been brief chipmunk chatter from what sounded like two of them, and was now quiet. Aunt Madge spoke first. "Thank you Adam, now I know where they both are."

Scoobie was still on his knees, staring up at us. "You want me to move the washstand?"

She shook her head. "They're too fast. I thought they'd be easier to corner in the closet. If I put a couple of sunflower seeds under the washstand they'll stay put." She picked up the pet carrier and walked through the swinging door into the kitchen.

I stared down at Scoobie and he grinned. "I bet they'd be good in soup."

CHAPTER EIGHTEEN

NO MATTER HOW HARD I tried not to think about it, I was mulling over a plan. I say tried not to think of it because it involved criminal activity – breaking into what would soon be Annie's campaign headquarters. I figured it couldn't be that hard to locate a closet. If Annie hadn't stopped by when I was doing the appraisal I could have looked harder. My guess was that the door was behind the wallpaper and that was why Annie had not taken it down from the wall near the kitchen door. *Though if she knew it was there, so what?"*

In the warmth of Aunt Madge's great room I looked at the small ledger in my lap and wondered what someone had wanted with the ones stolen from the old trunk. The one I had most recently looked at was dated June 2, 1929 – January 4, 1930. I had selected it because it had entries just before and after Richard's disappearance. The entries up to October 4, 1929 were mostly in what I assumed was his writing – at least it was not Peter Fisher's precise lettering. After October 4, all the writing was Peter's. Looking more closely I realized that the erasures and write overs stopped after Richard quit making the entries. Either Peter's math skills were better or Richard had been altering the entries so he could take some money from the till.

It looked as if Peter Fisher suspected that Richard Tillotson was cooking more than bread and cookies and had taken over the bookkeeping to get a better sense of the business. Idly I wondered what the exact date was for Audrey Tillotson and Peter Fisher's wedding and went in search of an article I had printed from the microfilm at the library. October 12, 1929.

I tried to put myself in Peter Fisher's place. He would have been furious if he verified that his future brother-in-law was stealing from the business, but might not have wanted to confront him before the wedding, which was only days after the ledger switched to all-Peter authorship. Could they have fought after the wedding? Mary Doris had been convinced Peter killed Richard, and it could be true.

Maybe Richard took off for a long drive in his Model T, had an accident and had not been discovered for a week or two. By then bugs and weather had done their work and his body was too hard to identify. No, his car could likely have led police back to the Tillotson family.

Or maybe Richard didn't really want to marry Mary Doris and just took off. That seemed least likely. Even in the days before Social Security numbers it would be hard to disappear and still make a living. *Unless he went to Montana or someplace.*

I pushed the thoughts aside. Richard had not left of his own accord, died later, and arranged to have someone place his skeleton in the wardrobe in the attic.

A glance at the clock on the microwave told me it was almost midnight. Scoobie had left about 9, after he thrashed Aunt Madge and me in a game of Scrabble, and Aunt Madge had gone to bed more than an hour ago. Scoobie would never agree to break into the Bakery at the Shore building. He had a couple of marijuana arrests before he changed his habits and he wouldn't want to risk his freedom for something like breaking and entering a decrepit building. But, maybe Ramona would be willing to help. I would, after all, need some kind of a lookout partner.

RAMONA'S NONTRADITIONAL AURA did not extend to B&E, but she did have an idea. "Why don't you ask my Uncle Lester? He'd love to investigate with you." The last line was said with some tongue-in-cheek humor. Ramona knew that I–as did most people who knew him–found Lester to be a bit brash. Or, at least forceful.

But, she was probably right. He'd go with me. I guess I stiffened, because Ramona looked at me with a concerned expression. "Is your back hurting more?"

"No, I just realized…" *Should I tell her? Why not?* "Lester probably has a key. He was the realtor who listed the place before Mary Doris died."

Ramona and I both broke into broad smiles.

LESTER WANTED ME TO MEET HIM at Java Jolt, but I suggested his prior site for meeting clients, the Burger King near his office. I thought it would be noisier and we would not be overheard. I wasn't worried about my volume of conversation, but Lester can be boisterous.

As I outlined my thoughts about looking for the old closet I realized how outlandish the idea of breaking into the building was. Even Lester looked skeptical, and he fancied himself a sleuth. "Sooo, you want me to use the key, which I do still have, to enter a building, but you don't want me to tell the building owner we're doing this or why?"

I nodded, sure he would say no.

Lester slapped his hand on the table. "Why not?"

"Why not," I was seriously reconsidering, "is that you could lose your real estate license."

He shrugged. "I'll say I went in to get the paperwork I left there for people I showed the place to, and then I was gonna give Annie the key back."

"And why would I be with you?"

This stumped him for a moment, then he brightened. "You're thinking of using your old real estate license here in Ocean Alley instead of doing the appraisal crap, and we were going to talk about a building I had listed and you appraised." He looked very pleased with himself, and added, "On account of you're tired of working for that goody-two-shoes Harry Steele and want to be my partner."

I gave him a dour look and he barked his laugh. "Yeah, I know. You like the guy."

NEEDLESS TO SAY, I was not going to tell Aunt Madge where I was going, but planned to strongly imply that I was going to Lakewood to do some Christmas shopping with my sister and might spend the night.

I did tell Scoobie, who was against it. We were in the library, talking in whispers. "I'm not asking you to go." I met his cold stare with one of my own.

"Oh, yeah. I'm going to let you go with Lester to break into a building. He wants to break into your pants, you know."

I laughed loudly, and Daphne gave me a raised eyebrow.

"How do you know that?" I asked, reverting to a whisper again.

"Ramona as much as told me." He scowled. "He's old enough to be your father."

I snorted, but quietly. "He's Ramona's father's youngest brother. He's only about ten years older than we are." As he continued to frown at me, I added, "And I think you and Ramona are wrong. I'd be able to tell if he were…" I groped for a word, "flirting."

"I'll tell Madge," he said.

My eyes widened in disbelief. "Traitor."

We glared at each other, and his expression softened a bit. "OK, I won't tell, but I'm your lookout. Get me one of those burn phones."

"Burn phones?"

"You gotta watch more CSI, too." He began putting his notebook and pens in his knapsack. "Prepaid phones, throwaway phones, whatever you want to call them."

I needed to go to the Wal-Mart on the highway anyway, to ask them for food for the pantry for the holidays or a dollar donation. I knew it was late to be asking, but the gig is new to me.

In retrospect, I should have gone alone. The store was crowded, and Scoobie's enthusiasm for helping me pick out a 'burn phone' had waned within minutes of being in the packed store. "You want to wait in the car while I talk to the manager?" I asked.

He gave a quick shake of his head and moved over to the TV area, where it was less crowded. I paid for the phone and walked over to tell him I was going to the manager's office. "OK, Alex and I will miss you," he said, not looking at me. I glanced at the TV and saw he was watching *Jeopardy*.

The harried-looking Wal-Mart manager clearly did not believe me. Why would he? I was forty years younger than anyone he would have previously dealt with at the food pantry. "Would you mind calling Reverend Jamison? He'll vouch for me. My name's Jolie Gentil."

The manager, Philip M., according to his name badge, looked at me for a moment. "Have I seen your name in the paper?"

I sighed. If I'd been in one of the smaller stores in Ocean Alley someone would have asked me if I were Madge's niece. "Do you remember the woman who was cleaning out an attic and found a skeleton?"

He started to laugh and checked himself. "Not someone you know, I hope?"

"No. An old murder case."

"Oh dear." He gave me a look that boded skepticism. "I'll give Reverend Jamison a call and be right back."

I watched him walk into a narrow hallway behind the customer service desk. Philip M. was probably in his late thirties and had the beginning of a pot belly. Hard to imagine how he got it walking around a store as big as this one.

As he walked back toward me, two employees stopped him with questions and a young mother with a baby in her arms went up to him to complain that the store did not have a brand of formula she preferred. "The reverend vouched for you. I apologize for doubting you."

"No problem. You haven't dealt with me before." He spent a couple of minutes telling me that he would give us some food the next day and a $200 donation. "I can't give more than that without you applying for one of our community grants, which I encourage you to do." He signed a paper on a clipboard a stock boy thrust at him. "What I will do later is give you a lot of baking materials, but I can't do it until a couple of days before Christmas. Depends on what we sell."

I made arrangements to have the first round of food picked up and said I would stop back the next day for the check. And thanked him, of course. As I walked back to get Scoobie I reminded myself that Dr. Welby, Lance and Sylvia Parrett were talking to other groups about donations. I had thought about doing a food drive before Christmas but decided we needed more time to plan and get volunteers.

Scoobie was watching for me. "What's another term for housebreaking?"

"Are we talking puppies or burglars?" I asked.

He glared at me.

"Uh, breaking and entering," I said.

"You forgot to say "what is breaking and entering"? He sidestepped a child of about seven who was running toward the exit.

"Very funny."

It had started to snow lightly. We were going to Aunt Madge's to set up Scoobie's phone. I had suggested the library, thinking it would go faster using the Internet rather than using a land line phone, but Scoobie nixed that idea. "I don't want a lot of people knowing I have a phone."

As I programmed the phone he swept the fast accumulating dry snow off the porch and the small sidewalk, despite Aunt Madge telling him we were supposed to get less than an inch. He declined dinner and said he'd see me tomorrow.

"What's with Adam?" Aunt Madge asked.

"We were at Wal-Mart. I guess he doesn't like crowds." She nodded as she opened the sliding glass door to let Mister Rogers and Miss Piggy into the yard. I felt a bit guilty lying to her. The crowds at Wal-Mart were less of a worry to Scoobie than what I had planned for the next night.

LESTER THOUGHT WE SHOULD both dress in black, but I pointed out that we didn't want to look as if we didn't want to be seen. He agreed, but reluctantly. We had decided to go about five-thirty. A lot of people would be eating dinner – hopefully Annie among them – and yet there would still be enough natural light that we might not have to turn the overhead lights on. And if we looked as if we weren't breaking in maybe no one would call the police to say they'd spotted burglars.

I parked across the street from the former Bakery at the Shore. Scoobie would sit in my car and call my cell phone if anyone seemed to pay a lot of attention to us. I walked through the narrow alley to the back of the building, where I was to meet Lester, who had keys to the front and back entrances. The buildings in the short block were flush with each other, and there were two between the alley and the back of the old bakery building. Lester saw me coming and got out of his car and walked toward the back door.

He said hello and handed me a clip board and kept one for himself. "Carry a clip board and you look like you're working."

I glanced at it. Lester had placed a copy of the building's former listing sheet on top of a couple of pages of blank paper. He was smart, no doubt about it. Devious, but smart.

The smell of must greeted us. "Nuts. It's darker in here than I thought it would be."

"Not to worry, kid," Lester said. "I came in a few minutes ago and set up a lamp on the bar. Give us a little light, but won't let every Tom, Dick, and Harry see in too good." Lester flicked the lamp switch and it spread a dim glow.

"And what will you tell people when someone asks why you aren't using the main lights?" I asked, mostly teasing.

"Christ. Have you seen how old the wiring is in the place? Could start a fire if you put your average computers and a fridge on at the same time."

"You neglected to mention that on the listing sheet," I said dryly.

He gave me a quick smile and we both turned to look at the wallpaper-covered wall where I thought the closet had been. "You know," Lester said, running his hand along the wall, "there's a thin crack here…and here." He had reached to his left about two-and-a-half feet.

"Maybe they took down the molding around the door frame and took off the door knob and covered it over," I mused.

Lester took a box cutter from his pocket and began to make a tiny slit in the spot where he had felt the crack. "What are you doing?" I shrieked.

Without looking at me or seeming ruffled, he said, "I thought you wanted to do this kinda quiet like."

"But she'll know someone's been in here." I spoke more quietly.

"Maybe. I'm trying, if nobody else screams in my ear and makes me go crooked, to follow the outline of what mighta been a door here." Lester isn't tall, but neither was the supposed door. In less than a minute he had traced its outline and gestured to me to come closer. "Your fingers are smaller. See what that feels like. If it's not a door we'll seal it back up a little." He pulled a plastic prescription bottle from his pocket. "Wallpaper paste. Pretty slick, huh?" He grinned.

"Very." I could feel the clear, straight line of what could easily be a door. I put my nose on the wall paper to see if I could see through to anything, and immediately sneezed three times in quick succession.

"Great, get snot on the wallpaper."

I sniffed loudly and held my nose as I tried again. "I can't see anything. I think someone put some really thin wood here to fill in the door crack."

"Yeah that would work." He peered more closely. "See these little nail marks?" He pointed to a spot on the wall that was just below my waist and had a few tiny holes in an even horizontal row. "I think they had a piece of molding here, like a chair rail, to hold the door up."

"Why?" I asked.

"Cause they had to take the hinges off the door to hide the entrance. Needed something to hold it upright or it would fall backwards." He glanced up at me. "Unless you can think of another way to keep it standing up with no knob or hinges."

"Nope."

"I'm thinkin' they just took the molding off. If they did it awhile ago, the places where the nails made holes probably woulda ripped by now."

I nodded, thinking. "You can't smell it now, but when I was in here doing the appraisal I thought I smelled something that reminded me of the old rubber cement."

He shrugged. "Maybe somebody started to tear down the wallpaper, found the door, and glued the paper back on."

That someone would pretty much have to be Annie. "I wonder why Peter Fisher didn't just plaster over it," I mused.

"Dunno." He started to put a dab of wallpaper paste here and there. He stopped for a second, thinking. "I guess they coulda glued the door to pieces of wood that filled in the cracks around the door, but glue woulda maybe gotten old after a bunch of years."

"Maybe." I thought some more. It took a lot more effort to put up wall plaster than it does to hang dry wall today. "He wouldn't put up plaster if he had to do it fast."

"Or maybe whoever did it wanted to be able to get back in. Like, to retrieve a body." He grinned at me.

I remembered Scoobie's comment. "If he had a body in there wouldn't it smell awful?" We both seemed to agree that I was talking about Peter Fisher hiding Richard Tillotson.

Lester was thoughtful, something I had not seen him be previously. "They wouldn't have had plastic to wrap it in. Maybe in a canvas tarp in a trunk? Put a lot of vanilla on the floor, something else with a strong smell."

"Vanilla. I guess bakers would have that. Scoobie said he didn't think even lime could hide the smell."

Lester snorted. "He an expert?"

None of us were experts in hiding the smell of a dead body. At least, not that I knew. "I guess there are lots of strong-smelling things in the universe. Lavender, maybe, cinnamon."

He shrugged. "Or use a combo of ten different things. So, now you know there's a door here, what are you gonna do?"

My cell phone rang before I could respond. "Annie," was all Scoobie said.

"Crap!" I unplugged the lamp and made sure I had both clipboards. "Run!" We went quickly down the hallway and out the back door. I hoped Scoobie hadn't seen Annie drive toward the back of the building. Surely he would have said something. I hoped she had walked over from her office.

"Around the corner, quick." Lester said.

"You didn't lock the door." I whispered.

"Screw the door." He walked fast toward the corner of the alley that was away from the courthouse.

When we reached the alley and were well out of sight even if someone peered out the back door, I said, "I didn't even think of an escape plan." And I started to laugh, covering my mouth with my hand.

Lester just shook his head.

"Jolie." Scoobie's whispered voice came to us. He had entered the alley from the street.

I motioned him over.

"We can't drive off in your car, she might see us," he said.

"And she'll hear mine if I start it," Lester said. "There's no one in any of these old buildings now, no reason for me to be driving outta there."

"Newhart's," I said. "My treat."

CHAPTER NINETEEN

I DON'T THINK LESTER or Scoobie liked the idea of having dinner together, but they didn't mind me paying for it. Women truly are liberated.

I was into my second helping of fried shrimp – it was all the shrimp you can eat night – when Aunt Madge and Harry came in. *Uh oh, I told her Christmas shopping.*

Scoobie waved them toward the three of us, but they just waved back and sat at a table close to the door. He turned to me, grinning. "You didn't exactly tell her where you were going, did you?"

I shook my head. "I said Christmas shopping in Lakewood."

Lester, who was on his third helping, shrugged. "Tell her you got done early."

"I'm not lying to her for you," Scoobie said.

I knew he meant it. "I'll think of something."

"I'll lie," Lester threw in.

"The hard part for Jolie will be figuring out a way to explain why she is with both of us."

From his grin, I could tell Scoobie was enjoying this.

Lester shrugged. "Just say you ran into me here."

"I should have thought of that," I said.

Aunt Madge was coming toward us. "I didn't see your car, Jolie."

The jig is up.

"Around the corner," Scoobie said. "Lot was packed when we got here."

"And how are you, Lester?" Aunt Madge asked.

"Doin' great. Talked these two clowns into sittin' with me."

Aunt Madge smiled slightly as she turned to go back to her table. "Jolie is very funny sometimes."

We were all silent for a few seconds.

"You did lie," I said to Scoobie.

"Crud," he said, and Lester barked his laugh.

THE NEXT DAY WAS kind of anticlimactic. Aunt Madge didn't mention she thought I got back early from Christmas shopping. I sent Renée an email asking her to cover for me if Aunt Madge mentioned Renée and I had been shopping together. Renée would probably hope I had a hot date I didn't want to talk about with Aunt Madge.

If Annie suspected anyone broke into her building I didn't hear about it. *Like she'd call and talk to me about it.* I wasn't sure what to do next. As I saw it, my options were talk to Morehouse about the closet or talk to Annie. Likely neither one would appreciate my efforts. I picked Morehouse.

"You did what?!" Morehouse's voice could easily have been heard throughout the police station.

"Do you need to shout?" I asked, trying to act as if my behavior of the night before was what any citizen concerned about a crime would do.

He walked over and shut the door to his small office. "I could arrest you, you know."

"Based on what? Did you just have a tape recorder going?"

He sat back in his chair and stared at me. "Why do you care about a maybe seventy-year old murder? It's not your family."

I had prepared a response. "I could let go of it..."

"Yeah, right," Morehouse said.

"...if it were just Richard Tillotson's skeleton. It's Mary Doris."

"As far as anyone knows, nothing in that closet relates to Mary Doris." He pulled a notebook toward him and took a pen out of a drawer.

"What are you doing?" I asked.

"Taking your statement."

"My statement is that I came in here to wish you a Merry Christmas." I stared at him, careful not to blink.

He ran the fingers of one hand through his hair, then tried a 'be reasonable' approach. "Why are you concerned with a closet you found on seventy-five year old drawings?"

I outlined my thinking that it was a logical place for Peter Fisher to hide a body. "He could have papered over the entrance, but he'd still have had access to move the body years later."

"I could never prove that," he said.

"I know," I paused. "It's like Watergate, it's the cover-up."

His look said he thought I was mad. "Uh huh. Now we're into politics."

It came into place, just like that. *How could I not have thought of it earlier?* "Annie is running for prosecuting attorney. Mary Doris left her the building and Mary Doris dated Richard Tillotson, whose body was just found. He was clearly murdered, and now she's been killed." I had to choose my words carefully so I didn't disclose Mary Doris' secret. "Maybe Annie doesn't want anyone to talk about all that when she's running for office."

"Who would give a rat's ass?" Morehouse asked. "It doesn't have a damn thing to do with Annie Milner – Assistant Prosecutor Milner to you.

You think I'm going to talk to Annie about this? I'm not about to do anything to piss off the prosecuting attorney's staff."

I stood up and picked up my donut. "Okay."

"What does that mean, 'okay'?" he asked.

"Just okay. I hear you."

"Like hell you do," Morehouse stood. "You never listen to me. You almost got yourself killed awhile back playing detective. You stay the hell out of this." His voice was rising again.

I could feel my face reddening. "You asked me to come to you, if I found something. I did. I'm done." I put my hand on the doorknob, then turned back to him as I opened it and gave him my best smile. "Merry Christmas." I said it loud enough for anyone nearby to hear.

BACK TO SQUARE ONE. Sort of. Maybe I don't care. *Of course you care.* The terrible thought that had been in the back of my mind pushed forward again. Would Annie have killed Mary Doris to hide Richard's decades-old murder and the fact that Annie's grandfather was illegitimate? That just didn't make sense. I couldn't remember what percentage of today's children were born outside of a marriage but I knew it was large. It was part of almost everyone's family, if it had enough people in it. No one would care.

Maybe Annie thought that once Mary Doris was certain about the skeleton being Richard's that Mary Doris would make a big stink. The focus would probably end up on Annie. Maybe it had nothing to do with the election and unwanted publicity. Maybe she just didn't want to be on center stage because of someone else's action. *I can relate to that.*

On most levels Annie's involvement made no sense. Aunt Madge thought Annie was closer to Mary Doris than her parents. Annie probably didn't even know Mary Doris was her great grandmother instead of her great aunt. *Or did she? Mary Doris told Lance.*

I sat at Aunt Madge's kitchen table, Jazz on my lap, thinking about the last couple of days as I had an afternoon cup of coffee. Harry had asked me to appraise a house about ten miles out of town, someone he'd known years ago who'd found out he'd opened Steele Appraisals. I was glad to do it, but it was ten miles closer to Lakewood, and I'm still not anxious to run into people who know me from my commercial real estate days; more accurately, my days married to a gambling embezzler. I sighed and stood up, which annoyed Jazz. I had to get over those thoughts. I knew I hadn't done anything to be ashamed of. What bugged me was the idea that everyone knew I'd had the proverbial wool pulled over my eyes.

I made a decision. *Annie did not kill Mary Doris.* It was ludicrous to even think it. No one running for public office would add murder to their resume.

CHAPTER TWENTY

IT WAS FOUR DAYS BEFORE CHRISTMAS. If I'd known how much work the food pantry chair had to do I would have moved. I'm not sure where, anywhere.

In fairness, a lot of people helped. Lance said that the cash donations were more in one month than in the entire last year. That's what asking does. Really, it was no different than being a commercial real estate agent in Lakewood. You had to look for donors as much as clients.

Scoobie, Megan, and I were taking an eyeball inventory of what was left on our shelves. We were also checking dates on cans of some of the recently donated good. "Who eats asparagus soup?" Megan asked.

"Same people who eat all the sweet potatoes," Scoobie said. He was unpacking a large box of sacks of flour that Wal-Mart had sent over. They'd also sent a few boxes of sugar, brown sugar, cooking oil, and chocolate chips. Manager Philip had been true to his word, and had actually sent things over earlier than he said he would. I had asked Megan's daughter Alicia to walk over to Midway Market grocery to buy some baking soda, baking powder, and powdered cinnamon, which Mr. Markle was giving us half-off. He was donating twenty small turkeys on Christmas Eve.

We were opening a half-day each day through Christmas Eve. A couple of people on the board thought that was too ambitious (think Sylvia and Monica), but Reverend Jamison agreed with Scoobie that you had to be open enough hours for new customers to hear about us and come in. Usually recipients have to have been vetted by Salvation Army or the state welfare office, but we had decided to relax that policy until after Christmas. As Dr. Welby said, anyone who came asking for food at this time of year had to be pretty desperate.

And there were a lot of desperate people. Half of me was almost glad to be getting the food pantry more active, and the other half didn't want to know how many people didn't have enough to eat. People who looked normal, whatever that means, said they didn't have enough food to get them through until the end of the month.

A rubber band went whizzing by my ear. Given that there were three of us in the room, I knew who had shot it, but Scoobie ignored me when I turned around.

I WAS SURPRISED ANNIE called me that night. "I don't understand what you mean on the appraisal, the part about the electrical system, and why that makes the property worth less."

I thought for a minute, not wanting to scare her. "It's old knob and tube wiring, and it was used oh, up to the 1930s, maybe…"

"But why can't I use it now?" she asked, her tone showing exasperation.

Thank goodness Aunt Madge redid her wiring about ten years ago. "Obviously, it still works, and it was fine for its purposes back then. When your building was constructed electricity was mostly for lights. In fact, my Uncle Gordon called the electric bill the light bill, I think."

"Mary Doris did, too," she said.

"You probably will want to do more than turn lights on and off." I thought fast. "If it were me, I'd want to redo all the wiring, and this might be a good time to do it." *Maybe I can get back in there with her and we can 'discover' the closet together.*

"Why now?" she asked.

"If you plan on keeping it, you're probably going to do some remodeling anyway, right?" I didn't wait for an answer. "When they put in new wiring and a circuit breaker box they might have to poke some holes in the walls. Might as well get it done before you paint and stuff."

She sighed, "I hadn't planned on this. Timing is not good."

"Christmas and Mary Doris' death." I assumed this was her thinking.

"Umm. A bit. I was going to move some things into the building between Christmas and New Year's." She paused. "Would you mind showing me what you're talking about?"

"I might be able to…"

"If you want me to pay you for your time…"

"No, of course not. It's just the wiring is behind the walls, and the walls are still up..." I thought for a moment. "If you think you will get the rewiring done, we can poke a bigger hole around a plug or light switch and probably see what I'm talking about."

We agreed to meet when she got off work. Now I wished I had talked to Aunt Madge about the closet. She was the handy woman, and I wanted her to come with me when I met Annie. In the end, I didn't tell her about the closet, just said that I wanted her to help me explain the old electrical wiring to Annie.

IT WAS THE FIRST TIME I'D seen anyone appear to be less than happy to see Aunt Madge. Why is that?

Annie recovered quickly and thanked us for coming. True to her reputation, Aunt Madge had brought a small tool box, from which she pulled a screwdriver to take off the plate that surrounds a socket and a small hammer. After she took off the wall plate she placed the business end of the screwdriver on the plaster near the wall socket and began tapping and then gently removing small pieces of plaster until she had about a two inch by three inch hole. I felt as useful as salad dressing at breakfast.

"Sit here, Annie." Aunt Madge patted a spot on the floor next to her and pulled out a flashlight. Annie did so and her gaze followed the beam of light. "See those little knobs that are nailed into the boards?" Aunt Madge asked. When Annie said yes Aunt Madge continued. "They're ceramic, and you can see the wire runs through them to keep the wiring away from the boards."

"What are those flakes of material on the wires?" Annie asked.

"The wires were originally wrapped in cloth – this would have been before the kind of sheathing used now. Over time, the cloth disintegrates."

"Oh dear," Annie said.

Aunt Madge shrugged as she began to pack her tools. "The wiring is still OK, the knobs keep the wires off the boards. It's just all around better to get a circuit breaker system put it if you're going to have much plugged in. You're better protected from fire, too." She stood. "Now, how about a tour? I haven't been in here since it was an insurance agency about twenty years ago."

I trailed after them as Annie explained which of the small offices would be hers and that she envisioned campaign staff sitting in the larger room. "And I'll have some campaign literature along the bar."

Aunt Madge stood in the middle of the large room and turned a full circle. She glanced at the large mirror behind the bar. "That thing will weigh a ton. Make sure you have several people help you if you take it down." Annie agreed, and Aunt Madge asked, "You need some advice on getting that old wallpaper down?"

Annie's no was said very quickly and Aunt Madge looked at her as she walked over to the wall I was convinced hid a closet. She ran her hand over the paper. "Looks as if you've already scored it." She nodded to the razor thin cuts that Lester's box cutter had left.

"Yes, now I really do..." Annie began.

"The glue's really dry." And with that my aunt, the one who believes in minding her own business, put a fingernail under a piece of the wallpaper and yanked.

The three of us stared at the partially exposed door. "Goodness," Aunt Madge exclaimed, "I bet you didn't know you had a built-in storage cupboard." She smiled at Annie, who did not return it.

"It appears I do," Annie said, stiffly. But, while she was probably annoyed, her expression did not betray any anxiety, or even curiosity.

"It's on the original floor plans," I said, and they both looked at me. "The drawing is in the Registrar of Deed's Office." I moved closer to the door, trying to think of something neutral to say. "Most people would kill to find such a big closet." *Damn, that's not neutral!*

Annie looked at her watch. "I need to get going." She took out her key ring, apparently hoping this would hurry us.

Instead, I ran my fingers over the exposed part of the door and peeled back a couple more inches of wall paper. "You can see the end of the door. It looks…"

But, I didn't get to finish my thought. "I'm going to have someone take that down, thanks." Annie's voice was sharp. "I really appreciate the advice on the electrical system, Madge."

Is Annie really in a hurry, or is she antsy about the closet?

When we were back in the car, Aunt Madge said, "You should never entrust a secret to Lester, you know."

SO, PETER COULD HAVE PUT Richard's body in that closet at some point, assuming he had a lot of old fashioned deodorizer. *Where does that leave me?* "Nowhere," I said aloud. Jazz, who was lying next to me in bed, rolled toward me and stretched, expecting an ear rub.

"We're going to the food pantry today and that's all we're going to think about." Jazz yawned and stretched some more. *We. Great, I'm talking to Jazz like she's a person.*

It's a good thing that's all I planned, as we had literally dozens of people bringing in canned goods all morning. One sweet woman even brought in a plate of brownies, "For the hard working volunteers," she said.

About ten o'clock George Winters called. "I heard my story worked."

"What story?" I asked, holding my cell phone to my ear by balancing it on my shoulder so I could write the name and address of a donor in the notebook on the counter.

"The one about the rejuvenated food pantry."

"Wait, no, I got here early. I didn't read the paper."

"Oh, you didn't read it?" he sounded disappointed.

A short, very plump woman set a box of canned goods on the counter and said, very loudly, "Good thing I saw that article before I went shopping." She turned to leave.

"Would you like to leave your name?" I called.

"Merry Christmas," she said, not turning around.

George had heard the conversation. "See, I wrote something you'll like. When you get a paper, look at page three." He hung up.

I relayed the short conversation to Megan, who put on her sweater and went to the newspaper box a couple doors down and came back reading the paper and smiling. "Rejuvenated Food Pantry Helping More Residents."

It was a short article, and to the point. George had apparently been by when I was out – which was much of the time, since I was entreating churches and stores for donations – and had taken a photo of Alicia on one side of the counter talking to a young pregnant woman standing on the other side. In the background you could see Scoobie's back; he was stocking shelves. I skimmed the article. No mention of Scoobie. That was probably good.

I looked up at Megan. "This is really great. Uh, where is Scoobie?"

She shrugged and turned to the counter to accept two large plastic bags that I could see had stuffing mix. "I need a receipt," the elderly man said, and I wrote one for him and stapled his grocery receipt to my note.

When Scoobie did not show up by eleven o'clock I called Daphne at the library. No Scoobie. Not at Java Jolt and Mr. Markle said he had not been in the grocery store, either.

Aretha Brown came in to relieve Megan and she picked up on my anxiety right away. "Maybe he just slept in."

"He's been here every morning at nine o'clock sharp." It was the day before Christmas Eve. Scoobie seemed to be having the time of his life working at the pantry. Half the people who came in knew him and were delighted to see him. I had the sense that several of them had known him before he stopped using marijuana and drinking too much and liked what they saw now.

After I'd called Scoobie's 'burn phone' several times without an answer I asked Aunt Madge to relieve me for a while so I could look for Scoobie and left as soon as she got there. I pulled up outside the ancient old house where Scoobie had a room and stared at the place, willing him to come out. If he were in there he'd be furious at me for knocking on his door. Not that I knew which one it was.

It was as I was leaving the library a few minutes later that I decided to ask Sgt. Morehouse. He and Scoobie were not always on the best of terms, but I'd heard him once tell Scoobie he was "doing good," which I took to mean not using drugs for good while.

Morehouse wasn't in, but Dana Johnson told the counter clerk she would come out to the front desk. I took a minute to take in the transformation of the normally drab waiting area. There was a small artificial Christmas tree in the corner, but it was the walls that were most colorful. Apparently decorating them had been an elementary school project, for there were at least fifty colorful drawings taped to the walls. I noted a couple of Menorahs, but most were snowmen, trees, or wreaths, and often they thanked "the policeman" for protecting them.

Dana walked out and nodded to the officer at the counter to buzz me in, which he did. We talked in the hallway, which was quieter than the volume in the large open area that had desks for just about everyone on the small police force. "If you saw him yesterday he isn't a missing person," she said, not unkindly.

"I just want," I paused, not sure what I wanted, "you to know I can't find him. He's with me almost every day and..." I stopped. If I said more I thought I'd cry. *Where did that come from?*

Morehouse came in through the back door, which led to the parking lot, and our eyes met. Dana had seen my attention was drawn elsewhere and she and I both greeted him as he walked up to us. "What have you done now?" he asked.

That banished any tears of worry. "Nothing! I'm looking for Scoobie."

"Scoobie? You don't know where he is?" As I shook my head, he said, "He's been working with you at the First Prez Pantry, right?" I nodded. "Wasn't that his backside in the paper today?"

"Yes, and he was supposed to meet me there this morning. He always comes."

Morehouse's interest had gotten more of Dana's. "He didn't act like he was coming down with anything, did he?" she asked.

"No, and I know he'll be mad at me for looking for him, but I've checked everywhere I can think of."

Morehouse thought for a minute. "OK, I'm not going to do anything official, but I'll ask the guys to keep an eye out for him and just call me if they see him. Not talk to him or anything."

I don't think he expected me to kiss him on the cheek, because I think if he had he would have deflected it.

"Don't you know it's flu season," he grumbled as he turned to walk toward his small office.

Dana smiled at me. "I bet he's okay."

"I hope so." The officer at the counter buzzed me out and I walked into the light snowfall that had started while I was in the police station.

When I got back to the food pantry there were stacks of food behind the counter, and so many sacks and small boxes that it was hard to move around. Aunt Madge offered to stay so I could be free to come and go, but I said no. I had done all I could. It was time to practice Scoobie's Serenity Prayer. "Go on home. He might even show up there."

CHAPTER TWENTY-ONE

IT WAS AFTER SIX O'CLOCK when I locked the door. I had sent Megan and Sylvia home at four-thirty. We were supposed to close at four but there was still a line, so we stayed open longer. Even after I locked the door at five people would peer in and I'd let them come in. I had spent the last hour and a half restocking the shelves and worrying.

I was halfway to Aunt Madge's when I pulled over to let two fire trucks roar past me. Idly I hoped it was just a grease fire or something small, nothing to disrupt a family's Christmas. When I turned onto D Street I saw the plume of smoke rising from the business district. Damn. That would ruin a ... In the middle of my thought I gasped and pulled behind the second fire truck, matching its speed. The smoke was coming from an area near the old Bakery at the Shore.

IT LOOKED AS IF THE FIRE had started at the back of the building and was moving toward the front. I couldn't think of anything in there that would start a fire, and I thought Aunt Madge had talked Annie into doing nothing until the building was rewired.

When you read about a chill running through someone when they're scared, it's true. I ran up to a firefighter who was pulling on his boots. "There's a closet. Look in the closet!"

"Stand back, miss." He put out an arm to block me from going further.

"You don't understand, someone might be in the closet."

The next two minutes were a blur. The firefighter hollered at the man who was directing the effort and they asked me exactly where in the smoke-filled building the closet was. I stood with tears running down my hot face until a hand pulled me backwards and I saw Sgt. Morehouse. He said nothing.

About ten seconds later two firefighters came out, each holding one side of Scoobie, who had his arms apparently tied behind him and was unconscious. Morehouse kept tight hold of my arm until I stopped screaming, and then he turned me to face him. "Let 'em work on him," he said, referring to the paramedics.

I nodded, not speaking, and turned my head toward the ambulance.

"Can I let go?" he asked.

"Yes." All I could do was stare as a paramedic put an oxygen mask on Scoobie and another one yelled, "Let's go!"

I turned to my car. Morehouse said, "I'm driving." He took my keys from me and tossed them to a bystander. "Move that car down the way and drop the keys at the station." The man caught the keys and nodded.

"Buckle up," he barked at me as he started to drive the police car. I began to sob and couldn't stop.

"Jolie, listen to me. If he was dead they wouldn't be in such a hurry."

It took me a couple of minutes, but I got control of my sobs and fished in my pocked for a tissue. "Thank you."

Morehouse parked right by the emergency room door and kept his hand on my elbow as we walked in. I guess he thought I'd try to get into the patient cubicles. He asked the clerk at the desk to keep him posted on the guy they just brought in. When the clerk looked confused, he added, "The one from the fire."

Morehouse's phone buzzed and he picked it up, listened a moment, and said, "She's with me." He shoved it back into his pocket. "Two guesses. Well, one."

"Aunt Madge," I whispered.

Even before she got there a man in scrubs opened the locked entrance to the patient area and motioned to us to come in. "Looks like he'll be okay," he said to Morehouse, "but we need to watch him. Quite a bump on the head."

He gestured us into Scoobie's area. I almost burst into tears again. Scoobie had an oxygen canella in his nose and his face was darkened with soot. One nurse was wiping soot off his face and another was adjusting an IV.

Scoobie saw me and tried to sit up. The two women each threw an arm across his chest and the taller one said, "Down!"

He obeyed and looked at me without saying anything. He looked exhausted more than anything.

"Your buddy here knew something was wrong," Morehouse said, tilting his head in my direction.

"I figured you would," he said, his voice hoarse, "then it got later and I smelled the smoke..." His voice trailed off.

"If you hadn't talked about that damn Serenity Prayer I would have kept looking."

At that he gave a full smile and looked at Morehouse. "And you thought she wasn't teachable." His voice was still hoarse, but his words sounded more like Scoobie.

Both nurses had stepped out by now, and Morehouse pulled his notebook from a pocket. "What can you tell me?"

He closed his eyes. "Not a lot. I remembered Jolie and Lester saying they left the back door unlocked, and..."

"Lester, Lester Argrow?" Morehouse turned to me, the more familiar look of irritation on his face.

"He's the real estate agent for the place." I said, defensively.

Morehouse snorted. "Go on."

"I couldn't sleep. All keyed up from working at the food pantry, I guess." He took a breath. "Went over there about seven-thirty this morning, and the door was open. I wanted to look around for myself." He stopped to swallow and asked for some water.

"He didn't go in with us," I explained to Morehouse as I took a Styrofoam cup next to the sink, filled it, and plopped a straw into it. As Scoobie took a couple of sips, I added, "He thought going in there was a bad idea. I should have listened to him."

"Should have listened to myself." He put his head back onto the pillow and winced. "Got a bump on the noggin."

"Did you see who hit you?" Morehouse asked.

"No. I was standing to the side of the bar, looking at that great old mirror, and that's the last I remember."

"And you woke up before the fire?" Morehouse asked.

"Yeah, hours ago. But my hands were tied behind my back and there was a gag in my mouth. I kept kicking the wall, but the buildings on either side are vacant."

You couldn't stand up, let someone see you from the street?" Morehouse asked.

"I was in that closet, and the door wouldn't push open."

Morehouse made a note. "Locked you think?"

"I couldn't tell..." his voice trailed off.

"Adam." Aunt Madge was in the curtained doorway. She looked much more distressed than any time I'd been in the hospital.

"He'll be all right, Madge," Morehouse said. She nodded and sat in one of the two plastic chairs. I avoided her eyes.

"So, you smelled the smoke or what?" Morehouse asked.

"I heard the crackling first, I guess I'd been dozing." He opened his eyes. "I think I smelled gas, well, not really gas, but something sort of like gas."

"Yeah, not likely natural causes," Morehouse said, dryly. "Anything else?"

Scoobie started to shake his head and winced again. The blood pressure cup on his arm started to inflate and he asked me to take it off. "No," said Aunt Madge. And that was that.

CHAPTER TWENTY-TWO

THE DOCTORS LET US TAKE Scoobie back to Aunt Madge's late in the day on Christmas Eve. I remembered Aunt Madge had spoken harshly about his parents, so I gathered he did not spend holidays with them. Without really discussing it, she and I had brought him back to the B&B and put him in the room, next to mine.

"I can stay on the couch," he said as we climbed the stairs.

"You don't go with the Christmas décor," Aunt Madge said. She had placed a pair of men's sweat pants and a t-shirt on the bed. "Jolie and I will step out while you get changed."

We waited outside, not speaking, while Jazz pawed at Scoobie's door. I knew Aunt Madge was really mad at me, even though she said she wasn't. I figured she thought that Scoobie wouldn't have been almost killed if I hadn't led him astray.

Thank goodness for Megan taking charge at the food pantry. She called every member of the committee and they all came in to work.

I fielded calls from people all morning. Even Joe Regan had called. Ramona had been at the hospital for a few minutes the night before. Daphne wanted to know if she could put up a sign at the library saying Scoobie was okay and would be back after Christmas. I told it was probably all right, but to be sure to take it down before he did get back.

Even Gracie heard and called. She also informed me that neither she or her mother had found the deed for the Fisher house and she was going to "let go of it." I suspected the happy pills enabled this attitude.

"I'm dressed," Scoobie called, in a silly falsetto. I gestured that Aunt Madge should go in before me. He was lying on the top of the quilt, and Jazz ran in before either of us, hopped on the bed, and walked up to Scoobie's head and sat down on his neck, seemingly daring Aunt Madge to make her move.

"At least she's not putting her b...tail in my face," he said, pushing her to the side, but rubbing the top of her head. He looked at both of us. "I really am okay. I'm just here so you'll have company at Christmas."

Aunt Madge looked out the window. "It will be a quiet one," she said.

My parents are in Florida. My sister Renée and her husband and two children were supposed to come down for Christmas lunch, but there were about three inches of snow on the ground accumulating toward a foot of the white stuff. Aunt Madge insisted they not be on the roads and we said we'd get together New Year's Day instead.

"I'll make us a pot of tea with honey," she said, and left the room.

When she was gone Scoobie looked at me. "How pissed is she?"

"I think we really scared her. But it's me she's angry with, not you. She figures I got you into this."

He looked at Jazz as he stroked her. "I should have followed my own advice and stayed out of there." Jazz walked onto his chest and plopped down. "On the other hand, we know for sure someone has something to hide." He gave me a grin that was more like his usual self.

"I FIND IT ODD," Aunt Madge said as we ate crab soup for Christmas lunch, "that Annie Milner hasn't called. You'd think she would want to know why Adam was in there, if nothing else."

"Me, too," Scoobie and I both said. We were sitting at Aunt Madge's large oak table, which had a poinsettia and set of Christmas candles festooned in the center. Aunt Madge had gone to church that morning, saying that eight to ten inches of snow wouldn't stop her. I had planned to go with her, but we agreed that someone should stay with Scoobie.

"I suppose Annie could be away." She stirred a few oyster crackers into her soup.

Scoobie's and my eyes met and looked away. We had talked at length in the morning, before going downstairs. Who else but Annie would be in the building? Though, as Scoobie pointed out, the door had been unlocked. Several homeless people stay in Ocean Alley during the winter – most go south – but even if one of them had come into the building to sleep they wouldn't have any reason to hit Scoobie, much less tie him up and set the building on fire.

Suddenly she gave us both a stern stare. "What do you know that I don't?"

Under normal circumstances I'd give her a smart answer, but this time she wouldn't have stood for it.

Scoobie spoke first. "We don't really know anything." He looked at me and I shrugged. "Jolie and I thought maybe Peter Fisher killed Richard and put his body in the closet. But how that relates to what's going on now beats me."

"What I care about," I said slowly, still thinking," is who killed Mary Doris."

There was a loud bong from the front door chime, and we looked at each other. Aunt Madge does not accept B&B guests between Christmas Eve and New Year's. She started to get up, but I gestured she should stay down and I went to the door. The dogs seemed to know this was an odd time for a visitor and escorted me, one on each side.

Lance Wilson stood there, collar turned up against the wind and what looked like a tin of fruit cake in his hand. As I greeted him Aunt Madge and Scoobie came out and she and I made a fuss over him, telling him to come in and get warm and have some crab soup with us.

He agreed with no hesitation and as Aunt Madge was ladling his soup he turned to Scoobie. "I'm so sorry about what happened to you."

"Thanks." Lance continued to look somewhat uncomfortable, so Scoobie added. "I'm going to be fine."

As Aunt Madge sat back down he smiled at her and said, "I make a mean fruit cake. They usually get eaten before anyone can use them as a hammer."

I couldn't imagine why Lance had come. You generally don't just drop in on someone on Christmas day. I broke the silence. "You did a lot of work at the pantry this week, you must be tired."

He swallowed some soup. "Yes, but not from that. I'm just…bone tired."

I didn't say anything. I could guess what was weighing on him, and he finally spoke. "You see, I knew some things I should maybe have told a couple of people. But, it didn't seem right." His voice trailed off.

Aunt Madge reached over and put a hand on his. "Lance. Whatever it is, I'm sure you did the right thing."

He set his spoon down. "I thought I did. Well, how could I have known?"

"Known what?" Aunt Madge and Scoobie said together.

He cleared his throat. "You see, Mary Doris, well a long time ago she had a baby."

"Had to be a really long time ago," Scoobie said.

Aunt Madge gave him a look.

"She had Richard Tillotson's baby and gave the little boy up."

Scoobie and Aunt Madge stared at him for several seconds. "Those were," Aunt Madge seemed to look for words, "different times."

"Yes, they were. The thing is, it was not what you would call a stranger adoption."

I could see Scoobie wondering where this was going, but Aunt Madge got it right away. "Annie's father, no have to be grandfather."

He nodded. "I thought I was the only person she told. She only told me about ten years ago maybe. About the baby. I didn't know who it was until after she died; she left me a letter. Now I'm wondering," he paused.

"If Annie knows, maybe she doesn't want all this brought up if she wants to run for office," I said.

"That doesn't make..." Aunt Madge began.

"It makes total sense," Scoobie said, at the same time.

"Yes, it does," I added.

Aunt Madge gave me a sharp look. "You knew."

"I told her a few days ago," Lance said, "and made her promise not to tell anyone. It was selfish of me, but when Mary Doris died the way she did..."

Aunt Madge's expression relaxed, but Scoobie kept staring at me. All he said was, "Wow."

"Where is Annie?" Aunt Madge asked. "They said in the paper this morning that Mary Doris had owned the building and it would likely pass to Annie, but I don't recall her being quoted in the article."

"I saw Sgt. Morehouse after church this morning, and he said she can't be found. But," Lance took a spoonful of soup, "If she was going to be away for a few days for Christmas she may not be following local news."

Lance stayed until early evening. He said he had had lunch with Mary Doris at the nursing home for the last several Christmases, and he hadn't realized how lonely he would be without her.

We were in the middle of a two-team Scrabble game – girls against the boys – when Harry Steele called. I remembered Aunt Madge said he was going to spend Christmas with a son and his family in Maryland. Aunt Madge looked a little flustered when she came back to the table, but all she said was that Maryland was getting a lot more snow than we were.

I took the dogs for a walk in the snow about four o'clock, and while I did that Scoobie napped for a half-hour. At supper time we had grilled cheese sandwiches and more crab soup. Aunt Madge had decided to leave the turkey in the freezer until New Year's Day dinner, and I had stowed the pecans and molasses I'd bought for pie until then as well. After we each had one more piece of Lance's fruit cake he headed home. He said it had been a very nice day.

Scoobie went to bed early, saying his head didn't so much hurt as throb.

"I'm still mad at you, you know," Aunt Madge said as I wiped the counter in the kitchen. "I figured I wouldn't say anything until after Christmas."

"I don't blame you. I should never have gotten Scoobie involved in any of this."

"It was one thing to help Gracie with the attic, but anything beyond that was just busybody work. And then some."

"I know. I just…" I stopped for a few seconds. "I guess I should learn to leave things alone. It's just hard for me to walk away sometimes." I crossed the room and gave her a hug. "Don't stay mad too long, okay?"

"It's not likely I will." She walked over to the pantry and took out a box-shaped item that looked like some sort of a cage. "Live animal trap," she said. "I'm going to get those chipmunks one way or another." She put a few sunflower seeds in it and set it next to the washstand in the hallway, with much help from Jazz, who kept trying to get in the trap.

CHAPTER TWENTY-THREE

SERGEANT MOREHOUSE called the day after Christmas to say he was stopping by. He accepted a cup of tea from Aunt Madge and complimented her on her red hair.

"I think it embodies the Christmas spirit," she said.

As we settled around Aunt Madge's large table he pulled several photographs out of a folder. It looked like early twilight and the picture of the person in them appeared to have been taken from a distance.

"There were no cameras on any of those old buildings, but I asked the manager of the Happy Dollar Store if any of his could get anything as far away as Mary Doris' building. He thought they got a bit of the area the fire was in, and he spent part of Christmas Eve working with a couple of students in the college photography program, and they made these stills from the video."

He had photos of several different views of the person, who was wearing a hip-length coat with a hood that was trimmed in something furry. It was impossible to see the face. I held one up to the light and Aunt Madge pulled a magnifying glass from a kitchen drawer.

Scoobie shook his head. "I can't even tell if it's a man or a woman."

"Me either," said Morehouse, looking glum. "I'd guess only about five feet, six inches, judging by where the head comes to on the building. But, there's plenty of people that height."

The camera only took in one spot near the Bakery at the Shore building, pretty close to the back of the building that abutted the alley where Lester and I had run to avoid Annie. I asked why Morehouse thought that person had started the fire.

He shrugged. "There's no one behind those buildings except this person between about three p.m. and when the fire started. And if you look close," he pointed to a spot near a gloved hand, "he's carrying something like a small box. About the size of charcoal lighting fluid, which was the accelerant used to start the fire."

"Damn," Scoobie said. "They meant business."

"They did," Morehouse said. "It was two days before Christmas, the block has only vacant buildings, and nobody had any reason to be back there." He collected the photos. "It's just a shot in the dark. Didn't expect you to recognize anyone."

"What's funny," I said slowly, "is that the person found Scoobie early in the morning..."

"By 'found' you mean accosted, right?" Scoobie asked.

Aunt Madge shook her head. I thought she looked pretty upset, so I reached over and squeezed her hand.

"I hear you," Sgt. Morehouse said to me. "Where did the person go between seven thirty or so and maybe five or five thirty?"

I thought some more. "Maybe they went there to burn the building and weren't expecting anyone else to come in."

"And they had to figure what to do once they hit Scoobie," Morehouse said.

"That's a pretty evil person, to plan all day and come back to kill Scoobie," Aunt Madge said.

"You got that right," Scoobie said.

We were all quiet for a few seconds. "Did you find Annie?" Aunt Madge asked.

"Yep. She went into the city with some guy she works with. I gather," he gave a small chuckle, "staff in the prosecuting attorney's office aren't supposed to fraternize."

"Hubba, hubba," Scoobie threw in.

"She spent the twenty-third with him, had dinner with him and his parents Christmas Eve, and got back here early Christmas afternoon. Fit to be tied, is how I hear it."

"If you tell Ramona half the town will know by tomorrow," I said.

"Nothing funny about this," Morehouse said.

Aunt Madge said, "Get a grip you two."

Scoobie looked directly at Morehouse, "I probably know best that it's not funny."

Morehouse ran one hand through his hair. "Sure you do. I just want to get the bastard who did this." He nodded to Aunt Madge, "S'cuz me."

"Did Annie have any ideas who would do this?" I asked.

"Nope. And she is going to be all over this. That windbag boss of hers called already, too. Offered to get any paperwork fast if we need to go to a judge for search warrants or anything."

"I was just in there a couple of days ago," Aunt Madge said. "She could have done a lot to bring that building back to good use. It wasn't that far gone." When Morehouse looked at her with a question in his eye she explained that I had taken her over there to talk about the wiring with Annie.

Morehouse stood and put on his coat. "I ever need a house inspected I'll call you, Madge. You're a better carpenter than half the guys on the force."

"You should hire more women," she said.

ANNIE CALLED LATE ON DECEMBER twenty-seventh. "I've been very upset, but I'm also so glad Scoobie wasn't hurt."

I started to say a mild concussion was hurt, but stopped myself.

"I assume," she continued, "that he went in to get warm. He doesn't have a home, does he?"

I explained where he lived and repeated the story Scoobie and I had agreed on. He saw the back door wide open with no evidence anyone was in the vacant building. He knew it was Annie's because I had gone to her campaign meeting there, so he knocked on the door and walked in. He was admiring the mirror behind the bar when someone hit him from behind.

"So...I guess the person must have been in there, and he didn't see them," she said.

"I suppose. I still get a chill every time I think he could have died in the fire."

"It's almost enough to make me rethink running," Annie said. "Maybe someone saw the article in the paper about the candidates and decided to target me."

It had not occurred to me that this would be Annie's reaction. Certainly she hadn't wasted a lot of time wishing Scoobie well. "I guess you've prosecuted all kinds of cases."

"That would be an understatement." Her voice sounded grim.

"I hope you were insured."

"The executor continued the policies on everything Aunt Mary Doris owned. My problem is she only owned that building and the fire marshal says the damage to the buildings on either side of it was substantial. The city wants the entire block torn down."

"Gosh, I'm sorry. I hope it doesn't get to be some drawn-out court fight."

"It won't. The prior owners hadn't paid taxes for years. The city owns the other two buildings."

"You know," the former real estate agent in me perked up, "as a vacant lot that site could bring you a lot of money. It's only three blocks from the beach."

That seemed to cheer her. We talked for a couple more minutes and hung up. If she had knocked out Scoobie and set the fire, or hired someone to set the fire not knowing Scoobie would be there, she was a terrific actor.

NEW YEAR'S EVE WAS quiet. Last year I'd been married to Robby and we went to the Florida Keys with two couples we were good friends with. I had no idea my husband had a gambling problem, and certainly didn't know he had borrowed money from some true New Jersey gangsters. This year, I did not know where Robby was, since he was supposed to go into the witness protection program after ratting on said bad guys. And, of course, he's not my husband anymore.

I try not to think much about all that. It's done, I have more or less landed on my feet, I like working with Harry, and I consider Scoobie and Ramona good friends. I had a lot of holiday cards from my Lakewood friends. I gather most of them called Renée to get my address. My plan is to do a "Happy New Year, I'm better than you think I am" letter – when I get around to it.

NEW YEAR'S DAY WAS not quiet, but it was fun to be around my sister and her family. I burned the crust on the pecan pie, but they swore it was good. My nieces seemed uncertain about why I had moved from an 1,800 square foot apartment to a single room, and the youngest asked where Robby was. Renée just said he couldn't be here today, which I guess is good enough for a four-year old.

I DIDN'T SEE SCOOBIE until a couple of days after New Year's. I think he had had far more human interaction than normal for him and he needed a break. He did promise – because Aunt Madge asked him, not me – to call each day. He opened every phone call with, "Scoobie here." Or Adam if Aunt Madge answered. "I'm not in a burning building today."

On his own Scoobie had Reverend Jamison let him into the food pantry and he counted the leftover cans of sweet potatoes. He told me Lance won the guessing contest, but would not accept the prize, which was the leftover cans.

I got up the Monday after New Year's feeling rested and ready for my first full year as a post-divorce, unmarried woman who had plans to make. That lasted until about noon, when I realized that staying in Ocean Alley doing appraisals and watching out for Mr. Rogers' chipmunks was my world at the moment.

After doing an appraisal in the morning I went back to the B&B to make a sandwich for lunch. Aunt Madge was just hanging up the phone. "You'll never believe who called."

"I can't guess, but I might believe it."

"Sophie Tillotson. Morgan, that's her married name."

I stopped with my hand on the refrigerator door. "You're kidding, right?"

Aunt Madge ignored my question. "She's in Cape May now, and said she's been upset ever since Richard's skeleton was found, and the fire in the old Bakery at the Shore just made it worse."

"I didn't know you knew her." I wouldn't have forgotten that!

"I wouldn't recognize her, and I can't actually remember meeting her." Aunt Madge thought for a moment. "Her family went to First Prez, so I may have met her, oh…forty years ago. I didn't even know she was still alive."

"Why did she call you?"

"Because of you," she said, simply.

"Me! Why me?"

"Because," she said, dryly, "you're the one who fell out of the attic with her brother."

"Oh, right." I sat on one of the chairs at the oak table and placed the bottle of milk I'd been holding on the table. "So, I wonder why she didn't call before?" I didn't really expect Aunt Madge to know.

"She didn't say. Just said she'd been reading the *Ocean Alley Press* on line ever since Gracie's mother called to tell her about Richard, and was upset about the fire. Apparently she doesn't know many people who live here now, and Gracie's mother suggested she call me if she wanted to talk to someone local."

I gave myself a head slap. "I completely forgot. Mary Doris said Sophie had her grandson drive her over here after she heard the news about Richard."

"That's odd," Aunt Madge said. "I had the impression she hadn't been here in years." She shrugged. "I didn't ask her that, of course. We only talked for a few minutes."

A couple of thoughts were brewing. "Do you suppose she knew about the baby?"

Aunt Madge shrugged. "Does it matter?"

"I guess not. I remember Mary Doris saying that Sophie's visit was the only good thing to come out of finding the skeleton. Other than closure for herself."

Aunt Madge gave me one of her looks, and I rose to my own defense. "I didn't ask her about any of it. Anyway, when I talked to Mary Doris I had no idea she'd had Richard's child." I stood to get a glass for my milk and my incomplete thought matured. "Hey, maybe she'd want the albums." I didn't mention that I'd like a chance to talk to her.

"It's Gracie's house, you better ask her," was all Aunt Madge said.

SCOOBIE ANNOUNCED HE DID NOT WANT TO discuss anything more about Richard's and Mary Doris' murders or the fire. "We know what we're going to know," he said, when I tried to coax him into a conversation one day at Java Jolt. "You remember that bit about accepting what you can't change?" he asked.

"I remember it, I just don't like it."

After that, he didn't call or drop by for a couple of days, but I knew he wasn't mad, just tired of me bugging him.

So, I tried Ramona. I went to the Purple Cow to see her, since she'd been away since her brief visit to Scoobie in the hospital. She'd gone to visit her parents in Florida for the holidays. As I walked into the store the white board reinforced that Scoobie was just fine.

He had apparently erased Ramona's daily quote and replaced it with, "Why do you call them hemorrhoids instead of assteroids?" I was laughing as I went into the Purple Cow, but Ramona was ringing up a customer so she didn't see me at first.

The office supply store owner, Roland, was in his small office, so I had to pretend to be looking at something. I picked up some paper clips.

"Sophie," I was saying, "knew Mary Doris from a long time ago. Maybe she would know if she had any enemies."

Ramona was skeptical. "And these enemies waited until now to kill her?"

"I know, it's lame." I thought for a minute. "Although the person I care about is Mary Doris, I'm still curious about what happened to Richard. Maybe Sophie will have some ideas, now that she knows he didn't just run off."

"Doubt it," Ramona said. "I went to the library to look at those articles, too. She was just a kid. Maybe ten or so."

I sighed. I'd forgotten that. "Oh well, she wouldn't want to talk to me, anyway."

IT TURNED OUT THAT Sophie Tillotson Morgan did want to talk to me. I answered the phone at the end of the week, and Sophie said she was going to have her grandson bring her back to Ocean Alley and she would stay at the B&B a couple of days while she made burial arrangements for Richard now that the police were willing to release the body to her. "They were going to do it earlier, but then when dear Mary Doris was killed they said they wanted to hold onto it in case there was a link between...between the two." Her voice caught.

If I had not known her age I would have thought I was talking to someone my own age. Her voice was firm and purposeful. Only the mention of having her grandson drive her gave away her age.

"Has anyone set a time for Mary Doris' memorial service?" she asked.

"Not that I know of. I'll call her niece, Annie Milner, and ask her."

Aunt Madge was pleased to have a guest at Cozy Corner B&B, since winter is a slow time for business. She suggested I let Gracie know Sophie was coming. "From what you've said about that attic, there could be some of Sophie's old toys up there."

I called Gracie, who said she was back on her happy pills since the kids were back in school; she had stayed off them when they were home. "They can get in trouble in five minutes." She giggled. "Kind of like you." It turned out she didn't mind if Sophie took any of the pictures or toys. "I wish the damn attic had been empty. Except I like the quiltsh I took."

SOPHIE MORGAN WAS IN terrific shape except for "a touch of arthritis in the knees," as she put it. Her grandson worked as a nurse in Cape May, and was to come back for her in two days. She and Aunt Madge had talked until about ten the night before. For two women who didn't know each other they knew a lot of the same people, many of whom were long dead.

We were having our coffee and rolls later than usual – all of eight o'clock. The weather was mild, with temperatures expected to go up to near forty degrees. I drove Sophie around town, and she commented on a number of changes. "Almost too many to count. I was here a long time after the Great Atlantic Hurricane in forty-four, but in my mind Ocean Alley looks the way it did before then."

"With the big pier and the Ferris wheel?" I asked, smiling. When she agreed I told her that Uncle Gordon had spent an afternoon on the boardwalk with me when I was five or six, and he described the pier and its Ferris wheel and small merry-go-round. "I went home and demanded to be taken to the 'place with the rides,' according to my mother."

Sophie specifically asked to see the burned out store, so we parked across the street from it and stared at the charred wood and police tape. I explained how it was laid out now, and she told me it used to have two chimneys instead of the one.

"There was one in the kitchen for that monstrous stove Richard insisted on buying. Luckily it was delivered before they had the glass in the main window, because it wouldn't go in the door."

"Now I get why it's still in there. It doesn't look as if it's been used in years."

She nodded. "Peter closed the bakery about the time the war started. Started for Europe," she amended. "He rented it to several different businesses and finally sold it."

"He sold it to Mary Doris?"

She shook her head vehemently. "Oh, no. He didn't like to be around her. He knew how she felt about him."

When I asked what she meant, Sophie added, "Mary Doris never said so directly to him, but I know she held him responsible for Richard's disappearance. She told me once that he may not have killed Richard himself, but he perhaps had someone else do it. After that I did not contact

Mary Doris too often." She paused, "My brother-in-law may not have been a saint, but I cannot believe the Peter I knew was a murderer."

"I'm glad you have good memories." I didn't know what else to say.

Sophie peered out the car window. "Looks as if anyone could go in there."

I followed her gaze. "I think it would be pretty dangerous. You can see how half the back has collapsed." On impulse, I added, "It was very nice of you to visit Mary Doris after Richard's remains were found."

She stiffened. "We weren't close for years. But I always liked Mary Doris. I know my brother's leaving – I didn't believe he was dead for a long time – was really hard on her." She thought for a moment. "But, if that hadn't happened she likely would not have gotten her teaching certificate and taught all those years."

Yeah, she'd have been married and raising a son.

I dropped Sophie at the funeral home. She didn't want to be accompanied, and I was glad of that. I popped into the library for a few minutes and sat with Scoobie as he worked on a poem. Given that there were two notebooks on the table, I gathered he had spent a lot of time writing recently. I suppose near-death experiences give you a lot to write about, if that's your thing.

As I stood to go, he looked up. "Hang on one second." He finished a line, and then opened the other notebook to a page marked with one of the library's free bookmarks. He shoved it toward me.

The snow will melt and we will see
that the rivers will always flow to the sea.

The tide will always ebb and flow
the sun will rise and set aglow.

The rain will come and the wind will blow,
thunder and lightening will hit below.

The earth will tremble and start to shake,
our homes will sway and begin to break.

And when the mountains decide to explode,
we will have a sea of lava, without a road.

This one I could almost understand. I reread it. "You don't usually use rhyme so much." I looked up at him. "I like it."

"Why?" He asked.

I had not expected his question. "Umm. I think I might get what you are saying. Maybe that things are inevitable?"

He shrugged. "I don't always have a message that I know of, but I have been thinking a lot about how you can make all kinds of changes in your life, but if your time is up, it's up."

I shivered. "I'm glad yours wasn't up."

He placed his hand on his neck and stretched it. "I still have a headache, but it's a lot better."

"Seems like a long time. Should you go back to the…"

"No more doctors," he said. "Took me a long time to explain to the guy in the hospital why I wouldn't take the crap medicine they wanted to load me up with."

I smiled. "Congratulations." I looked at my mobile phone. "Almost time to pick up Sophie at the funeral home."

He grinned. "I'd say it's nice of you to take her around, but I'm familiar with your ulterior motives."

"She doesn't know anything about Richard's disappearance; at least not that she's talked about. And, believe it or not, I'm not asking a lot of questions."

Scoobie gave me a smirk and went back to his writing.

WHEN I GOT BACK TO THE FUNERAL HOME, Sophie was sitting on a small loveseat outside the funeral director's office. Across from her, on a chair that looked too dainty to hold him, was George Winters. It occurred to me that he must have spies all over town that let him know who was where or what was going on.

They both looked up at me, and George had the decency to look guilty. "Mr. Winters has given me a copy of all the articles that mention my family through the years," Sophie said. "I shall treasure them."

I know George better than he thinks I do. He wanted to jog her memory. "How nice of him." I tried not to sound as venomous as I felt. *Bothering an elderly woman while she was making her brother's funeral arrangements!*

Sophie looked back at George. "You see, young man, I was only ten the day my sister got married." She got a far-away look. "I remember many things about that day. For one thing," she gave both of us a bright smile, "it was the first time I had a bouquet of flowers of my own. I wasn't truly a bridesmaid, but my sister was very thoughtful. I had a dress like the grown-up girls and my own bouquet."

I could sense George's impatience. He had not come to hear of a little girl's first bouquet. "Did you see Richard and Peter Fisher quarrel at the wedding?" he asked.

Sophie gave a dismissive wave. "They didn't really *quarrel*, just a bit too much to drink, I think. They were very close friends." She paused. "I think someone thought that would sell papers. You know, after he went missing." She leaned over to pat his hand. "You can't believe everything you read in the papers, you know."

To his credit, George did not get churlish.

SOPHIE WENT TO BED by eight-thirty that evening. She said that the day's activities had worn her out. Though we didn't do a lot of walking, I figured she had run an emotional gamut. I was in bed by ten-thirty, but woke up abruptly about one o'clock. "Did you hear that?" I asked Jazz. No response.

After about ten minutes of tossing and turning I got up and went downstairs to heat some milk in the hope of falling asleep again. Mr. Rogers and Miss Piggy were asleep on a throw rug near the washstand. They generally slept in Aunt Madge's room, but I figured she let them out to stand guard over the chipmunks. I started to continue into the kitchen when something about their breathing struck me. It seemed a lot more shallow than usual.

I bent over and said both their names softly, then more loudly. Neither stirred. Gently, mindful that a startled dog can nip or bite, I scratched Mr. Rogers' head, then Miss Piggy's. No response from either of them. These are dogs that can hear a squirrel on the patio from two rooms away. I shook them both, still nothing. *They're breathing, they must be okay.*

I studied them some more. *Somebody drugged these dogs.* I sat on the bottom step leading upstairs and considered waking Aunt Madge. Sophie's face popped into my mind and I stood up. She was the only unknown person in the house. *She had seemed to like the dogs, why would she hurt them?*

I walked quietly up the steps and stood outside her room. If I opened the door and she was asleep I could startle her greatly. On the other hand, if she had drugged the dogs, Aunt Madge might do more than startle her. I eased open the door.

The bed was empty.

CHAPTER TWENTY-FOUR

I THINK I STARED at her bed for a full fifteen seconds, then took in the rest of the room. There was an adjoining bath, a so-called Jack and Jill bath shared with the next room's guests. But, there were no other guests, and no light in the bathroom. I peeked in, hoping not to find her on the floor. No Sophie.

In ten seconds I realized there were no shoes in the room and the clothes she had worn earlier were not on hangers or in her small suitcase. *She drugged the dogs so she could sneak out.*

I pulled on jeans and a sweat shirt and picked up my shoes so I didn't wake Aunt Madge as I descended the stairs. I knew exactly where Sophie had gone. The driveway was on the opposite side of the house from Aunt Madge's bedroom, so I wasn't too worried about her hearing my car start.

As I pulled out of the driveway I pushed the speed dial for Scoobie's so-called burn phone. Amazingly, he picked up, sounding sleepy. "Jolie?"

"Who else?" I talked fast. "I think Sophie went over to the old Bakery at the Shore building. Can you meet me outside your building, like now?"

He hung up. Either he had gone back to sleep or I'd see him in a minute.

I rolled down my window so I could rub the outside mirror. It had been warm enough to rain sometime since I'd gone to bed and the air smelled of rain and sea. Usually I love that smell, but now it brought no comfort.

Scoobie was coming out the front door of his rooming house as I pulled up and he slid into the front seat. "Are you out of your mind? Wait. Is she?"

There was no one else on the roads so we made good time going the eight or nine blocks to the old bakery. I parked on a side street. "Pull the flashlight out of the glove box, okay?"

Scoobie did so without comment and we walked toward the front of the building. "At least we don't have to worry about what door to go in," he whispered.

The building didn't have enough wood left to pound plywood over a window or door. Still, if it had been summer, with hordes of tourists, the fire department would have found a way to more fully secure the building.

Now there were several orange and white sawhorses and a lot of police tape.

When we got to the front of the building we could see a pinpoint of light moving in the area that had been the large front room. I thought Sophie had some guts. She had to walk about four blocks to get to the fire-ravaged building, and here she was wandering around with a flashlight after one in the morning.

Scoobie knelt and I followed suit. It took a moment to adjust my eyes to the near-total darkness. Sophie had what looked like a metal tape measure that was extended at least a couple of feet and she was sliding it behind the mirror, near the bottom. Scoobie and I looked at each other and shrugged.

After about a minute, during which time my knees began to protest their position, she gave a quiet, "Aha!" She worked the tape measure up and down and sideways, and finally something white appeared behind the mirror. She tugged and a long piece of paper appeared. I drew in a breath, and Scoobie stared at me.

I stood up and spoke in a normal tone of voice. "Sophie?"

"Oh my God!" she turned toward us and dropped the paper.

"I saw you were gone." Scoobie moved closer to me, so that our shoulders touched. "Thought you might have taken a night walk until I saw you drugged the dogs."

"You forgot to mention that little detail," Scoobie said.

"Sorry." My eyes never left Sophie. She stooped and picked up the paper.

"It's the deed, isn't it?" I asked.

"How did you know?" She looked truly flabbergasted.

"I suggested that Gracie look for it, and she and her mother had no luck. I figured it had been so long since the house was built that it had been thrown away decades ago."

She gave a harsh chuckle. "Not thrown away. But my dear brother was determined to use it as leverage against Audrey's husband."

I nodded. "Peter Fisher figured out Richard was embezzling."

She walked a few steps closer. "I don't think Richard looked at it that way. I was just a little girl, so I don't really know what was going through his head. Not long before the wedding I heard him tell Audrey that he thought Peter didn't appreciate all the time Richard spent at the counter." She smiled. "I do remember that everyone liked my brother. He had a smile for all the customers, and he'd give children pieces of cookie that broke." Her countenance darkened. "Peter hated that."

"So, how did the deed get behind the mirror?" I asked.

"Who cares?" Scoobie's voice was harsh. "It's cold. We should get out of here."

"But then you'll never know how Richard died, will you?" She spoke softly.

She had my attention. "You know?" I asked.

She nodded. "Richard had me walk down here with him. We had a lot of out-of-town company, so we were all awake very late even the day after the wedding. Me latest of all. I was still so excited."

"Peter and Audrey had gone to the hotel, and I read in the paper – the very paper that your friend George Winters gave me – that Richard sang under their window on their wedding night."

I nodded. "That was supposed to be the last time anyone remembered seeing him with Peter, so to speak."

"Except me," she said, sadly. "Mother put me to bed, but I couldn't sleep. My big brother came home late the night after the wedding. He was probably out with Mary Doris." She said the name almost as a sneer. "When he saw me sitting on the couch with my little bouquet, he didn't look too pleased."

She glanced at the deed. "I would guess he did not expect to see anyone up. He said we'd go for a walk after he went upstairs. And we did, to the bakery."

"We should really go," Scoobie said, in a singsong voice. I ignored him.

"We walked down, everybody walked back then, and when he opened the door you could smell that fresh bread smell. Until that night I really loved it."

She glanced toward the mirror and back at me. "Richard went over to the mirror and took a piece of paper out of his pocket, and he slid it behind the mirror. It was a tight fit, and he was probably a little drunk, but he did it."

She pointed to a spot across the room. "And then he sat me in this little wire and wood chair at the edge of the display case, and gave me a cookie. And I sat with my big brother, and…" Her voice choked.

"And then what?" Scoobie asked.

Her tone grew bitter. "Then Peter Fisher came in. He said he'd looked out the hotel window and seen Richard go by. I don't think he knew I was with him until he got to the shop. He was as mad as a hornet that just had its nest knocked down."

"Did he say why?" I asked.

"It didn't make a whole lot of sense to me until years later. I just knew Peter was mad about something with money. Later on I figured he was accusing Richard of stealing money." She sighed. "If Richard had kept his temper in check, maybe... but he was never very good at that. He told Peter that if Peter 'went public' that he'd have a heck of a time selling the building because he'd never find the deed."

She reached into her pocket and took out a tissue to dab her eyes. "I was scared. I'd never seen two people so mad. Richard started saying things like Peter had no idea how much work Richard did and Peter said something about putting up all the money. And then they just went at each other."

She shook her head, then looked at me again. "I was crying by then, I can tell you. They didn't really punch each other much, but there was a lot of pushing. And then," she gave a strangled sob, and I started toward her, but Scoobie put an arm in front of me.

"And then Richard kind of lost his balance, he was still tipsy, and Peter gave him a hard push." She pointed toward the bottom of the bar, across from the closet. "There was a glass display case there, and the corner was quite sharp." Her voice dropped to a whisper. "There was so much blood. All over the floor, just outside that stupid mirrored closet where they hid all the alcohol they were selling."

I remembered that the floor there had wider boards than the rest of the floor. You probably couldn't see the difference now, the entire floor was covered in soot and tiny pieces of burned wood. I had a quick thought that Peter must have replaced the boards that had blood on them.

"And then what?" I asked.

"Then Peter said he was going to take me home and come back to help Richard. He said tomorrow it would be like a bad dream, that I should never again stay up so late. And I was never to talk about what happened." She shivered. "It was very clear to me that Peter had hurt Richard and was letting me know he could hurt me, too."

We were all silent for perhaps twenty seconds, then Sophie spoke again. "I left that house the day after I graduated from high school and I hardly ever came back."

"That's a long time to live in fear," Scoobie said, quietly.

"And I kept that secret," Sophie said, "and I intend to keep keeping it."

"That would be fine, if it weren't for Mary Doris. And I bet you started the fire." I looked directly into Sophie's eyes and saw a pair as resolute as my own staring back. Could this elderly woman really have killed Mary Doris? How on earth could she have done it? What would she know about making a poisonous alcohol?

"I know what you did," Scoobie said softly.

I looked at him, amazed. "What?" I asked.

"I bet you had some old bottles of alcohol, spirits, whatever you want to call it, from Peter and Richard's so-called bakery. Or maybe something they bought from somebody else to sell." Scoobie's voice had a bitterness I'd never heard before. "You went to see Mary Doris, and you gave her some to drink. Only you didn't drink any, because you knew it was wood alcohol, not grain alcohol. You also knew it would take someone several days to get sick after she drank the bad stuff. No one would associate her death with your visit."

After a long ten or fifteen seconds, Sophie spoke. "You are either a very smart man, or a very devious one."

"Smart enough to recognize your deviousness," he said, calmly.

Sophie's voice was almost a hiss. "We helped her. My mother gave her money so she could get her teaching certificate. She owed us."

I gave a violent shiver. I had been so focused on Sophie's story I had not realized my feet had become blocks of ice. It was a warm night for January, but it was likely just below freezing and not a night to stand in the cold as long as we had. Scoobie put one arm around my shoulders and gave me a quick hug.

She continued, more calmly. "Peter kept a lot of the old bottles as souvenirs. Hid them in the basement in a wooden crate. It even said 'poison' on the top of one of the crates. Audrey told me, this was years later, that some of the last stuff they bought to sell was bad. Bad hootch, she called it."

Sophie paused for a moment. "Pretty dumb to keep it around, with Peter and Audrey having kids. I took a few bottles as souvenirs after Audrey died. I can't begin to tell you why I kept a couple of the poison ones." She shrugged. "The labels were a bit different, I guess I wanted samples of each label.

She smiled sweetly. "You'll be pleased to know I made sure the other poison bottles were emptied.

"So, you took a bottle to Mary Doris. But why? What did she ever do to you?" I had a catch in my voice.

"After everything we did for her, everything, that silly old woman was going to tell the whole story, let everyone know Peter killed Richard. As soon as I heard she knew the DNA results, I was sure that's what she'd do."

"So what?" Scoobie said, stomping his feet a couple times. "There's no one to arrest, the sins of the father don't always pass to the child."

"That's what you think. It wasn't just Richard. That bad hootch killed several people. You know City Councilman Grooms?"

I nodded.

"His grandfather. Not that he knows the bad alcohol was from my family. The names Fisher and Tillotson mean something in this town. My mother and Audrey gave most of the money for Ocean Alley's library. There's a huge plaque."

"Yeah, there is," Scoobie said. "I'll see it comes down."

"And that's the point!" Her voice was strident. "If people find out about this," she gestured around the ruin of Bakery at the Shore, "they'll put it together. All the good, our reputation, it will all be down the drain."

"Actually," I felt my blood about to boil; if only it would get to my feet. "If you hadn't murdered Mary Doris, all people would guess, if they even thought about it, is that Peter killed Richard. And it was an accident you said."

"Oh, there's more to it than that. You don't know about her bastard baby." Sophie had a look of something close to hatred.

"Actually, I do. We do." I tilted my head toward Scoobie. "She left a letter with one of her good friends, to be opened after her death."

That seemed to truly shock her. She reached to what was left of the old mahogany bar to steady herself, then looked down at her dirty gloved hand. "Then you know what I have to protect."

"What do you mean?" I asked.

"The family money. We had a lot, but it's dwindled over time as everyone's heirs got a piece. Those damn Milners will want a share now. And we'll all have to give some to them." Sophie had a hard, angry look now. "That money's for *my* grandchildren, not Mary Doris Milner's."

My sense was that if she were a man she would have spit on the floor.

"So," she pulled something from her pocket. "I'm not going to ruin our name, and I'm not going to give a dime to Matt Milner and his wife and daughter."

I looked at her hand. She held one of the smallest guns I've ever seen.

Scoobie started to laugh. "That's a twenty-two. You wouldn't be able to hit us." He started backing up.

Sophie's expression looked like a mad woman's and she raised her arm to shoulder height. "Watch me, I can…"

There was a humongous blast. I jumped and landed on my knees. Scoobie darted forward. He picked up the small gun from where Sophie had dropped it when she sat down hard.

I looked at Sophie. She was sitting on the floor, her hands at each side, balancing herself, looking around. Together our eyes traveled to a hole in the wall above her head. There was still sawdust swirling.

I looked behind me for the source of the noise. Aunt Madge was lowering Uncle Gordon's old hunting rifle. "I might have let you get away with aiming at Jolie, but no one hurts my dogs."

CHAPTER TWENTY-FIVE

I STOPPED BY Annie Milner's office later the same day, to apologize. She didn't know the evil things I'd thought about her, so I didn't really have to. But, it seemed right. She took it pretty well. I didn't say anything about Mary Doris being her great grandmother rather than a great aunt, but she brought it up.

"My dad was mad at Mary Doris one time, I was maybe fourteen. He thought she spent way too much on me at Christmas, it was a lot more than she spent on my brother."

I didn't even know Annie had a brother. And why would I?

She looked at my puzzled expression. "My brother wasn't her grandchild. Technically he was my half-brother, mom's son from when she was married before." She gave a small wave. "We never thought about half brother and sister stuff."

"Anyway, Dad didn't know I could hear what he said. I was at the top of the steps. I'd gone to bed, but I heard them arguing. Mary Doris started to say something about me, and he told her to leave her granddaughter out of it."

"It took me awhile to understand, but I eventually worked it out. I realized my grandfather was born a couple months after my great grandparents got married. We had those wedding photos. Great Grandpa John's wife, Irene was her name, wasn't pregnant." Annie stopped.

I wasn't sure what to say. But, being me, I plowed on. "Was Mary Doris happy that you knew?"

Annie shook her head. "I never told her. My parents were furious when I asked them about it, and they said I had no business talking to her about it, that it was her secret to keep." Annie paused for a moment. "I never really understood her thinking, but I eventually accepted it."

"You know a single woman with a baby would have been a pariah in the late 1920s."

Annie nodded. "For her, she did the right thing. I was furious with my parents for not telling me, for telling me I shouldn't talk to Mary Doris about it. That's why I came here at the end of my junior year of high school." She gave a small smile. "I wanted to get to know her better."

I smiled slightly. "Did your parents get any smarter as you got older?"

She returned the smile. "I got over being mad, if that's what you mean. The more I learned about Mary Doris' life, the more I realized my grandfather was better off in some ways with her brother John and his wife. Not," she said quickly, "that I think Mary Doris wouldn't have been a good parent. But she worked; she lived in small apartments until she was maybe forty." Annie shrugged. "By the time I knew her she had plenty of money, but she would have had a horrible time raising a child on her own back then. And Grandfather Brian would have suffered, too."

"Kids can be mean." We both nodded.

CHAPTER TWENTY-SIX

LUCKILY THE OCEAN ALLEY police chose not to press charges against Aunt Madge for firing a gun within city limits, a pretty serious crime. Sgt. Morehouse gave her a heck of a lecture though, told her she was "taking a page out of Jolie's book" and it should be the other way around. She sat calmly at her kitchen table, and when he was done she offered him some tea. He accepted.

If Sophie Tillotson Morgan had let things be, no one would have paid much attention to how Richard died. Peter Fisher probably had not meant to kill him. But killing Mary Doris was unforgivable in the eyes of everyone in town. What was most mentioned was the sheer malice that went into Sophie's plans, including trying to burn Scoobie alive.

She'll never get out of prison. The judge denied pretrial release, citing her wealth and lack of remorse. He thought she would do whatever she could to flee.

Annie told me they hoped to reach a plea deal so the prosecuting attorney's office didn't have to use all its resources on one mega-trial. Annie, of course, cannot work on the case. Conflict of interest.

They'll probably never prove she started the fire. It turns out Sophie was perfectly capable of driving herself, and she came to Ocean Alley at least three times before her stay at the B&B. Her grandson drove her when she poisoned Mary Doris. She drove herself to take some of the ledgers from the attic trunk and again when she tried to burn the old Bakery at the Shore -- neither of which she would admit to.

Her daughter said that Sophie said she was going Christmas shopping the day of the fire, insisting that Sophie wanted to finish her shopping on her own. Sophie, of course, was smart enough to have bought a bunch of presents that day, and had the receipts to prove it. As Aunt Madge said, Sophie was perfectly capable of shopping and trying to murder Scoobie in the same day.

Sophie was more than just strong-willed. To hit Scoobie and drag him into the closet took more strength than most people decades younger have. Perhaps we should all walk two miles a day when we're her age.

We guessed that Sophie worked out that Peter Fisher must have hidden Richard's body in the closet. We figured he moved the remains to the attic about the time he sold the building, and she wanted to be sure there was no evidence in the closet.

Scoobie maintained that if Sophie had watched CSI she'd know there wouldn't be anything left to implicate Peter Fisher. That was his only comment on the whole affair, and he went back to his rooming house as soon as Sgt. Morehouse questioned us the morning after Sophie would have killed us.

It still gives me the willies to think that Peter must have had to scrub the remains to make the skeleton so clean. *Yuck*.

George Winters did a decent article that linked the death decades ago to the current murder and fire. He titled it "Rekindling Motives." He had a detailed sidebar on Prohibition and the dangers of methyl alcohol, which was cheap to make back then but as deadly as arsenic. More so, actually. If the conversations in Java Jolt were any indication, everyone read both articles.

SCOOBIE CAN BE WITHDRAWN, but I thought he was burrowing in way too much, even for him. Aunt Madge reminded me that his parents were "severe alcoholics" and perhaps that was part of Scoobie's need for solitude. He didn't even go to the library.

Finally, Ramona and I went together to his rooming house. Sgt. Morehouse told us which room was Scoobie's, and we had to knock for two minutes before he came to the door.

"Have you heard of the right to privacy?" he asked, blocking the door so we couldn't go in.

I didn't want to go in, I wanted him out.

"Yes, we have," Ramona responded.

"We just don't respect it," I threw in.

I saw the beginning of a smile, but it left quickly. "You know I like time to myself. Everything that went on, it's a lot to process."

"You're isolating."

He looked astonished. "Since when did you get familiar with danger signs in recovery?"

"Gambling is an addiction, you know. I read all that stuff when Robby got in trouble." I stared at him, not flinching.

"The question is, did it sink in?" He looked at us for another couple of seconds. "I'll tell you what, I'll meet you at Newhart's in a half-hour. You," he pointed at me, "are buying."

WE HAD THAT LUNCH, and at seven o'clock that evening Scoobie, Aunt Madge, Ramona, Harry, and I went to the memorial service for Mary Doris Milner. Annie held it in the ballroom at the hotel because no one thought that St. Anthony's Catholic Church could hold everyone. It was a good decision; even at the hotel it was standing room only. Lance Wilson sat next to Annie.

I studied the faces I could see without craning my neck too far. I recognized the mayor, several high school teachers, a couple dozen people who'd been at the reunion, everyone I'd ever met through Aunt Madge, and a lot of faces that I'd seen around town but couldn't associate with a name. George Winters caught my eye and winked. I actually smiled at him.

Mary Doris Milner's life turned out a lot differently than she expected when she was Richard Tillotson's girlfriend, and I'm sure there was a lot of sadness for a time. But her life after Richard seemed to have taken some happy turns. If the number of people at the memorial service was any indication, she had a lot of friends.

I take heart from her life.

Read all the books in the
Jolie Gentil cozy mystery series

Appraisal for Murder (first of the series)
Rekindling Motives (second of the series)
When the Carny Comes to Town (third in the series)
Any Port in a Storm (fourth in the series)
Trouble on the Doorstep (fifth in the series)
Behind the Walls (sixth in the series)
Vague Images (seventh in the series)
Ground to a Halt (eighth in the series)
Ocean Alley Adventures (boxed set of books 1-3)
Jolie Gentil Translates to Trouble (boxed set of books 4-6)

Find out where to purchase Elaine's books at:
www.elaineorr.com
www.elaineorr.blogspot.com

AUTHOR BIO

Elaine L. Orr is the Amazon bestselling author of *Trouble on the Doorstep* and other books in the Jolie Gentil cozy mystery series, which now has eight books and a prequel. She wrote plays and novellas for years and graduated to longer fiction. *Biding Time* was one of five finalists in the National Press Club's first fiction contest, in 1993, and *Behind the Walls* is a finalist in the 2014 Mystery and Mayhem Awards. She is a regular attendee at conferences such as Muncie's Midwest Writers Workshop and Magna Cum Murder, and conducts presentations on electronic publishing and other writing-related topics. Her nonfiction includes carefully researched local and family history books. Elaine grew up in Maryland and moved to the Midwest in 1994.

Made in the USA
Middletown, DE
15 April 2017